The Path Divided

by Jeanne Moran

For Fox,
Choose the green path.
Jeanne Moran

ISBN: 9781728729152

Cover design by Michael Rausch
www.michaeljprausch.com

Back cover photo by Daisy K Photography
www.daisykphoto.com

Every attempt has been made to portray locations and historical events accurately. The author accepts sole responsibility for errors.

For my husband Michael, with whom I share
this secure green space.
All my love.

We are not to simply
bandage the wounds of
victims [caught] beneath
the wheels of injustice.
We are to drive a spoke
into the wheel itself.
—*Dietrich Bonhoeffer*

Humanitarianism is the
expression of stupidity
and cowardice.
—*Adolf Hitler*

Chapter One
Rennie

Until the picture frame showed me otherwise, I thought my corner of the world was green. I didn't know I'd already colored the paths in front of my best friend, my unsuspecting brother, and me.

None of us would ever be the same.

Freising, Germany
25 July 1938

I eased the screen door closed behind me and slipped into the dewy grass. A few dozen meters from the farmhouse, I sat atop a rock and opened *Julius Caesar.* It's not like I planned to audition for a starring role. Those parts were for experienced actors, not a fourteen-year-old like me. But I wouldn't settle for a voiceless face in a crowd scene either.

I paged through the script in search of a supporting character, one whose role was small but essential. The part I played had to make a difference.

And there it was—the Soothsayer! I hissed the famous warning of Caesar's day of betrayal and death, "Beware the Ides of March." Hunching forward, I tried the line with a growl and then rose and straightened to deliver it with a shout. "Beware the Ides of March!"

I was startled by the approach of rumbling wheels and clomping hooves. A dusty workhorse pulling a gypsy wagon stopped in front of me. A woman climbed down from the wagon driver's seat. She was short and soft, as if a feather pillow were stuffed in her faded blouse and crumpled black skirt.

A small door on the wagon's roof pushed open and clanked backward as the head of a dark-haired boy popped out. He looked at me and grinned. "That's her. Rennie, she calls herself. Renate Müller, from Munich." His head disappeared, and the door banged shut.

I slid from the rock and stepped closer. "Have we met? Frau…"

"Wait here," the woman ordered as she entered the wagon's back door. "I have something for you."

So, I waited. The wagon's peeling sides exposed patches of weathered wood, yet freshly painted flowers and scrolls decorated the roofline. From what I knew of these travelers—Roma, they called themselves—they lived in wagons like that. The whole family and everything they owned were crammed into that narrow rectangle. Where did they store winter clothing? Where did they keep their grandmother's dishes?

The woman stepped out of the wagon with the boy—her son, I assumed—at her heels. His stained white shirt and dusty trousers sagged from his thin frame. Poor kid. Not more than ten years old, wearing someone else's clothes and living in a wagon.

The Romany woman approached me and swept both hands forward in a grand gesture. A dull silver object sat on her open palms. I stated the obvious. "It's a picture frame."

"I told her you wanted one," the boy said.

How did he know? I stepped back, ready to bolt to the Huber's farmhouse.

He tugged at his pants as he spoke. "I saw you in town a couple days ago. You asked the shopkeeper about picture frames." That was true. I'd visited a shop in search of a frame for my favorite photo of me and my best friend Sophie. In case one the right size turned up, I'd left my name with the store's owner. The boy smiled. "Shopkeeper shooed me out, thought I'd steal something. But I don't steal. I get leads."

"Leads," I repeated.

"Like this. You need a picture frame." He gestured to the item still in his mother's outstretched hands. "A special one."

Actually, the frame looked quite ordinary. The sides of the empty rectangle were dull silver with engraved vines that were partially worn away. But when the Romany woman shoved the frame into my hands, I felt a connection. Familiarity, maybe. For the photo of Sophie and me in happier times, best friends together, the frame was perfect. "If you'll wait here, I'll get the money…" I began.

The woman drew her face close and examined me for several moments. I was about to pull away when she snapped, "It belongs to you."

I shook my head. "I'm afraid you're mistaken. I've never seen it before."

"The frame is yours. Look how you cradle it. As if holding a babe."

Sure enough, it was nestled into the crook of my arm. I even swayed a little, rocking it. I froze.

"The photo you want the frame for, it is special to you?" Her face wasn't as close as it had been, but her eyes continued their fine examination of me.

"Very special."

"And a person in the photo, something has happened to her, *ja*?"

I was about to answer yes, my best friend Sophie had gotten polio a few months earlier, but I clamped my slack jaw shut. This woman, this entire encounter…

She continued, her tone urgent. "Any picture frame shows what is real. This"—she poked a finger at the frame even as I tugged it close to save it from her jab—"this frame shows what is possible."

"I…I don't understand."

"The past is past, paved in stone. But the future—that is mystery. All depends on which path you choose." She climbed to the wagon driver's seat, then clucked her tongue and snapped the reins. "Let's go, Bruno." The boy hurried through the wagon's door.

As the horse started walking, I called out, "Wait! I need to pay you!"

For the first time, the woman smiled at me, a sad, tight smile. "Oh, you will pay," she said. "Be careful, Renate Müller. Once a path is chosen, there is no turning back."

She may as well have said "Beware the Ides of March." I shivered.

The door on the roof opened, and Bruno popped up, calling, "I'll watch for you in town." He waved, and the wagon rolled on, spewing dust.

From the farmhouse up the hill, I heard the stirrings and voices typical of every morning. The four Huber children were waking. Time to start my day's work. I hurried to my room and tucked the frame in a drawer. I'd puzzle over the Romany and her odd words later.

I'd finished stocking the pantry with fresh-made jam when eight-year-old Conrad flung open the back door. Grinning all the while, he shoved the largest basket I'd ever seen into the kitchen. "It's a two-bushel basket," he announced.

Anticipating more jam making, I groaned. "What's in there? Peaches?"

"The basket's not for you, Rennie. It's for Ada." He stepped past me in search of his little sister.

I blocked his path. "Show me first."

Conrad whipped off the basket's gingham cover. Empty. Then I heard it—a dry scrape like footsteps through autumn leaves.

I followed the sound to the basket's base, squatted, and squinted into the space created between the woven fibers. Something moved. I jerked back and bolted upright, then peered inside the basket again. Empty. I used my best threatening tone. "Conrad."

Still grinning, he reached deep inside the basket, stuck a finger in a small hole, and lifted. "A false bottom." Coiled at the basket's true bottom half a meter lower lay a thin black snake. Before I could speak, he reached in, grabbed the creature, and dropped it at my feet. Somewhere behind me, little Ada squealed. Her footsteps skittered away.

I wished I could join her, but I was in charge until the children's mother returned home. I willed my voice steady and picked up the horrid thing. "Nice snake. Weren't you afraid it would suffocate in there?"

"There's space between the weaves. Air holes." The boy's eyebrows pulled together. "Why didn't you scream? Girls always scream at snakes." He sounded disappointed.

Good. I fixed my gaze on him. "This fellow's mother will come looking for him soon. I hope she's not mad." I shook my head. "A mad mother snake." Conrad's eyes widened, so I embellished as if I were onstage. "I wonder how big she is. Maybe she's—" I spread my arms and let the snake dangle from one hand, suppressing a shudder as the creature squirmed and tried to gain purchase on my arm.

"I…I better put him back," Conrad stammered. He grabbed the snake and raced outside, leaving his precious trick basket behind.

While I scrubbed my trembling hands, Ada peeked around the doorframe. "He's gone," I said. "The snake too."

She drew close to me and whispered, "Why does Conrad do that?"

I kissed the coiled braids on top of her head. "Because he's eight and you're five."

"How old are you, Rennie?"

"Fourteen. Fifteen next month."

Ada peered up at me. "I want to be just like you when I'm fourteen, fifteen next month. Not afraid of anything. Not even snakes."

"Can you keep a secret?" She nodded and used a finger to draw a cross on her chest. "I was just acting brave. I'm scared of snakes too."

"You are? Does anyone else know?"

"Nope. Our secret. Grab your book. I'll give you a piggyback ride to the couch."

When I was halfway through reading "Cinderella," the children's mother came in. "Frau Huber," I said, rising to greet her.

She pulled off her kerchief and smoothed her brown waves. "How's my Ada?" she said, opening her arms to the little girl's embrace. She lifted Ada against a hip and peppered me with questions. I detailed the chores I'd done and told her of the snake incident. Frau Huber tipped her head and smiled. "I don't know how I managed before you came, Renate."

I liked my summer Youth assignment at the Huber's farm. Herr Huber oversaw the farm itself—the crops, the animals, and the machinery. Between eight and twelve Youth worked with him and lived in the farm's bunkhouse. Since I was mother's helper, I lived in the family's home. Daily household chores and childcare were my jobs.

Frau Huber sold the farm's goods at the town market a few mornings a week. Ten-year-old Otto usually went along to help with lifting and toting. That left me in charge of the house and three younger children, Conrad, Ada, and Martin, a toddler with a constant runny nose and full diaper, until Frau Huber returned midafternoon.

The woman smiled at me. "There's mail for you on the kitchen table."

The word "mail" brought a lump to my throat. "*Danke.* I'll take it to my room." I didn't want to get teary-eyed in front of Ada—not when she thought I was so brave.

As I raced upstairs with the two envelopes addressed to me in hand, Frau Huber called, "When you're done, take the other mail to the bunkhouse."

In my stuffy attic room, I kicked off my shoes and climbed on the bed, nesting both envelopes between my crossed ankles. One had been posted back home in Munich a few days earlier. I didn't recognize the handwriting.

Dear Rennie,

I am Luana Weber, a nurse at University Hospital, writing this on behalf of Sophie Adler. Because of her arm injury and surgery, Sophie could not write you herself.

I almost dropped the letter. What arm injury and surgery? When did my best friend leave the polio hospital and go to University Hospital?

I thought you would want the enclosed letter Sophie and I began, even in its unfinished state. She began to dictate it late one day but grew tired and asked to finish another time, so I placed the letter in my uniform pocket and took it home. When I returned for my next shift, Sophie had been discharged. The cleaning staff found some personal correspondence stuffed under her mattress, including a letter with your return address on the envelope.

Sophie spoke of you often. She treasures your friendship. When you see her, give her my best.

L.W.

I removed the second sheet of paper from the same envelope, also written in Nurse Weber's hand. I knew who had dictated those words. Sophie!

Dear Rennie,

I found the missing items and sent them on their way! But I think the Pied Piper figured it out. All of it. Can you

I turned the paper over. Blank. I looked inside the envelope. Nothing else.

My stomach lurched. Had Werner really figured it all out? Even my role in helping Sophie?

And can I what?

The second piece of mail I'd received was written in my own hand. I'd addressed it to Sophie at the polio hospital, and it was postmarked two weeks earlier. Stamped across the envelope's front was **Return to Sender. No forwarding address.**

No forwarding address? If Sophie wasn't at the polio hospital and wasn't at University Hospital, she must have gone home. Why didn't they send her mail home?

From the doorway of the converted barn the Hubers used as a bunkhouse, I hollered, "Mail's here!" In moments, six girls appeared. As I called names, the girls crowded me, snatched envelopes, then darted off. Before I called two of the girls, Uta and Marie, I asked to speak with them in private. They were from my Munich neighborhood and had been childhood friends of mine and of Sophie's. With the others out of earshot, I handed Uta and Marie their mail and asked if they'd heard from Sophie.

"Um, no," Uta said. "Not for weeks."

Marie shook her head. "Me neither."

I shared the incomplete news I'd received. Marie was dating Sophie's stepbrother Klaus, so I was disappointed when all she offered was, "Klaus didn't mention her. I know he's back in Munich taking care of the bakery." She glanced around and lowered her voice. "You know, because of their parents' arrest."

Poor Herr and Frau Adler. Treason charges. I shuddered. "So, if Klaus is back home," I asked, "is that where Sophie went?" The two girls stared at me. I couldn't tell if they thought I had a point or if they thought I was a fool for asking. "And if she's home, why didn't the hospital forward her mail?"

Uta dismissed this with a wave of her hand. "Clerical error."

Marie chimed in. "Yes. Hospital staff saw an empty bed and didn't look further." They both turned heel and walked away.

That evening, I opened a drawer to get a nightgown and stopped short. The picture frame. I'd forgotten! Now I could display my favorite photo of Sophie and me.

An avid photographer, Sophie had snapped the photo several months before she got sick. We'd been on a Youth outing to the Neuschwanstein Castle. She posed me before a castle wall, set a timer on her camera, then hurried beside me. The photo captured us in profile, pointing and laughing at little brown birds that pecked at her nearby lunch. Our shared delight was as genuine and comfortable as our friendship.

I slid the precious photo into the Romany woman's frame and settled it in view on my nightstand. It was the last thing I saw when I turned off the light.

The next morning, I wrote two letters to try to learn Sophie's whereabouts. One was to my mother back home in Munich, asking her to inquire of Klaus at the Adler's family business, the *Bäckerei* Adler.

As I began the second letter, the one to Erich Fischer, I worked to steady my thoughts. Erich was a classmate of ours, a fine, handsome boy. He and Sophie were sweet on one another. Neither of them knew I was sweet on Erich too.

I kept the tone of my letter to Erich friendly. I shared the information I'd gotten from the nurse and asked if he'd heard from Sophie. After sealing the envelope, I held it to my chest, wishing, hoping. But I would never betray Sophie. A wish would have to do.

I busied myself with duty. From breakfast until midafternoon each day, I cared for the children, canned fruit, mended clothing, and kissed scraped knees. I delivered mail to the bunkhouse, weeded flower beds, and bathed the little ones. Before I collapsed into bed each night, I said my prayers, always including one for Erich and one for Sophie.

Sometimes, I was convinced Uta and Marie were right. Sophie had to be home with her brother, and "address unknown" was a clerical error. Other times, when the children's demands grated me raw and prevented my rest, a dark dread found its way into my heart. What if Werner really did know what Sophie had done? And what if he knew how I helped?

A day or two later, I auditioned for *Julius Caesar*. The director told me I was too young for any speaking part, even the role of the Soothsayer. I was to be part of the crowd scenes. No lines to learn and only the tiniest bit of makeup and costume. Nothing to practice. I thanked him for the chance to be onstage and kept my disappointment to myself.

About ten days after I mailed my letters, three envelopes arrived addressed to me. In the privacy of my attic room, I read my mother's letter first. I scanned her typical courtesies, asking about my health, that of the Huber family, the weather, and all manner of ordinary things. Then,

Regarding your friend, Sophie Adler. I stopped at her family's bakery to get some stollen. Sophie's stepbrother Klaus was there. He is running the shop by himself now, working dawn until dusk every day to keep the business going. Such a good boy. His parents' arrests have driven customers away, so the shop is not as busy as it had once been. Klaus closes for a few hours every day to make deliveries.

I inquired about Sophie. The last Klaus knew, she was at University Hospital. When I explained your confusing correspondence, he said she is not home and must have gone back to the polio hospital. Being such a hardworking boy, he hasn't had time to visit.

No help there.

The second letter was unexpected. It was from my troop leader in BDM, the League of German Girls.

Greetings, Renate.

I'm going to the Nuremberg Rally for the Hitler Youth Day in September. I've arranged for you to join me to represent our troop. This is a real opportunity for BDM to be part of the Rally's festivities.

We will stay at the home of my Tante Sabine right in Nuremberg. Enclosed please find the rail tickets for your round-trip passage.

Helga

While thrilled to be asked to represent my troop, I wondered—why me? Older members had put in more time and were more committed to the Movement than I was.

Getting to the Rally wasn't cheap either. Many Youth collected bottles and cashed in tin cans to fund their way. Here

Helga had gone and bought my rail ticket and provided housing too. Was she buttering me up because of the positions my brother and my uncle held?

I didn't know if my *Onkel* Edmund would attend the Rally, but I knew for sure my brother Werner would. Werner was the local *Scharführer,* the Youth Master Sergeant for our Munich neighborhood. He was always just so, all spit and polish and proper behavior. He demanded the same of me, urging me to tame my short, curly hair into impossibly neat braids, wondering aloud how I got gray eyes when our parents' eyes were blue. Everything about Werner shouted Party loyalty. Now, with the possibility he knew what Sophie and I had done…

I couldn't think about it.

I allowed the prospect of adventure in Nuremberg to bubble and energize me. I'd speak with Frau Huber about time off as soon as the children were in bed.

Seeing my name written in Erich's hand on the last envelope sent a little thrill through me. There, in the privacy of my room, I relished each word.

Dear Rennie,

Great to hear from you! Sounds as if you're busy this summer too.

To answer your main question, no. I haven't heard from Sophie, not since I saw her in July back home in Munich. Something happened that day. It's a long story, and I'm not fond of writing.

Are you going to the Nuremberg Rally? If so, perhaps we can meet so I can tell you the whole tale in private. Let me know so we might arrange a place and time.

Erich

I could picture it. There, in the midst of tens of thousands of people and a schedule jam-packed with parades and competitions and speeches, Erich would pull me away and walk with me, alone. Maybe our arms would brush, ever so lightly. Maybe as his gentle voice washed over me, I'd sink into his coffee-colored eyes…

I checked myself. My feelings couldn't interfere. Something important happened to Sophie in July, something Erich knew about. I'd listen to all he had to say. My emotions would have to stay locked inside my heart.

I touched the framed photo of Sophie and me on the nightstand. "Don't worry," I whispered. "I won't…" I pulled back and stared, then drew the frame close.

The image of Sophie and me seemed right, her arm outstretched and pointing, both of us laughing. But something was off. The individual stone blocks of the castle wall behind us were blurry, out of focus. I'd never noticed.

As I reached to replace the frame on the nightstand, I stopped midair and pulled it close a second time. I was certain that when the shutter clicked, I had been standing in place. Yet there in the photo, one of my feet was a bit ahead of the other. As if I'd taken a step.

I stared at the image for another few moments, then shrugged it off.

Chapter Two
Werner

West Palm Beach, Florida
2005

I hurl the TV remote across the room. Documentary, my ass. The person behind the camera chose the story. American television—all drama. Fairness and facts be damned.

The people they interviewed, they want to find their long-lost parents. More like long-dead parents. Why, they'd be dead, too, if it weren't for loyalists like me. Now we're to blame? We're to be charged? For what? For saving their sorry selves? Pah.

They'll never pin the blame on me. There's no proof. Words on paper—those are proof. My papers say I'm Willi Knox from Munich. All is in order. Has been for decades.

I work my way to the lumpy chair near the window and ease my bones into it. The sun warms my face. Reminds me of my youth—mountain hikes, campouts, boating on crystal blue lakes. The days when millions of us believed. When I close my eyes, the old excitement flutters within reach. Our vision of greatness. The prosperity we deserved.

A voice startles me. A nurse hovers in the doorway, flanked by a tall, thin woman in blue jeans and sandals. "Sorry to wake you, Mr. Knox," the nurse says, picking up pieces of the broken remote. "You have a visitor."

I peer at this stranger, this woman with salt-and-pepper hair. "What do you want?" I snap.

Her dark eyes scan me. No expression. "I'm Susanna Docken." British, I'd say from her accent. She extends a hand. Unlike her voice, her hand trembles as it comes near me.

I take in her bone structure, her dark skin tone. She's a *Mischling,* a mixed breed of half Negro and half white, I suspect. I don't shake her hand. "Willi Knox," I say.

She raises an eyebrow, then pulls up a chair and sits facing me. "Mind if I sit?"

Pah. Modern woman. Doing what she wants and asking permission afterward.

She settles something in her lap and taps it. "I've come to deliver this."

I focus on her face. She's in her fifties, about the same age as my purebloods are now. "Do I know you?"

In answer, she lifts a clear, zipped plastic bag from her lap and shakes it. "This has been in our family's safe-deposit box for years. Belongs to my sister. I believe it will be of interest to you."

I keep my hands limp in my lap. "Do I know her, your sister?"

She hesitates. "She'll visit in a few days. And yes. You knew her from Munich."

Memories surge, and I close my eyes to blot them out. Last time I saw my hometown of Munich, it was unrecognizable. Streets clogged with rubble. Medieval churches blasted apart. Windowless, roofless shells of homes. Smoldering ash and stinking, bloated corpses. No power, no food, no clean water. Shuffling hordes of vacant-eyed people. Stunned. Starved. Desperate. Like me.

Must be the sister knew the real Willi Knox, maybe even lived near him. Which means she lived near me too, in our *Altstadt* neighborhood. But I don't ask the name. I doubt I'll recognize it. Too long ago.

A small sound, and my eyes fly open. Susanna Docken still sits, watching me. "I considered mailing this to you"—she pats the plastic bag—"but I'd always hoped to deliver it in person. When my work called me to the States, well, I took advantage of the opportunity."

I clench the bottom of my shirt and raise my voice. "What is it you want?"

She purses her lips, then rises and places the bag on my lap. The bag holds a picture frame and a dark book. "I want you to read this journal," she says.

I wave her away. "Can't read much. Bad eyes." I'm lying, but she doesn't know that.

"Then I'll read it to you." Before I can object, she unzips the plastic bag and pulls out the book. She squats beside my chair, opening the book so we can both see the handwritten first page. My heart jumps. It's written in German. This woman, this stranger with the British accent, reads to me in my native language.

If I am accused of illegal or treasonous activity, I write these words on behalf of others. Any consequence for my actions must fall only on me. I have acted alone. My late father's friend, whom we called Onkel Edmund Koch, my mother Liesel Müller, and my brother Werner Müller were, to my knowledge, unaware of my involvement in said activities. Likewise, my employer, Klaus Lange of die Bäckerei des Volkes, my friends, and my neighbors were not part of my scheme. They are blameless.

I shoulder sole responsibility for what I have done. With the grace of God, I accept whatever path my life now takes.

Renate (Rennie) Müller

3 January 1939

I'm stunned. After all these years, a letter from my sister.

If this had come to light in '39, all would have been different. I might have had a legacy.

If only.

Oh, Anna.

"There's a bit more. A postscript," she says. "A quote from *Julius Caesar*: 'For let the gods so speed me, as I love the name of honour more than I fear death.'"

My hand trembles as I press the journal's cover closed. I recover my breath and force stiffness into my voice. "Why bring this to me?"

"I've done my research," she says. "I've spent years tracking down this person, this Werner Müller." She gestures to the page. "He was from Munich, as you were." I must look confused because she clarifies. "Databases. Birth and death records, military service, baptisms, marriages—it's all out there. There's even a computer program to show how a person will look as they age."

Such nonsense. As if some newfangled machine tells the truth better than my paperwork.

"I've come to meet you and share this journal with you. To tell you what I know and to hear what you remember of my origins. You see, my sister and I believe you are Werner Müller."

My breath comes short. Right on the heels of the documentary. Another wave of Nazi hunters. Not now, not when this endless life is almost over. I gather my voice and wave her off. "You are mistaken. I am Willi Knox."

"What a shame. I wanted to thank Werner Müller."

I'm curious, but I dare say nothing.

Doesn't matter because she continues. "Werner Müller saved my life."

I stare at this woman, that skin like toast, those dark eyes and hair. Certainly not one of my Aryan purebloods. And yet her unexpected visit has cracked my shell. "He...he saved your life? This Müller fellow?"

She tips her head, and the fluorescent light picks up gray streaks. "When I was an infant."

I continue to stare at her. The words "How can that be?" exit my lips without my permission.

She gestures with the book. "My sister and I have pieced together much of the story. Everything is documented here, right after the letter I read to you. Shall I continue?"

I'm tempted, but it's too much. "No."

Again, she ignores my command and does what she wants. "There's also a photo." She pats the plastic bag. "And the picture frame, of course."

"Ach!" I wave her away.

"My sister will bring another photo or two from those years. We can slip them in this picture frame and..."

"Get out! Get out!" With effort, I rise and lurch a step or two toward the door. "And take that book with you!"

She stands and brushes off her lap, unaffected by my outburst. "I'll leave everything with you." She slides the book into the plastic bag and places it on the empty chair. "About the picture frame. When you're in a better mood, I'll show you how it works. The result is quite remarkable." She turns to the door and pauses, looking back at me. "Rest easy, Werner Müller." Then she is gone.

I'm trying to recover my breath when a nurse barges in with that wheeled blood pressure contraption. She smiles. "I hear you had a visitor."

I roar at her. "Every five minutes someone bothers me. First her. Then you. Mosquitoes."

She clucks her tongue and goes about her nurse business. When she finishes, she says, "Did your visitor bring you a gift?" She peers at the plastic bag and its contents. "Looks old."

"Like me." When she leaves, I climb in bed and tug the blankets over my shoulders. I'm treated to memories—or are they dreams?—of sunny Alpine campsites, lines of fit, disciplined Youth. We march and sing, filled with the joyful promise of our future, of our value to our leader's plan. Even now I mouth the words that defined the dream, words I pledged so long ago: "In the presence of this Blood Banner, which represents our Führer, I swear to devote all my energies and my strength to the Savior of our country, Adolf Hitler. I am willing and ready to give up my life for him, so help me, God."

The Allies, they destroyed the dream. Traitors like my sister and her crippled friend helped them.

The familiar weight of loss crushes me. Loss of the greatest leader the world has ever known. Loss of my role as Youth Master Sergeant, the Scharführer, a title I held until age eighteen. Over one hundred young people under my command back then. I encouraged their skills, exercised their bodies, and focused their energies. I shaped their loyalties down to their very thoughts to create a disciplined machine. Under my leadership, we answered our country's call.

Does that role connect me to this Susanna Docken and her sister? Why do they have a letter from my sister, a letter that could have—that should have—vindicated me decades ago? If only…

I must know what this book contains, what damage might result if it came to light. Nazi hunters are still around. They're everywhere. The documentary I just saw proves that. I climb from bed, tuck the plastic bag bundle under my arm, and shuffle down the hall.

The solarium is filled with plants and sunlight. No people. Perfect. I sit with my back in a corner and pull the bag's plastic zipper. A scent emerges, dust and age, like the clothes in the back of my closet. With it comes more memories. Renate weeping when *Vater* died. My sister again—I don't want her so close in my thoughts!—as a young teen the last time I saw her at the rail station, ducking into a black sedan. My teeth grind.

I reach in the bag and pull out the cold, rectangular picture frame. It's small, about as long as my hand. Each side is two fingers wide with a worn engraving of twisted vines. I close one eye and turn it this way and that, inspecting for engraved initials, perhaps a small cleft that might hold a note or a key. Nothing. An ordinary picture frame. Glass front. Leathery backboard with one of those foldout wings to stand the frame up. Damn thing's not even real silver.

The family kept this in a safe-deposit box? They thought this was valuable? Pah. Fools.

I shove the frame back in the bag and pull out the book. Eyeglasses perched on my nose, I tip my head this way and that to read the first page again. There it is. My sister absolved me of blame way back in '39. The truth of it rushes through me.

I press a hand to the wall and bolt upright, sending my lap's contents to the floor. I begin to pace. If only I were young and fit enough to run.

One of those flitting nurses walks past. "Mr. Knox," she says as she rushes in and grabs my arm. "Settle down. What has you so upset?" I bark at her, tell her I can walk. Two more people appear and force me into a wheelchair. "Here, you dropped these," one says. She slips the book into the plastic bag and plops it on my lap.

These bits of my past crush me, burn me. I must destroy them. They must never be found.

Without my permission, I'm pushed to my room. "Into bed you go," a nurse says, almost lifting me from the chair and depositing me there.

When she starts to place the bag on a shelf in my closet, I yell, "Ach, too high," and gesture to the windowsill. She complies and closes the door as she leaves.

Those nurses are informants. They'll tell that Susanna woman I was upset. She'll know she's right. I am Werner. She'll tell someone who will tell someone else…

The evidence must be destroyed.

I shove the bag under my arm and shuffle to the bathroom. The nurses leave a box of gloves near the sink, and I pull on a pair. I cover the closed toilet with layers of clean paper towels, then sit on the lid and start the shower.

Water. The great purifier. Many times, I've seen water used to purify a litter, to eliminate imperfect, unwanted creatures. So must this unwelcome book be eliminated.

As the water warms, I open the plastic bag and slide the contents out again. The book's cover is burgundy leather, chipped at the edges and veined with yellowed cracks and creases. I press the cover back. It crackles like my knees. With the thick stack of pages against my leg, I tug at the cover, but it holds tight. That old picture frame—I use a corner of it as a knife. In less than a minute, I cut through the front cover's binding and free it from the pages. The brittle pages are bound by a stiff net along the spine, tan and mottled as a brindle underbelly. Most sheets are curled at the edges and smudged with dirt. Contaminated. I'm glad for the gloves.

I'm ready to cut off the back cover when I notice—the entries are handwritten in German. With an inexplicable hunger, I read a few pages. The entries are a series of dates with a notation below each: *11/12/45, No response to my Red Cross enquiry. 01/02/46, Ad posted in seven German newspapers...* That sort of thing.

I shake myself back to the present. I will not be distracted from my task. Again, I raise the frame's corner and prepare to cut. Again, I halt. The book's pages have shifted, and something dark sticks out between them. It's a photograph, a faded black and white. A water stain mars part of the image, but recognition slams me. A wiry adolescent holding the hand of his curly-haired sister. Me and Renate. The loyalist and the traitor.

I have been found.

I must destroy this photo. I will tear it to shreds.

I want to caress it, keep it at my bedside.

I remember.

I must forget.

There's a knock, and the door behind me opens. A nurse pushes into the bathroom saying, "You know better than to shower without help." She sees me clothed, seated on the closed toilet lid, elbows on knees, a sharp metal object clasped in my hand. In a flash, she grabs the frame away and pushes a red button on the wall. A burly orderly appears from nowhere.

I shove the photo inside the book and protest that I want to be left alone. The nurse will have none of it. She carries on—sharp objects, harm to myself, wet floors, risk of falls. Pah. Such nonsense. I tell her I wasn't going to hurt myself, wasn't taking a shower in my clothes. She doesn't listen. The orderly shuts the spigot and hauls me to bed.

The nurse continues to scold as if I were a child: I should never do myself harm, I'm to rest, she'll call the doctor and have him prescribe something to settle me down. On and on. She tells the orderly to stay with me and bustles from the room.

A bodyguard I have now.

"Bring my things from the bathroom," I tell him. He obeys, and places the plastic bag, the book with its half-removed cover, and the old photo on my lap. The metal picture frame he places on a high closet shelf.

That won't stop me.

A stooped woman comes in pushing a cart of paperbacks. If she wore a kerchief, she could pass for a Polish peasant. I tell her no, I don't want her *verlaust* books. But when I hear her voice in the next room, I tell the orderly to get me a National Geographic magazine.

Those are kept in the hospital library two floors down. That'll keep him busy.

When he leaves, I use one of the long-handled reachers they give us old people to grab the frame. I shove it in the plastic bag with the rest of my former life and shuffle from the room, scanning the walls for the incinerator chute. The nurses ignore me, chattering and buzzing, clacking their computer keys and talking on the phone.

I pass the front of the station and start to circle one side. One of the nurses looks at me, and her mouth moves, but I can barely hear her words. Something about the doctor and my blood pressure. She's mumbling. I wiggle a finger in my ear. Doesn't help.

My foot drags. I glance down. My slipper is stuck. I can't lift it.

The hall tilts.

I can't move my foot. I reach for the edge of the nurse's station. My hand touches nothing. My vision blurs.

Damn nurses gave me bad pills.

The glaring tile floor rushes toward my face.

Pain.

Darkness.

Silence.

Then. Rest.

Blessed rest.

Quiet.

Peace.

I'm aware of the passage of time. A minute? A week?

Doesn't matter. I'm content. Neither here nor there. Floating between.

A sound breaks in. No, a series of sounds. Faint.

A voice, I think. Yes, a voice.

The voice grows louder. It fights its way through my silent darkness. It disturbs my rest, but I'm happy to hear it. Eager even. The voice speaks words I've missed hearing. Words I haven't spoken openly for decades.

The voice speaks German.

Chapter Three
Rennie

Freising, Germany
3 September 1938

From her bed, Frau Huber said, "I'm too sick to work at the market today." The sun had risen an hour before, and Otto stood dressed and ready at his mother's bedroom door. "Bring me some water, would you, Son?" He obeyed, and she lifted her pale face to meet the cup he brought. She sipped, then collapsed back on the pillow.

I kept my place in the doorway. I'd heard her retching during the night and didn't want to get too close. "How can I help you, Frau Huber?" I asked.

"Pack a bag for the two little ones. Drop them off at my sister's, then go with Otto to the market." The woman lifted her chin to Otto. "Get Conrad up and dressed. He's going with you too."

Otto's eyes widened. "I can't watch that little troublemaker while I work the stand."

Frau Huber wagged a finger at her son. "No back talk, young man. Conrad can help. Renate will keep an eye on him."

Otto, Conrad, and I opened the Huber's market stand at ten *Uhr*, a full two hours later than usual. Otto arranged produce in the center of the sloped display, his movements practiced and precise. A line of homemade bread and rolls fronted the produce, and a raised shelf of jarred pickles, red cabbage, and kraut provided a backdrop. His finishing touch was to unroll and hang a fringed canopy to protect the goods from the elements. The overall arrangement was pleasing to the eye—not too cluttered, not too sparse. I smiled at Otto and said, "You've got quite a knack for this." He beamed.

Conrad watched his older brother for a time, but in fewer than five minutes he grew restless. "What are we supposed to do all day?" he asked. "Stand here and look at onions? I'm going exploring."

I grabbed his arm. "Not alone, you're not." I turned to Otto. "Are you all right here for a little while?" He assured me he was, so Conrad and I left to explore together.

Compared to the huge *Viktualienmarkt* back home in Munich, the farm market was small—only a couple dozen carts and booths. At one cart, a lovely young woman stood behind a colorful array of cut flowers, arranging baskets and wrapping stems. As we approached, she paused and smiled, reaching a daisy to Conrad. He reddened and hurried past. I caught the woman's eye and shrugged. "Boys," we said at the same time, laughing. She gestured with the daisy. "For you then." I thanked her and tucked its stem behind my ear.

Pungent smells drew us to a canopied booth. A large-boned woman with a huge knife stood behind a full round of cheese, carving off slivers and offering samples to passersby. Conrad gulped his piece without chewing. Not me. I let the buttery tang melt on my tongue so the taste would linger.

We continued this way around the market, stopping at the sausage maker, the confectioner, and a small eatery whose entire menu was coarse, dark bread and soup. We strolled past other customers—a waddling woman with bulging shopping bags, a bicyclist with leafy vegetables protruding from a basket.

A few meters ahead of us, a knot of people clustered near a wagon. Some waved their arms and pointed; others spoke in raised voices. Conrad leaned forward as if to bolt into the fray. I grabbed his shoulder to slow him as we approached.

Two figures carried a table through the wagon's back doors and placed it in line with the booths around the market square. Gestures and grumbled words of protest formed an undercurrent among the folks gathered there.

Conrad and I moved closer. I knew that wagon's peeling sides, the bright scrollwork along the top edge. I knew the short woman who reemerged through the doors. I knew the skinny boy carrying a box behind her.

The Romany woman settled a basket on the table and began unpacking and arranging its contents despite the crowd's objections. One man stomped away, announcing, "*Zigeuner*! I'll be back with the authorities!" Several people stepped back, arms crossed, their expressions satisfied. Others hurried away, heads down.

I turned to Conrad. "Go on back to Otto. I need to speak with these people."

His voice was filled with wonder. "Gypsies! Will they tell your fortune?"

I laughed. "No. I've met them before. I want to see what they're selling."

"Why do I have to leave?"

"Because when security comes, there might be trouble."

Conrad's grin spoke of curiosity and excitement. "Mother said you're to watch me today. I have to stay with you."

I hesitated, then consented. As I approached the Romany, Conrad slowed until he fell half a step behind me, clutching my skirt and almost hiding in my shadow. That boy.

The table displayed dozens of squat, lidded jars and glass bottles of all sizes, each labeled and topped with a cork. Their colored contents ranged from chalky white and sea green to brick red and black as coal. The labels indicated these were medicines—herbal remedies for fever and stomach ailments, syrups for coughs and colds, ointments for warts and bruises, potions and infusions for body aches and gout. "Nice to see you again," I said. "I'm Renate Müller."

The woman set her dark eyes on mine. "I remember." She didn't smile as she said it but kept her expression serious and her gaze steady on mine.

I tried to meet her stare, but it was like playing the "who blinks first" game. I dropped my eyes to the goods on the table and cleared my throat. "So, do you make these remedies?"

"I do."

The young boy reappeared lugging two chairs that he placed alongside the table. As when we'd met before, he grinned, hitching up the back of his ill-fitting pants every few steps. "I find the plants," he announced, "and *Dya* makes the concoctions. Then we sell them." I smiled at the boy, trying in vain to remember his name. He and Conrad introduced themselves. Bruno—that was it.

I gestured to the goods on the table. "I've never seen remedies in so many colors."

"Color tells us much." The woman touched one vial. "Red. The color of war and power. Good for a sluggish system." She tapped another. "Green—stability and safety. When a body needs to maintain good health." And lifting another, she said, "Black" and placed it back on the table.

"What does black medicine do?" I asked.

She frowned. "Black is for serious illness. Even in your culture, black means death, *nicht*?"

I blinked, then tried to change the subject. "What's your favorite color, Conrad?"

"Brown. Like mud." The boy grinned.

"And like chocolate," Bruno added, nodding. "What's yours, Rennie?"

"Yellow. Blue is a close second."

The Romany woman smiled, perhaps for the first time. "Yes, yellow for joy and energy. That you have in plenty." Her gaze settled on my face, then bored deep again. I shifted. "Blue. Blue is your challenge." She broke her gaze and turned to her wares.

I was almost afraid to ask. "Why blue? What does blue mean?"

"Trust. Loyalty."

Why would she say that? I was trustworthy. What I'd done for Sophie proved I could be loyal.

During our conversation, a dozen people had continued to huddle and mutter nearby without approaching. An older man shuffled past them to the table of goods. With a nod to the Romany woman, he picked up a jar of liniment. "For rheumatism?" he asked.

She nodded. The old man then asked for an elixir to help him sleep. The woman asked him to turn in a circle and studied his size and shape a few moments. Then she pursed her lips and plodded into the wagon, returning with two amber vials topped with tiny corks. "For a man your size, this will last a couple weeks. A spoonful before bed. No more. No less. Wash it down with water. You'll sleep like a baby." Smiling, the man paid for the vials and the liniment and went on his way.

Conrad and I stepped aside as the security guard arrived. “Your papers, please,” he asked the woman, his hand outstretched. He scanned each page, nodding. As he did, I saw more shoppers stop to watch, waiting and pointing. They hovered like vultures ready to pounce at the first sign of weakness. I shuddered.

“All is in order,” the security guard announced. He turned to the bystanders. “She has a permit. Go about your business.” Seeing no prey, the vultures dispersed.

The guard turned back to the woman’s goods, lifting jars and reading labels. “I’m glad you’re here today, Frau Lunka. We’re going to my mother-in-law’s next week.” He groaned and patted the roundness of his belly. “Which is the one I’ve bought before, the one for indigestion?”

She handed him a tallish brown bottle. He read the label, nodding. “That’s the one.” He tapped the bottle with one finger and winked at Bruno. “This stuff is magic.” He dug in a pocket and paid for the syrup, then tucked both the bottle and his change in a pocket. The woman, Frau Lunka, I now knew, nodded, expressionless.

Conrad and Bruno had chattered together during this exchange. When an engine roared overhead, their attention shifted skyward. Pointing in excitement, the boys traced the plane’s track. Once out of sight, Conrad asked Bruno, “Have you ever been in a plane?”

“No. Have you?”

“Not yet. But I’m going to be a pilot when I grow up.” Conrad spread his arms and zoomed around the display table. After one pass, he stopped and faced Bruno. “You could be my copilot.” Again, he zoomed off, this time with Bruno right behind him, their arms spread and lips vibrating to imitate a motor. The guard watched their antics, then strolled off, chuckling.

One corner of Frau Lunka's mouth was lifted in amusement, but in moments, her expression tightened. Her icy focus trained on the laughing, chattering boys. The words she spoke were to no one in particular. "Not a plane. A train. Yes. Trains for both of them." She stiffened, then in a whirl of skirts, she turned and bolted into the wagon. In moments, a howl erupted from within the wagon. Bruno stopped short, then rushed into the wagon too.

I started after them, but Conrad tugged me back, his gaze darting from the wagon's closed door to the open marketplace. "Let's go," he said. "We…we have to check on Otto." The woman's wail softened, and I heard Bruno cooing to her.

"Wait here." I gestured to their table of medicines. "Guard this."

Bruno answered the wagon's door, his brow glistening with sweat. Behind him lay his mother, curled on the floor, writhing, sobbing. I asked, "Should I send for a doctor?"

He stepped forward and closed the door behind him. "What did she say before she"—he hesitated as another howl rose—"before she got this way?"

"You boys were talking about planes, and she sort of froze."

The boy squeezed my arm. "And then what?"

"She said planes weren't for you. Trains were. Then this."

Bruno glanced around the marketplace. The vultures had returned. "I'll pack up," he said. "No customers will come by now."

Conrad and I helped him collect the items they'd hoped to sell. In ten minutes, Bruno climbed into the driver's seat, and the horse and wagon pulled away.

Even by Monday morning, Frau Huber was not feeling herself. "What can I get you?" I asked from a safe distance. "Ginger ale? Tea?"

She waved the suggestion away. "Take the little ones to my sister's again. And please work the market stand with the boys."

"Of course. I'll get things ready."

When I turned to leave, she spoke. "Oh, and Renate? Your leave for the Rally. I doubt I'll be well enough to manage without you by midweek."

I nodded, arranging my expression to one of acceptance. In truth, I was crushed. I'd not only miss the Rally, I'd lose a quick visit home to check on Sophie's whereabouts. And of course, I'd miss the chance to speak with Erich alone at the Rally.

In less than an hour, I'd settled Ada and Martin at their aunt's house, and Otto, Conrad, and I were setting up at the market. I must have been quiet while we unpacked crates of peaches because Otto asked if I was feeling well. "I hope you're not catching the flu my mother has."

"No, I'm fine," I snapped, then returned to my work.

Otto scowled. "You're not fine."

"Yeah, you're grumpy," Conrad said. "Like this." He folded his arms across his chest.

Otto duplicated the pose, and the two of them faced me, holding the expression until all three of us laughed. "Sorry," I said. "I was approved for a visit home to check on…" I hesitated. "Well, things I need to attend to. Then on

Wednesday, I have tickets for the Nuremberg Rally. Guess I'll miss that too."

Conrad's eyes sparkled. "Oh, I'd love to go to the Rally."

Otto agreed. "It sounds so exciting, all those people in those huge stadiums. You know, they have tanks and rows of soldiers marching in formation."

"Plus music and parades," Conrad chimed in.

Otto nodded. "A boy from Freising's Youth troop went last year. He said the torchlight parade was incredible. Said you have to see it to believe it."

I'd heard similar tales. All I could say was, "Maybe next year."

Otto seemed lost in thought. "It seems a shame to miss it because Mother is ill. I can manage the market by myself for a day or two."

Conrad chirped, "I could take care of the house."

I laughed aloud. "Nothing doing. I've seen your bedroom."

He frowned. "Fine. Then I'll take care of Ada and Martin."

"This from the boy who won't change Martin's diapers and hides snakes in a false-bottom basket!"

Conrad gave a "humph" and kicked at little stones. I tousled his hair. Otto smiled at his brother, then returned to arranging the produce. Conrad looked up, his face bright. "What we need is some magic. And I know where we can get some!" He grabbed my wrist and tugged me along.

"Don't worry about the produce," Otto said, laughing. "I'll finish the display myself."

Conrad led me through the market until we reached the now familiar wagon and its table of medicinals. Bruno, wearing the same ill-fitting clothes he'd been wearing on Saturday, was arranging jars. He moved to the wagon door and poked his head in. "Dya? They're back, Rennie and that Conrad boy." Mumbled voices, then "Yes, the one who wants to be a pilot."

I feared a repeat performance of the woman's upset. "I…we don't want to disturb your mother if she's resting," I began, but Frau Lunka pushed through the door. She seemed to have recovered from the, well, whatever it was.

Conrad spoke to her with the confidence of one who knows he'll get what he's asking for. "It's my mother. She's been vomiting."

Lips pressed into a single line, the woman's dark gaze slid past me and focused on Conrad. He squirmed but to his credit, he stood straight and bore it. "Your mother, she is a big woman?" Frau Lunka asked. Conrad looked to me for help.

"She's my height, but she's had four children." I spread my arms. "Broader than me."

The woman nodded, twirling her finger to indicate I should turn. I complied. She nodded and lifted a tall orange bottle. "For vitality. A spoonful when her stomach is empty. Nothing with it. No food, no drink. Nothing. One hour later, a glass of water." She reached the bottle to Conrad but continued to speak to me, giving detailed instructions on medicine doses and the gradual increase of water and food intake needed. Her finger twirled, this time as the hands of a clock. "Every four hours day and night until Wednesday evening."

Conrad looked jubilant. "And then she'll be better?"

The woman nodded, her expression serious. "If she follows this."

If Frau Huber was indeed better, I could leave early Thursday. Sure, I'd miss the chance to visit home and check on Sophie's whereabouts, but at least I'd be to Nuremberg in time for Youth Day activities.

Frau Lunka turned her piercing gaze on me. "You have chosen your path."

"I beg your pardon?"

"The step you plan to take. You will move onto one of the paths."

"I'm not walking anywhere. I'll take the train."

Frau Lunka flinched at my clumsy word choice. I paid for the medicine and started away.

Not far down the market square, a shrill whistle sounded. A tall, thin security guard trailed by five or six uniformed Hitler Youth approached the Romany's table of goods. Two girls in white blouses and dark blue skirts waited behind the boys. Uta and Marie. Why were they here—and in their BDM uniforms?

"Where's your permit?" the security guard asked Frau Lunka, his tone demanding.

She produced it from an apron pocket. "The regular guard knows me. Checked my papers the other day."

The guard scanned the papers, his nostrils flaring. He thrust them back at her, then peered over her assortment of goods. "He's on vacation." Gesturing to the Youth who stood a meter behind him, he continued, "Today you deal with me and my helpers."

I grew uneasy and touched Conrad's shoulder. "Go to our stand. Stay there with Otto until I get back." Eyes wide, he scooted away. I approached Uta and Marie. "What are they planning?"

Uta tossed her glossy hair. "How would I know? Karl asked us to walk into town with him and his friends today. So, we came."

Marie shrugged. "It's our day off, and we're on an outing. No harm in that."

Their defensiveness spoke volumes. I turned to the Romany's table and inched toward it.

Frau Lunka faced the security guard. "I have a permit."

The guard snorted and flicked his hand at the wagon. "For today, maybe. You and your kind will be gone soon enough."

She pressed her hands against her table, leaning forward over her goods. The guard leaned toward her, their positions mirrored in a standoff. Seconds ticked. Neither spoke. The watchful Youth shifted, fists clenching and unclenching. The guard stepped away. "Boys, show this *Zigeuner* what we think of her kind."

With whoops of glee, they attacked.

One Youth upended the table, knocking it toward Frau Lunka. Bottles and jars crashed around her. Glass shards peppered her exposed shins. Multicolored liquids splashed every which way, staining her shoes, her shins, her clothes.

With eagle-sharp vision, other Youth scoured the ground. When they spotted an unbroken bottle, they raised it in triumph and propelled it to the earth, renewing the shower of glass and precious liquids. Each smash brought another howl of laughter.

Frau Lunka endured it all, flinching and startling with each new crash but standing her ground. Narrow crimson ribbons trickled down her legs and mixed with splotches of medicinal green, golden yellow, and black. In less than a minute, the destruction was over. The boys stood panting, their uniforms spotted and dripping with multicolored splatter.

After several silent moments, the Romany woman raised a shaky finger and pointed it at each of the offending teens.

"Stained uniforms," she said, her voice trembling. Her gaze bored into them one at a time. "Many boys. Many stains, dark ones. Much red. Much black. What you boys have done here, so it will be done to you."

A Romany curse. I backed away.

She then turned her penetrating stare to the snickering security guard. "And you," she growled. "May black thorns surround you, block your way. Beware the black thorns…"

I turned to flee the curse-filled air, but movement at the front of the wagon caught my eye. The poor horse was thrashing, no doubt frightened by the breaking glass and harsh laughter. Skinny little Bruno held her neck in a struggle to calm her. I hurried over. "What do you want me to do?"

"Stand by me and speak softly." I knew precious little about horses, but somehow, together, we soothed the old girl. Bruno bridled her, then hitched the harness to the wagon. He climbed into the driver's seat and grabbed the reins.

I started. "But your mother!"

As if in answer, the door in the wagon's roof pushed open, and Frau Lunka's head emerged like a turtle from its shell. Her ominous tone chilled me. "You have chosen your path, Renate Müller. Now you must face the consequences." The roof door slapped shut.

Laughing and shouting, the Youth picked up what few jars remained intact and hurled them at the retreating wagon. One hit its target and shattered on the back door, leaving a russet splotch over a painted wood panel.

The security guard and the Youth clapped one another on the back while dozens of silent gawkers stood nearby. A single figure strode through the crowd and saluted.

My brother Werner.

Chapter Four
Werner

West Palm Beach, Florida
2005

It's a woman's voice, speaking German. The words are unclear, but I long to see who is speaking my native language so close to my side. Anna? Could it be?

I try to rouse, to pull myself from the depths. The effort pounds against my skull. The throbs don't stop, so I give up and allow the words' familiar cadence to lull me to sleep. Sometime later, I hear one side of a conversation in English. A woman. "No, not yet. Soon, I hope." A pause, then, "I'll see you Thursday. Safe travels." A pause. "Love you too."

The voice is not Anna's, cannot be. She'd be my age, and this voice is younger and accented. I've heard it before. The pounding in my head is softer now, a rap of knuckles, so I work through it. My eyes crack open. Fluorescent lights over the bed blind me. The headache returns. I moan and shut out the world.

A whoosh of air nearby, then the same woman's voice. "Nurse? Yes, he's up."

Pah. I'm not up.

Now I recognize the voice. It's the *Mischling*, the one who figured out…

Soft-soled shoes squeak on the tile floor as someone approaches. "Mr. Knox, can you open your eyes?"

Can I? Yes. Do I want to? *Nein.* I want to go back to oblivion.

"Come on, Mr. Knox. The lights are off now. We've drawn the blinds."

If I don't respond, she'll leave me alone.

"Your visitor is here." A hand presses my shoulder, shakes it, taps it.

Ach. Nurses here are annoying as mosquitoes. I don't have the strength to swat her away. I take a breath and force my eyes open a crack. She's right, the light is softer. It doesn't stab. I take a few moments to focus.

A nurse hovers nearby, flicking the IV line with her finger. She glances down at me and forces a smile. "Lie still now. Take it slow. I'm glad you're awake, Mr. Knox."

Liar. She's not glad at all. Easier to poke and prod an unconscious lump. Do whatever you want to them. They won't know.

I wonder what they did to me.

I wonder what I said.

A voice comes from my other side. "Mr. Knox." I turn slowly and there she is, the Mischling. What was her name? Susan? Something like that. "Mr. Knox," she repeats. "It's good to see you again."

I open my mouth to speak, but pressure shoots into my skull. She lays a gentle hand on my shoulder and in German, says, "Don't try to talk. Rest. I'll do the talking."

A prison! I'm captive in this bed! Bound here by my feeble body and knocking headache. Forced to listen to a stranger who knows my true identity. I want to be gone! I struggle to rise, then collapse into the sheets.

The nurse clucks her tongue. "When I said to take it slow, I wasn't just whistling Dixie."

I sink into the pillow until the pounding stops. The nurse jabbers on, and her words echo inside me. I catch bits about my blood pressure, a fall, a concussion. It all comes back to me then. I was on my way to the incinerator with the book, the damn photograph, the decades-too-late letter.

When I peek from beneath my lids, the nurse is gone, but the other woman still sits at my bedside. In her hand, I see the yellowed back of a square of paper. It's the incriminating photograph of me and Renate. I open my mouth to protest, but I stop. I failed to destroy it. I must try again. And soon.

She regards me, this woman. My brows furrow in a vain attempt to tamp down the pain behind my eyes, so I'm sure I look angry. Pah. Don't care.

She glances behind her as if making sure she's not overheard. "Do you remember me then, Werner?"

"Name?" I croak.

"Susanna. Susanna Docken."

I give a small nod. Then I lift a hand to my chest. "Willi Knox."

She huffs. "Whatever you say." She turns the photo to me. I'm drawn to it like a magnet. There we are, my sister and me in our Sunday best at our home's front door. We both squint in the sunshine but we look happy, as if all is right with the world. Pah. I knew nothing then.

"Nice shot of you both," she says. She flips it over and reads, "At home, '33."

All of thirteen, I was. Before Vater's death. Before my role as Scharführer and the summer of '38 when Renate and her crippled friend turned against me. I took the blame for Renate, protected her as I promised Vater I would. Paid for it too. At first, Renate seemed to understand, appreciate what I'd done for her. Felt guilty—or so she said.

After Nuremberg, she promised —no, she swore—she'd be loyal to me. I took her at her word. I trusted her a second time. Fool me once, shame on you. Fool me twice…

Susanna's words interrupt my thoughts. "So, when my sister received this picture frame, it was in pieces. Four sides, glass front, leather backboard. She didn't know what to think." I peer at her. She notices and nods. "And she wondered—why was this important enough to pass on to her? There was only one way to find out.

"She snapped the sides together, added the glass front and the backboard. When she slid this photo"—she waves the incriminating item in her hand—"into the frame, it looked fine." She pauses there as if waiting for me to catch up. No need. I'm curious about the old frame too. "But within moments…well, you can see this for yourself." She slides the photograph into place.

It's been decades since I've seen that photograph in a frame. I've tried to forget. I allow my heavy lids to close.

"You're missing it. The transformation." Her voice demands my attention.

Doesn't she know I don't feel well? I'm recovering from a high blood pressure episode and a concussion. Does she think it's all right to harass an old man with her ancient history? I long to say all this, but exhaustion overtakes me.

When I awaken, the bedside chair is empty. The room is dark except for the thin beam of hallway light beneath my closed door. My head feels better. I'm thirsty. I prop on an elbow and buzz the nurse. And again. Finally, a skinny woman in a nurse's uniform pushes the door open, light pouring in with her. "What's up, buttercup?" she says, flicking on the overhead light as well.

I squint against the sudden brightness, waiting for the headache to start. It doesn't. I say, "Drink."

She peers at me, then winks. "Mm-hmm. No beer yet, Mr. Knox."

Some joke. I open my mouth to rage at her but stop. Because out of the corner of my eye, I notice something odd. The photo in the frame—it has changed.

Chapter Five
Rennie

Freising, Germany
5 September 1938

Werner lifted his chin and looked past his long nose at the mess of broken glass and splattered liquids. The Youth who had done the deed straightened and snapped to attention. "*Heil, Hitler*," they announced, almost in unison.

In the weeks since I'd seen him, Werner hadn't changed much. Even though he was short and wiry, his bearing, brisk walk, and crisp uniform still commanded attention. The Freising boys weren't in his troop, but they recognized his authority.

My knees trembled. "What are you doing here? I thought you'd be on your way to the Rally."

"I came to see you, little sister," he said in his high-pitched whine. "Walk with me." He strode a few steps from the broken bottles, then turned back to the Youth. "Get that cleaned up."

"Did you have something to do with this?" I said, matching his stride. "With the Youth wrecking Frau Lunka's table?"

He clicked his tongue. "Have you learned nothing, Renate? I sent you away from the bad influences of the city and placed you under the nose…"

"Under whose nose?"

Werner's lips drew to pencil thinness, and he lifted a finger to silence me. "Ah, little sister. As I suspected"—he gestured to the spot the Romany wagon had occupied—"you must be protected."

"Me? Frau Lunka is the one who needs protection."

"Your services will no longer be needed at the Huber's farm." I started, but his finger shushed me. "You are to return to Munich after the Rally and live at home with me and *Mutter*."

"But I have two months left on my assignment! Frau Huber and the children need me!"

"It's decided."

My face grew hot and I stood stock-still, arms folded across my chest. "I can make my own decisions. I'm staying at the farm until November, until the harvest. I just got a role in a community play." He didn't need to know it was a bit part. "Already have my costume and makeup and everything."

Werner stopped walking and faced me, tipping his head to one side in a gratuitous manner. "You'll go home. No argument."

I was stunned into silence, then gathered myself. "Who will watch the children? Frau Huber has been sick…"

He waved his hand. "One of the girls will transfer down from the bunkhouse. They'll be glad for the easy assignment."

My voice was loud and shrill. "Easy? You think it's easy to work from sunup until well past sundown? To feed and bathe the children, to cook and clean and fix bicycles?" Werner walked on. I followed, throwing my rhetorical questions at his back. "You think it's easy to put up pickles, make bread, and weed the garden all while the baby is napping? And wash clothes and settle children's arguments, fill the root cellar with potatoes and turnips?"

Tittering laughter nearby drew my attention. As I'd followed in my brother's wake, hollering and waving my arms, a dozen or so women had stopped their shopping to watch. Their expressions showed amusement. Two or three gave me nods of encouragement.

Werner must have heard the laughter too because he stopped and stiffened, his back to me and the onlookers. His voice dropped to a threatening timbre. "Renate, come here."

I took several slow steps to reach his side. His shoulders heaved, and he exhaled through pressed lips. With eyes straight ahead, he growled, "Don't ever challenge me in public."

"But…"

"No excuses! People laughing at me is…" He broke off. "I will not be humiliated, not by you, not by anyone." He took a shuddering breath and lowered his voice. "The extent of your fall has not been exaggerated."

"My fall?" I asked, but the brisk shake of his head meant he wouldn't explain further. As I watched him fight for control of himself, I struggled with my own emotions. I wanted to protest the unfairness, to argue my right to finish the job I'd started. Leaving the farm and the Huber children would break my heart.

"You'll receive your assignment when you go home after the Rally."

"I may not be going to the Rally. It depends on whether or not Frau Huber is well enough."

"You'll go. Pack your trunk and say your goodbyes Thursday morning. After Nuremberg, you'll go home."

At the farm, I'd felt free. Without Werner's judgmental eye on me, I'd just been Renate Müller, mother's helper, future actress, anything and everything I chose to be. An assignment in Munich would return me to life under Werner's daily commands and his endless expectations of what I'd do and how I'd do it. I wanted no part of it.

My brother began his usual commanding stride. "We must talk in private."

I matched him step for step.

At a small café off the market square, he settled at an outdoor table. A waitress hurried over and, accepting a nod from my brother as an answer for us both, poured two coffees. "I can't stay, Werner," I said as I slid in a chair across from him. "The Huber boys are alone. I'm in charge of them today."

He smirked. "You and your big responsibility." His expression hardened, and he peered past his pointy nose at me. "There are two matters of importance. First"—one finger lifted skyward—"Herr Adler has been convicted of treason. Sentenced to execution."

I bolted upright. Sophie's papa. The gentle man who gave away baked goods to the poor and the elderly, who loved Mozart and Chopin, whose eyes laughed before a sound came from his lips—he would be killed like some kind of criminal.

Herr Adler was a *Wehrmacht* photographer. What he saw, he photographed, even if it showed the Reich in a bad light. When photos of mistreatment of Austrian Jews ended up in a British newspaper, the photos were traced back to him.

"Sit, Renate. You're making a spectacle of yourself." I unlocked my knees and collapsed into the chair. "Here's the second thing we need to discuss." From a pocket, he pulled a folded sheet of newspaper and flattened it before me. "Look familiar?"

The collage of photos on the top half of the page took my breath away. At least four or five were familiar. They were the same photos Werner stole from Sophie and hid in our home. The same ones I'd stolen back from him and buried in the pickle jar where Sophie could find them. My head pounded.

Beneath the collage was a short article in English. Werner slid a handwritten sheet into my view. "The translation."

These photos were taken in recent weeks in Munich, Germany. They are printed here at the request of the photographer under the condition of anonymity.

The poster (below) was created using two of the above photos without the photographer's permission. It has been displayed in public areas throughout Munich as part of a new Nazi propaganda campaign against cripples.

My eyes dropped to the two-part poster and my heart sank. In bold print, the top half was labeled, **Should Germany's future look like this?** The image showed a dozen uniformed Youth members looking fit and disciplined as they lined up for target practice. The bottom half read, **Or like this?** I remembered that image. It captured one of Sophie's fellow polio patients while she danced. With her eyes half-closed, her mouth twisted into a grimace, her tiara askew, her lopsided body supported by a crutch and leg brace, she looked, well, ridiculous.

Poor, sweet Sophie. Her photos had been used to create something cruel, something that mocked her friend. Her own images had been twisted against someone just like her.

I steadied my voice and asked my brother, "Where did you get this?"

Werner snatched up the clipping, pressed it along its folds, and returned it to his pocket. "Two weeks ago, I received a summons to Party headquarters. I hoped it meant good news for me. Perhaps I'd been admitted to the Adolf Hitler School. So, imagine my surprise when I was given this." He tapped the pocket.

I propped my elbows on the table to keep myself upright.

"There I was at Gestapo headquarters, in Onkel Edmund's office."

The man we called uncle had been Vater's best friend. He was also Werner's godfather and a frequent guest in our home, both before Vater died and afterward. He always wore two things: a stern expression and his Gestapo uniform. I'd been wary of him since I was a child.

Werner was still talking. "Onkel had been tasked with finding the identity of this 'anonymous' photographer. Wasn't hard to figure out. The Party provided the film for Sophie to use at the polio hospital." He pointed to himself, face reddening. "But I was the one facing questions in Onkel Edmund's office. I"—a bit of spittle appeared on his lower lip—"was the one suspected of sending these photos to England. Onkel Edmund questioned my loyalty. Mine."

Despite my churning stomach, I worked to arrange my expression to a neutral one.

He leaned back in the chair and shook his head. "And after all I'd done for that little *Schwein*, that cripple."

I managed to say, "So…so you think these are Sophie's photos?"

He straightened and slapped his palm on the café table. "You know they are, Renate. I can't believe the little Schwein…"

I interrupted him. "Please don't call her names."

He continued, "…sent her photos to a foreign press. Which left me facing questions." He jabbed a finger into his own chest, his tone incredulous. "Me. I told Onkel Edmund what I knew to be true—the photos and the negatives were in my possession, in my home. When I was asked to produce them, I went home to do so."

My stomach and my resolve sank.

"Renate, the photos were not where I left them. Gone from my own home. From *our* home. The negatives too.

"Which led me to wonder—how could a crippled Schwein"—I winced at his cruel words—"steal photos and their negatives from our home? She couldn't, of course. She was in the polio hospital. She may have photographed the poster in any number of places when she was on a day pass for the *Tag der Deutschen Kunst.* But the original photos and negatives?" He tapped his chest. "They were in my safekeeping. They were property of the Party." Werner's chin dropped, and he glared at me from beneath his brow.

He knew I'd stolen the photos from him and returned them to Sophie. I slumped in the chair, wordless.

"Despite what you think, Renate, I'm not a stupid man. I pieced it together. When I realized the photos were not at our home"—he paused, tight lines forming at the corners of his mouth—"I had to report it to headquarters. So I returned there. As I entered, I learned I'd been admitted to the Adolf Hitler School. I was to report in early October."

I managed a tight smile. He'd accomplished one of his goals.

He continued, "Which made it difficult to explain why I'd returned empty-handed. I told Onkel the photos must have been lost on my way home from the polio hospital."

I started. "Wait, Werner. You lied to Onkel Edmund?"

"There was a price for what he perceived as my…my lapse. I cannot attend Adolf Hitler School."

"So you lost your dream, gave it up…"

His voice was soft. "…to keep them from learning your role in this matter. Yes."

My brother, my stiff, bossy master sergeant brother, had protected me. He lied and lost admission to the school of his dreams to save me. We sat in silence while our coffees grew cold.

"Why, Renate?" he asked, his voice full of hurt. "Why did you betray your own brother?"

Betray. The word slapped me. The truth of it stung.

Et tu, Bruté?

I stuck by friends, helped and stood alongside anyone down on their luck. Like Sophie. Like Frau Lunka and skinny little Bruno.

But Werner? He was self-confident—arrogant even. He was connected within the Youth's administration and held a position of authority. Certainly not down on his luck. He didn't need my help. But he did deserve my loyalty.

I admitted, "I didn't think of it as a betrayal, Werner."

"Ah. But it was."

Guilt gnawed at my stomach. "I see. I'm very, very sorry." If I didn't go to confession soon, I wouldn't be able to sleep.

"And now you've tangled yourself with that little crippled Schwein…"

"I asked you before. Please don't call her names."

He waited a few beats, his lips tight. "Here's what the Party is calling your friend: a traitor." My breath caught. "This"—he patted the pocket that again held the newspaper clipping—"is treason. Sophie Adler is a traitor to her country, as are her father and her mother. When she is caught"—he clucked his tongue—"she will be tried and punished as such."

I clapped my hands over my ears. It couldn't be! Sophie was only fourteen.

Werner reached forward and wrenched my hands from my ears, his touch so foreign that I startled at the contact. He pressed my palms to the table and covered my hands with his own. His voice was urgent, pleading. "Anyone who helps a traitor is themselves a traitor."

My head swam. I'd known Sophie would try to send the photos and the negatives on to England. That was the whole idea. I'd expected muss and fuss, some hurt feelings and bluster from Werner, but I'd never imagined this. I was a fool. A naïve fool.

The Party had followed the trail back to me. If not for my brother's help, I'd be facing treason charges like Sophie. Werner's lie saved my neck.

What's more, when I stole the photos from my brother, I made him an accessory to treason. His lie saved his own neck too.

My heart's pounding pushed the shocking news through me, reaching every nerve, every muscle, every fiber of my body. I'd been so sure of myself, so certain I was doing the right thing by supporting Sophie, by being a good, loyal friend to her. All I'd done was put her, Werner, and me in terrible danger.

I wondered what Onkel Edmund made of all this. He didn't really believe Werner was careless enough to lose the photos, did he?

In a drawer in the farmhouse kitchen, I rummaged through a pile of community flyers until I found the one I was looking for. After telling Frau Huber when I'd return to make supper, I hopped on my bike and took off.

At the little church in town, I slipped into an empty confessional, pulled the curtain closed behind me, knelt, and made the sign of the cross. Behind the carved scrollwork screen and layers of dark gauze, the vague silhouette of a priest was visible. "Bless me, Father, for I have sinned," I began with folded hands and a bowed head. I confessed small wrongs I'd committed—scolding the children, taking an extra helping of meat without permission, that sort of thing.

His voice held the tremor of old age. "What else troubles you, child?"

In a hushed voice, I told the tale to my shadowed confessor. "My friend, she is a photographer. My brother stole a number of her photos. He handed them over to the Party to make…" I shuddered, remembering the mocking distortion on the Party's poster. "Well, let's say the photos were used in an unkind way."

From behind the screen, the priest spoke in a gentle tone. "Go on, child."

"I stole them back. The photos and the negatives." I became aware of something, a small shift of air beyond the thick curtain that separated my confessional from the rest of the church. The priest's dark shape stiffened, and I fell silent. I lifted the heavy curtain to peek into the sanctuary. Nothing. I let the curtain fall into place and resumed, even quieter than before. "Taking back what my brother stole seemed so right. Now I'm not sure. He says I betrayed him."

"Your brother." The priest's tone was scolding. "Your own flesh and blood."

"Yes, Father."

"Look what betrayal did to Judas and to our Lord Jesus."

There it was again, the shifting air, the tiny breath of sound on the other side of the curtain. I froze. The priest sighed and waited. Half a minute passed before he spoke, and when he did, his voice was a tremulous whisper. "Watch yourself, child. These days, even confessionals have ears." Then, resuming his previous volume, he pronounced my penance.

Trembling, I slid into the back pew and whispered the prayers, my sweaty hands fingering beads, my head spinning. A familiar figure knelt in a pew halfway up the aisle. She tossed her long hair over a shoulder and glanced at me. A knowing smile formed on her lovely face.

Uta. I should have known.

Chapter Six
Rennie

For the last time, the farmhouse morning filled me. Scents of coffee, toast, and oatmeal drifted up the stairwell and mingled with the voices of the waking children. Outside, the pasture gates creaked while Herr Huber instructed the bunkhouse Youth on feeding and watering the noisy animals.

I'd miss the farm and the hard-working Huber family. My efforts, however small and insignificant to my brother, mattered to these good people. I dragged my trunk down the attic stairs without trying to soften its repetitive thuds.

As I neared the main floor, I heard Uta say, "No, I've never canned beans or made bread. How hard can it be?"

So Uta was to be my replacement as mother's helper. No doubt she'd asked for the assignment change. I tried to picture her responding to the many, varied demands she'd face—changing Martin's diapers, scrubbing breakfast dishes, putting up quarts of peaches, and settling sibling squabbles, all before ten Uhr. All I could do was smile.

Uta stood in the living room beside the still-pale Frau Huber. Martin, gnawing on Zwieback, grinned at me from his perch on his mother's hip. Sleepy-eyed Ada waited by the door in her rosebud-dotted nightgown. Conrad and Otto, wide awake and freshly groomed, were dressed in hiking clothes and holding rucksacks. Frau Huber pressed coins into the boys' palms and turned to me. "The boys were such a help when I was sick, I'm giving them a reward—a visit with their *oma* and *opa* for a couple days. They'll be on the train with you."

Otto adjusted his rucksack and straightened, nodding. "Just as far as Munich. Our grandparents will meet us at the station."

Conrad waggled his eyebrows. "I've got a deck of cards to keep us from getting bored on the train."

I laughed. "It's less than an hour's ride."

"Then we'll play fast."

Ada looked sad and serious, her dark hair a matted morning mess. I squatted to her level and opened my arms for a hug. Instead, she clicked her bare heels and raised her arm in a salute. Its skinny, outstretched length hovered over my head. I rose to my full height slowly, stunned.

"That's right," Uta said to her, with a sideways glance at the older boys. "Give Rennie a proper send-off to the Party Rally." Ada's cheeks brightened, and her arm stiffened more, if possible. Otto and Conrad started, then raised their arms in salute as well.

Frau Huber watched this tight-lipped. When she spoke, the spell broke, and everyone relaxed. "You've been a most wonderful help to me, Renate." Then turning to her boys, she said, "When you get to Munich, you will remind Oma and Opa to take Renate's trunk?"

Otto nodded and patted a pocket. "I've got the address right here."

"You're taking my trunk?"

Conrad turned to me, his face shining with pride. "Sure! Otto and I want to do a good turn for you."

Frau Huber planted a kiss on my cheek. "You will be missed, Renate. Please write."

I ducked out so she wouldn't see me cry.

I did indeed play cards with the boys on the train, betting with a couple dozen hazelnuts Frau Huber had tucked into Otto's rucksack. Through the magic of winks and nods between me and his older brother, Conrad ended up the big winner. Grinning, he scooped the pile of nuts into his hands. Then he popped one in his mouth, accentuating the crunch, eyeing us while allowing the *Mmm* of his pleasure to be heard. He licked his lips, ate a second and a third with the greedy delight of a pirate hoarding his booty. The rest he closed in his fist. When the train stopped, he straightened and turned to Otto and me. "Here." He thrust out his open palm. "Each of you take three."

That boy. Selfish one minute, tenderhearted the next. Otto and I thanked him and accepted his gift.

As always, Munich's *Hauptbahnhof* was busy. Ebony trains waited at a dozen platforms, huffing and steaming. People pushed luggage carts past shouting porters, shoeshine boys, and newspaper vendors. Departure whistles and a new arrival's squealing brakes echoed through the vast, glass-domed cavern. In the midst of it all, Otto and I each clung to a trunk handle and walked the length of the platform, Conrad close on my heels.

At the turnstile stood the boys' grandparents, a rather energetic couple. They hugged and kissed the boys and tousled their hair, remarking about their incredible growth and good looks in typical grandparent fashion.

I dreaded this last round of goodbyes. Otto shook my hand as if we were closing a business deal. He wished me good luck in my new assignment, then thanked me for my help at the farm stand and at the house. All business, as expected. I planted a kiss atop his bristled head. Even with Uta taking my place, he'd be fine without me.

Conrad hesitated. Following his older brother's cool approach, he reached out to shake my hand. It wasn't to be. Chin aquiver, he lurched forward and wrapped his arms around my middle, leaning into me with surprising and delightful affection. I met his embrace with my own, lifting him and spinning him full circle. I said a silent prayer that, even with Uta in charge, Conrad's conscience would stay tender and fresh. I'd miss that boy.

The boys' grandfather lifted one end of my trunk and gestured for Otto to lift the other. In a few steps, they fell into an even, although somewhat lumbering, rhythm.

I raced up beside them. "Are you sure? My house is a good eight or ten blocks from here."

Otto kept walking. "You have your clothes for the Rally in your rucksack, right?" he asked. I nodded, gesturing to the strap slung across my shoulder. "Then catch your train. In case your mother isn't home, who should we leave your trunk with?"

I gave him the name and address of our nosy next-door neighbor, Frau Knox. She'd see the group approach our door and bustle over to talk with them anyway.

After a quick wave, Otto and his grandfather continued across the platform. The boys' grandmother grabbed Conrad's hand and started after them. In moments, the four figures merged into the jostling crowd.

I wiped my eyes and started the lonely walk to my next train. Once at the correct platform, I settled on a bench and unpacked the cheese and bread Frau Huber had prepared.

I enjoyed watching the city characters who passed by, a bustling man in a tweed suit, a hunched woman whose shopping bag brimmed with yarn, a tight-lipped young mother who bounced a squalling infant on her hip. A dozen groups of uniformed Youth and Wehrmacht soldiers also rambled past. With multi-humped rucksacks bumping against their backs, they were probably headed for Nuremberg too, lugging camping and cooking gear with them.

I was lucky to be able to stay in a home in town because I only had to carry my clothes. I'd have to do something nice for Helga and her Tante Sabine to show my appreciation.

Someone slid onto the bench beside me and clasped my elbow. "Renate, I found you."

I wrenched my elbow free and feigned a smile at the young woman beside me. "Anna!" I said between gritted teeth. "Did Werner ask you to see me off?"

Her syrupy voice dripped. "He is very protective of you, Renate."

Anna was three or four years older than me. She'd been my troop's *Jungmädel* leader when I was younger. She ran hot and cold—kind and supportive one minute, throwing accusations around the next. When I moved up into BDM, the next age group of girls' Youth, I was excited to be away from Anna and her unpredictable backbiting. A few months ago, she started dating Werner. It didn't say much for his taste. Or hers.

Gesturing to the busy platforms around us, I asked, "Are you coming or going?"

"I'm headed to Nuremberg, same as you."

"To the Rally?"

"Of course. Didn't Helga tell you? She's unable to make it. She didn't want to disappoint you, so she asked me to take her place."

I waved a finger between the two of us. "So, you and I are..."

"Traveling together. Staying with Helga's aunt in Nuremberg. Isn't that nice?"

"Lovely." With deliberate breaths, I worked to regain my sense of calm. With any luck, the woman had a large home.

"Werner arranged for me to travel with you. He trusts his darling little sister to my care." She grabbed the bulk of my cheek and pinched as if I were a chubby baby.

I flinched and pulled away, rising and stuffing my food into my rucksack. A spy. My brother arranged for a spy. "If you're to be my traveling companion, you'll keep your hands to yourself."

Without acknowledging my comment, she rose and twirled, showing off the white cape around her shoulders. *Rotes Kreuz*. "I'm a Red Cross nurse now. With so many people at the Rally, emergencies happen. A broken bone, a heart attack, a terrible illness..."

Which made me think of Sophie. Since she'd been labeled a traitor, I had to be careful. I settled on the bench and worked to even out my breath. "So you don't work at the polio hospital anymore?"

"Oh, I'm still assigned there," she answered. Her pine green eyes followed two strapping young men in Wehrmacht uniforms, bulky duffle bags bumping against their thin hips. Her gaze snapped back to me. "Till November, I'm told."

"Do you enjoy it there?"

"Of course! I make things nice for those pitiful cripples." Then she giggled, a self-conscious, almost adolescent sound. "You should see your face, Renate! You look horrified."

I could contain it no longer. I burst out, "Sophie is not a pitiful cripple! She is a good, kind person. And she's my friend!" As soon as the words left my mouth, I chastised myself. If I were any kind of actress, I would have kept a neutral expression.

Anna leaned in and whispered, "You know she's in trouble, right?" I nodded. "And Werner told me you'd ask about"—she glanced around—"about her."

I waited for her to continue. When she didn't, I prompted. "And? Where is she?"

She turned to me and shrugged. "I wouldn't know. After she hurt her arm, she didn't return to the polio hospital." Something flashed across her face, an expression so fleeting it barely registered. Her gaze drifted away. "Last I knew, she was at University Hospital recovering from her injury."

"When was that?"

"July. The middle of the month."

Six weeks earlier! "Where is she now?"

She turned her gaze to me again. "She was my responsibility at the polio hospital. Once she left there"—she shrugged, her tone indifferent—"my job was done. But if I ever see her, I'll report it to the authorities, as is my duty."

I bolted to my feet and paced several steps, then spun to face her. "Sophie wasn't just another patient. You've known her for years, well before you were her nurse."

Anna stood and gathered her belongings, brushing imaginary dust from her cape. "You used to be so gentle and kind. Werner told me how outspoken you've become. Now I've seen it with my own eyes." She controlled a stray bit of hair with a swift stick of a bobby pin. "They're boarding soon. Come."

Again, I'd forgotten to use my acting skills. I'd have to do a better job of hiding what I really thought.

In silence, I trudged behind Anna and climbed on the waiting train. She stuffed her rucksack in the overhead bin, slid onto an empty bench, and patted the space beside her. I sighed and collapsed into the seat, hugging the rucksack on my lap. It didn't hold anything of value. I just needed to hold something. Anything.

Anna broke into my thoughts. "Too bad you had to skip your trip home before the Rally."

I started. "How did you know I wanted to go home first?"

"Werner and I talk about everything." Creases like parentheses formed around her mouth as she smiled.

"But," I started to say, then stopped. I hadn't told Werner my original travel schedule. Tears of frustration would pour from me if I spoke, so I pressed my lips closed.

By midafternoon, Anna and I joined the throngs as we bumped toward the exit at the Nuremberg train station. At first, I searched for familiar faces in the crowd. But when hundreds, then thousands, of faces blurred past me, I gave up. I focused on the red emblem on Anna's cape and followed it out of the station and into the streets.

A handful of SA officers in their mud-brown uniforms walked ahead of us. Here it was four years after Vater's death, and the sight of SA still twisted a fist in my gut. How could a strong, healthy SA officer leave for work one day and never come home?

A few years earlier, I'd asked Mutter. Her face had sprouted blotches, and she'd raced out and locked herself in the bathroom. I'd have to ask her again when I got home from the Rally.

Anna and I wove through the streets of Nuremberg, dodging hordes of people, packed sidewalk cafés, and clusters of boisterous *Brauhaus* customers. Within minutes, I was smiling. Despite the chaotic emotions of recent days, I was in Nuremberg, in the midst of the biggest festival in the history of our country. Might as well enjoy myself.

We ended up in Nuremberg's Altstadt, the old part of town. Its medieval architecture and cobbled streets reminded me of my own home neighborhood, Munich's Altstadt, where I'd be living again in a few days' time.

We stopped in front of a steep-roofed, gabled house and rang the doorbell. With a wide grin and energetic handshakes, Helga's Tante Sabine, a stout middle-aged widow, welcomed us into her five-room walk-up. The sharp smell of mothballs was masked by the hearty aroma of stew bubbling on the stove.

After we ate, Sabine pushed open a narrow door with a grand and unapologetic flourish. The room Anna and I were to share was a cluttered space built into the eaves. The sloped ceiling on two sides ended at low shelves of wool blankets, sweaters, and leather boots. Various dressers and armoires added their bulk to the taller walls. "This may be the last room available in Nuremberg. Make yourselves comfortable," Sabine said, squeezing out between a standing rack of coats and a precarious tower of hatboxes.

Once the door closed behind her, Anna and I giggled at our absurd situation, covering our mouths for fear of insulting Sabine. We restacked and cleared enough space to spread our blanket rolls on the floor. I sat on mine to rest.

Anna jabbed me with her toe. "Don't get comfortable. Let's go."

"Go where?"

"Out. Werner gave me money to make sure you're entertained while we're here." I must have grimaced because she hastened to add, "We could take in a movie."

"What's playing?"

"Triumph of the Will."

I groaned. That documentary about the 1934 Rally played everywhere the Party gathered. I'd seen it in school a year before and found it dull—long scenes with endless rows of marching soldiers. "We also passed the opera house," I volunteered.

Anna wrinkled her nose. "I'd rather the cinema. Get your sweater."

On screen, the image darkened. Hundreds upon hundreds of torch-bearing soldiers, their voices raised in song, emerged from the blackness, marching in complex formations. Their movement was choreographed, ever-changing but always organized, a dance not of graceful ballerinas but of fit soldiers amid glowing flames. Quite impressive.

The film's silvery flickers of light allowed me to see the expressions of Anna and a few others in our row. They watched the motion picture, posture straight, eyes wide and absorbing every detail. Entranced.

The last scene in the movie was the most famous—the Führer's speech to the tens of thousands of Hitler Youth during 1934's Rally. I'd heard similar speeches before, but in the darkened cinema in Nuremberg, the Führer's words seemed different. They tickled something inside me, as if trying to awaken my senses from a long sleep.

> "We want to be one people and through you, to become this people. We want a society with neither castes nor ranks. We want to be one country, and you must let that grow within you. You must be both peace-loving and strong. You must learn to sacrifice and to never collapse.
>
> "As we bind ourselves together, it cannot be any other way. You are flesh from our flesh and blood from our blood. The same spirit that governs us burns in your young minds. We know that Germany lies in front of us. Germany marches within us. And Germany follows behind us."

When the theater lights came on, Anna turned to me, her eyes sparkling. "Wasn't it incredible?"

I couldn't go that far. But it wasn't dull anymore.

The next morning, I joined Sabine and Anna at the small kitchen table. Sabine handed me a sheet of paper. "From Helga. The events you're to attend."

Anna spoke up. "Sabine will take us on a walking tour of the city before your first event. We leave in an hour."

My day was planned. "I'm to meet someone at eleven Uhr near the fountain in Adolf-Hitler-Platz," I said. Being a gentleman, Erich had chosen a public location.

"Oh? Who are you meeting?" Anna asked with more than casual curiosity. "Your Onkel Edmund?" She turned to Sabine. "You know of him, ja? Works with the Gestapo." Sabine looked impressed.

I hesitated to tell Anna the truth. She'd tell Werner everything I said and did, including who I met. Erich was a Youth member subject to Werner's authority. I didn't want trouble for him.

Sabine raised a graying eyebrow. "When a young girl won't say who she's meeting, there are only two reasons. One, she's planning to do something wrong." I shook my head. "Or two—she's meeting a boy." I poured a cup of tea so the redness of my downturned cheeks wouldn't be seen.

"Ah," Anna said, clapping her hands. "Renate is sweet on a boy." She leaned close. "Who is it? Someone I know?"

I stirred honey into my tea and looked up, working to keep my expression even, casual. "Erich Fischer." I turned to Sabine. "He's an old friend from our neighborhood." Anna sat back, her expression curious.

Sabine nodded her approval. "The fountain is easy to find. I'll make sure you get there on time."

Sabine was proud to show us her quaint hometown. Crisp curtains billowed from the open windows of trim, half-timbered homes. Bright clusters of geraniums lined walkways and spilled from window boxes.

Mitte, the central part of the city, was decked out for the weeklong Party Rally. Tall banners bearing red-and-white swastikas lined the streets. Flags hung from windows and along wires above the busy sidewalks. Ahead of us, two women squeezed through the crowded sidewalk to get close to the window of a ladies' wear shop. They peered over the top of a large image of the Führer to see the high-heeled shoes and patent leather handbags displayed behind.

Sabine pointed out various city landmarks as we wove our way through ever-thicker crowds. "There"—she pointed to a tall Gothic spire in the center of the town square—"is the fountain you need, Renate."

Sabine continued at a good clip, noting several beautiful old churches. "Nuremberg was chosen for the Party Rallies because the Führer loves it here so much," she announced. "He calls it the most German of all German cities, the Temple City of the Movement." I wondered if she'd ever been a tour guide.

As eleven Uhr approached, Sabine settled in an outdoor café at the edge of the Adolf-Hitler-Platz, ordered coffee, and announced she'd wait for my return. I thanked her and started toward the fountain to meet Erich. In moments, Anna was beside me.

I bristled. "You don't need to come."

"It's no bother. I'm happy to chaperone."

I swept my arms to the hundreds of people in view in the plaza. "Here?"

Sabine called after her. "Anna, nothing will happen to your charge. Let the old friends visit."

Anna sighed but did as the older woman asked. I thanked Sabine, which she acknowledged with a quick nod. And a wink.

Chapter Seven
Rennie

I recognized Erich right away—same tall frame, dark hair, gentle smile, and easy stride he always had. In the three months since I'd seen him, he'd grown into a young man. His jaw had squared, and courtesy of the Youth horsemanship program, his arms now rippled with muscle. He smiled and waved when he saw me, then wove his way through the crowd. My breath caught.

"It's good to see you, Rennie," he said, his now prominent Adam's apple bobbing as he spoke. Almost a head taller than me, he bent to plant a sisterly kiss on my cheek. His dark eyes and earthy scent were as familiar as my own skin.

I was glad he couldn't hear my racing heart. "It's good to see you too," I managed to say.

"I can only spare an hour. Have to meet my unit." He looked at the crush of people around us. "So much for speaking in private."

"No privacy for me at all." I jerked my thumb to the café table a dozen meters away.

Erich glanced at the table. His low voice matched mine. "Is that Anna Albrecht? Your old Jungmädel leader?"

I nodded. "One and the same. Werner sent her to spy on me."

His voice grew even softer. "Oh, Rennie. What's happened?"

Of the hundreds of people around us, none paid us particular attention. I hoped. "First, tell me what you know about Sophie."

Erich crooked one elbow, so I slipped my hand through. We set out on an easy saunter through the plaza, our heads tipped close. I breathed in his scent and felt my own rising heat. I leaned into him and…

…chastised myself. I wanted—no, I needed—answers about Sophie, my best friend, who was in terrible danger. I refocused and arranged my face into a sisterly expression.

Erich began his tale. "I was home for *Festzug am Tag der Deutschen Kunst.*"

I knew it well. The Procession for the Day of German Art was a huge parade every July, the big finale of an annual celebration of the arts in Munich.

He spoke just above a whisper, his voice so close and filled with breath it tickled my cheek. A sigh of pleasure tried to escape, but I disguised it by clearing my throat. "I was in the English Garden Park getting my horses ready for the parade," he said. "An old man with a cane hobbled up to a park bench to rest. He was still sitting there when a large group of horsemen came by. They held flags, so I asked the man to stand—you know, to show respect for the flag. Maybe he didn't understand, or maybe he was too tired. I don't know. All I know is…" He hesitated.

I waited. "What?"

"The man didn't stand. He sat on the bench, leaning forward on his cane. Then"—Erich's words came out in a rush—"your brother stormed over and kicked the cane out from underneath him."

I froze. I'd seen a photo of that in the British newspaper collage. A tall black boot was reared back and aimed at the cane beneath a smiling old man. That boot belonged to my brother. How could he be so cruel to that old man and yet so protective of me?

Erich tugged on my arm. "Keep walking. We can't call attention to ourselves." I gulped but willed my feet to move. Erich continued. "The man fell forward, had a bloody nose. I knelt beside him to help, to stop the bleeding, you know? From the corner of my eye, I saw this girl in a wheelchair taking photographs of him."

"Sophie."

He nodded. "She spoke to me. I'm not even sure what she said. I was such an idiot, crouching on the ground next to this bleeding man, gaping at Sophie." His cheeks tinged. "I had to return to my post at the front of the park. Then, out of nowhere, her stepbrother Klaus showed up." Erich shook his head. "He'd been away, building roads, I think. But there he was. Seems he'd been recalled early to take over the family bakery. You know, since the Adlers were…" He trailed off.

A wave of sadness for Sophie's parents, especially her sweet father, washed over me.

Erich continued. "Klaus said he needed to find Sophie. It seems the Scharführer—I mean, your brother—was looking for her. So, I pointed him in the right direction." Erich turned his dark eyes to search my face. "Maybe I should have said I hadn't seen her. Things may have turned out better." He fell silent.

I could only bear it a few moments. "Erich, please. Tell me everything."

He shot me an apologetic look. "Oh, sorry. It was easy to track Sophie—her wheelchair left a wet trail. When I caught up with her, Klaus was there. Anna too." He lifted his chin toward the café where Anna and Sabine sat. "Sophie was a little way off, rinsing her hands in a stream. Klaus and Anna were fuming. Seems a jar had been unearthed."

I drew a sharp breath.

Erich watched my face as he continued. "Klaus asked if Sophie and I had been passing secret notes in the jar. But we'd corresponded by post. Nothing in secret. Certainly nothing buried in a jar."

"Then the jar was empty?"

He continued to study me. "When I got there, yes." Erich narrowed his gaze, then glanced around before speaking. "But here's the thing, Rennie. There was something in that jar. Sophie took it out and hid it before anyone got there."

My stomach lurched. "Oh?"

"A little note." He searched my expression for a response.

I dropped my gaze to the cobblestones.

Without missing a beat, Erich continued. "And when your brother saw the note, he recognized your handwriting."

Guilt tugged at my stomach.

"Plus, Werner saw Sophie photograph the injured man. She had two rolls of film for the day, and Werner wanted her to hand them over right then and there. But he found only one roll—the one in Sophie's camera."

I looked up at him. "Where was the other?"

Erich shrugged. "She wouldn't say." He straightened a bit, then spoke to the crowded space ahead of him. "You know her, Rennie. She's timid, doesn't stand up for herself. But that day…" A sad smile quivered into place. "She had this determined look on her face." He did his best to set his mouth in an imitation of her firmness. "I could tell she had a plan. She didn't say what it was." He studied me, probably waiting for a reaction. "I suppose you know her plan, what with your note there and all."

I didn't respond, so he continued. "I tried to get your brother away from her, get everyone away so she could work her plan." He reached over with his free hand and ever so gently patted my arm where it lay entwined with his.

My mouth grew dry. A thrill tried to course through me, but I squashed it where it started. My own feelings, my own body's reaction to Erich's touch, would not betray me.

Erich was oblivious to my struggle. His feet moved beside mine, but his thoughts were separate from our time and place. Separate from me. As usual, he thought only of Sophie.

"Well, your brother sent Klaus, Anna, and me back to the park to look for the second roll of film. I knew we wouldn't find it there." His tone and expression dulled. "Later, I was told Sophie hurt her arm and had been taken to a hospital. Klaus told me she'd be at University Hospital for a few days and would then return to the polio hospital. I had to leave the next morning, so I never got a chance to visit. Now I hear she's been charged…"

I was glad his voice dropped off. I couldn't bear to talk about the treason charges either. "Did you write to her?"

"Yes. My letter was returned. No forwarding address."

"Mine too." I forced brightness into my voice. "Starting next week, I'll be home. I'll find out where she is."

He scoured my face, his expression a mix of anxiety, hope, and trust. "You'll let me know?"

I could have stared into those eyes all day. "Of course."

Suddenly, Anna stood in front of us, arms crossed on her chest. "Where do you two think you're going?" she demanded.

I hadn't noticed her arrival and wondered how long she'd been listening. Erich stammered. "Anna. Nice to see you. We're not going anywhere. Just catching up."

Her gaze fell to our linked arms. "How quickly a young man's heart can change."

Erich's arm dropped from mine. "Rennie and I are old friends."

The warm spot where Erich's arm had rested on mine cooled in a flash. Leave it to Anna to ruin even that small pleasure. "And now what, Anna?" I demanded without disguising my irritation. "Are you going to run to Werner and tell him I was talking with an old school chum? Going to pretend it was a secret liaison in full view of hundreds of people in the middle of Nuremberg?" How I'd ever managed a laugh with her the previous night, I didn't know.

Erich glanced from Anna to me, his discomfort obvious. "I don't want any trouble."

Anna tipped her head. "Trouble? Oh, there won't be trouble. You say there's nothing to tell Werner. And it's not as if your little friend will find out anytime soon."

My stomach flipped. "What do you mean?"

She shrugged. "No one knows where she is."

I scoured Anna's expression for any sign of a lie or a twisted truth. Her gaze was even, her tone sincere. She didn't know Sophie's whereabouts. Neither did Erich. The difference was Anna didn't care.

That evening, Sabine led Anna and me to the Rally grounds, an area over eleven square kilometers in size. I'd never seen such crowds, not even for Munich's *Oktoberfest*. "How many people are here?" I asked Sabine as we squeezed past another clump of people at a streetcar stop.

Sabine looked gleeful. "Officials expect a million. The most popular Rally yet. Stay together. We queue here for the Zeppelin Stadium."

Ahead of the thick, snaking lines of humanity stood an imposing white stone structure. It was square in shape and so huge the two corners nearest me were barely in view. Six flags sprouted from each of the dozens of towers along the top edge, creating an entire wall of stone and swastikas. I was dwarfed, insignificant.

Anna pointed to small openings on the ground level of each of the towers. "Where do those doors go?"

"Washrooms," Sabine said. "Most are for men. There's only one women's washroom, and it's—" She gestured to the far end of the stadium. I hoped I didn't have to use it. I might never find my way back.

Anna asked, "How many people does the stadium hold?"

"Fifty thousand on the main grandstand here." Her gaze swept over the stadium in front of us. "The field and side spectator stands hold another one hundred fifty thousand. It's bigger than the Municipal Stadium and the Luitpold Arena"—sites she'd pointed out on our earlier tour—"but not as large as the Deutsche Stadium will be when it's finished."

"How many will that hold?" I asked.

Her face shone with pride. "Upwards of four hundred thousand."

We became part of the queue, the river of people squeezed into a few thin lines. We pushed through the turnstile, climbed the stadium stairs, and slipped into our seats as dusk fell.

I'd never seen so many people in one place, rows upon rows all around the vast square. Most were so far from me they looked like tiny dots, indistinct and colorless in the fading daylight. The grandstand stood opposite us, straight across the stadium's width. It held a massive block of seats for the Party elite backed by pillars and flanked by tall columns—intimidating and unmistakable. In the gathering darkness, a huge brass swastika blazed above the grandstand. That Party beacon was probably visible on the other side of the city.

When the music began, the crowd stirred and rose to its collective feet. As in the film I'd seen, two wide columns of young men from the Reich Labor Service, the RLS, marched onto the field, long-handled shovels perched atop shoulders. For five full minutes, thousands of Youth filed in and filled the ever-darkening field, their feet pounding as a single heartbeat, their voices lifted in unison song. Those boys were my age. Gave me goosebumps.

From opposing sides of the field came columns of grown men holding torches, Wehrmacht from the left, Kriegsmarine from the right. As they marched in rhythm, their blazing torches bathing them in wavering golden bands of light, smoke trailing above and behind them, they sang one of my favorite national songs. I joined in.

> "Fall in, comrade. Pitch in, comrade.
> The fruit of our labor is bread.
> We battle for our land with peaceful intent.
> Work is our highest command.
> Fall in, comrade. Pitch in, comrade.
> We're tilling rich German soil.
> Our civic work ripens the seed,
> Feeding us bread, comrade of mine."

As when I'd watched the film the previous night, folks around me lifted chins and straightened shoulders in pride.

Now, seeing the spectacle in person, witnessing the grandeur myself while I sang with tens of thousands of my fellow Germans, I understood. Hard work and unity, our national principles, were alive. Those principles gave breath to our song, lived in our nation of willing workers. They were the lifeblood in which our country believed. Strength in numbers. The evidence was right in front of me.

I knew our country had struggled to recover from the Great War. Our nation had been defeated, our cities destroyed. Almost two million of our young men had been killed. Families shattered. Children left fatherless. At the end of it all, Germany lay in ruins—our patriotism destroyed, our people hungry and desperate, our government weak, our economy in shambles.

That night I saw change. I saw a willingness to work hard and bind ourselves to the cause of a greater good. I saw the drive to use our land and feed our people. We were recovering from the Great War. We'd continue to do so. We'd end up stronger and more unified than ever.

I was there to bear witness to the healing. I was part of the generation that would bring about change.

That knowledge flowed into me and merged with my lifeblood, coursing renewed energy into my every heartbeat. An unexpected result of this occurred deep in my gut—a loosening of sorts. I thrilled at the refreshing ease, the sheer joy, of being free from the pressure I'd made for myself, as if I lost the ache of a breath held too long. How foolish I'd been, fighting alone. I relaxed into the lightness, the exquisite relief of being part of the whole.

Soldiers lined up on either side of the grandstand's center, leaving a wide path between their ranks. The shovel-bearing RLS formation turned about face and marched along the path, disappearing in the golden torchlight. In moments, new columns of torch-carrying men marched in from my right and claimed the prime spot vacated by the RLS. I recognized their uniforms. SA. Vater would have been so proud of his SA, front and center before the grandstand. I swallowed, pushing against the lump in my throat.

The crowd shifted, and all eyes turned to the very gates we'd entered not thirty minutes earlier. A trumpet sounded. Sabine grabbed my arm. "Look! It's the Führer!"

Blue-white light burst around me. My hands flew up to protect my eyes from the blazing assault. I blinked into my palms, waiting for my vision to be restored, then raised my watery eyes to the spectacle before me. Through the open area between columns of soldiers, five men strode toward the grandstand. In their midst was indeed the Führer, right there, not fifty meters from my very seat. The masses of people around me, Anna and Sabine included, shouted and saluted, proclaiming their devotion to our country's leader.

But for me, the greater spectacle blazed all around us. Dozens and dozens of brilliant searchlights lining the stadium's perimeter pierced the night sky with wide columns of pure white radiance. Those luminous pillars surrounded us, enveloped us, created a protective shield around us. Past our vision, through the vast black sky, and onward to the great beyond, those beams of light stretched to the very heavens.

Below me, thousands of golden torches trembled on the field. Tendrils of smoke danced through the stadium and drifted into the path of those giant shafts of light. The silvery vapors quivered on their journey skyward.

I was suspended, happily adrift between two worlds in that cathedral of light. Men marched on the solid earth in front of me. Concrete lay beneath my feet. But the lights. Oh, the lights! The lights brushed the stratosphere like the fingertips of angels.

From somewhere across the stadium, drums beat out a rhythm, the heartbeat of those angels. The deep bass of tubas, the shrill of piccolos, the clarinets' melody, and the tinkle of glockenspiels surrounded the heartbeat and gave it a purpose. From the field, hundreds—no, thousands—of men's voices joined in song. The familiar tune was picked up by the spectators, and soon the stadium literally trembled as over one hundred thousand of us sang together.

> "We heeded calls to rescue you, our Fatherland.
> We're loyal in our duty.
> We're spending our lives building German might.
> We are the standard bearers of modern times."

Chills sparkled down my spine, and my chest filled to bursting. The familiar chant *"Sieg Heil!"* began. In moments, the stadium throbbed as tens of thousands of voices pulsed the staccato words. "Hail victory!" I shouted the chant into the night, dwarfed by its magnitude, accepting its pounding rhythm as my own.

I was so, so lucky. I was part of something great.

Chapter Eight
Werner

In the late '30s, I had the best of everything—food, beer, entertainment. I was among the chosen.

Given my champion bloodline, six generations of pure Aryan lineage, I was to be one-half of an approved couple. The promise of a future at the forefront of the Movement. All that remained was to decide on my breeding partner.

The woman I wanted for the job, the only one who appreciated my penchant for cleanliness and order, was Anna Albrecht, the nursing student I'd been seeing for some time. I cared about her, admired her commitment to our cause. The perfect wife to support my ambitions. When I broached the subject, her reaction was quick. "I'll need to see your ancestry."

"As I will need to see yours."

In the presence of her father, Herr Doktor Albrecht, we exchanged paperwork. Thus assured, Herr Doktor consented to our union. His daughter could bear my child for the Reich, but only if we married. Of course, I agreed. I'd fulfill my part in the ever-larger dream, uniting my life with the life of another pureblood. Together with thousands of other Aryan couples like us, our Germany would be strong, her future assured. The wedding was planned for the spring of '39.

Years later, I realized I'd never proposed. My engagement to Anna was arranged, more mutually beneficial business deal than the torrid love affairs of unseemly novels. During our courtship, I became comfortable with Anna's proximity, even learned to relax and enjoy her company. She told me stories of her past, old flames, disappointing friendships. I listened to her tales but revealed little of myself. Once we were engaged, she pried. Her questions became more direct.

Such was the case on a trip to Berlin in '38. Under clear autumn skies, we strolled arm in arm down Unter den Linden. We sat side by side at a sidewalk café and chatted over steaming cups of coffee. She leaned close and kissed my cheek, an intimacy I'd allowed myself to enjoy. I breathed in her scent—soap and fresh air. Wholesome. "So," she said, a soft finger stroking my cheek. "I've known you for years, Werner, but I know precious little about you."

I tried not to tense. "What do you want to know?"

She shrugged, her expression coy. "For instance, what are your career goals?"

I repeated what I'd always said. "I want to rise through the ranks, be a good, upstanding officer." I grasped her stroking finger and placed it on the table. I rested my hands atop hers. "And I want to provide for you and our children."

Her eyes took in our nested hands, then lifted to search my face. "What about personal things, things a wife knows about her husband?" She gave an endearing shake of her head as if "wife" and "husband" delighted her. "Such as, when you have spare time, what do you do?"

I wanted to share with her; I really did. But I wasn't sure how much to reveal or how to reveal it. Once she was my wife, Anna would see the real me, the fastidious man who hung his shirts all facing the same way, who sharpened kitchen knives after each use, who insisted his morning newspaper be ironed flat before reading. My family and neighbors would tell her stories. And Onkel Edmund—what would he tell her? Might it be better to leave certain matters unspoken until we were married? Or was it better to tell all now?

The small piece of me that had begun to soften threatened to build a wall.

How did people do this?

How could I do it?

Bonding with another person, it was difficult. Life would be simpler alone. Safer too.

But lonely. I was tired of being lonely, of never having an ally, of always being estranged and mocked and passed over. I took a steadying breath. "I organize…"

"Organize," Anna repeated.

I plunged ahead. "I sort coins according to size, make lists of tasks to be done, sort paperwork into folders. I take speeches and news articles and outline them." Anna tipped her head in an unspoken query, so I clarified. "I start by labeling the main ideas with Roman numerals, then break down…"

She interrupted. "You outline speeches? Even the Führer's?"

I was quick to answer. "No, those I commit to memory." I took a deep breath and risked a bit more of the truth. "I must have order."

Two lines formed around her mouth, a hint of a smile, and my insides cowered. "You prefer order. As do I."

I hesitated another moment, then risked a bit more. "I don't just prefer order. I need it. Crave it. Mutter always said order and organization are my food. You may as well know." I sat back, unsure what more I could safely share. Anna's smile was wide. "You mock me," I said, fighting the temptation to leave.

She leaned forward and squeezed my hand. "Not at all. It's just, I knew that already. Anyone who has known you more than a few days, a few hours maybe"—here she giggled—"knows you prefer things a certain way."

So, I was known. Accepted even. I relaxed.

"Tell me something else, something others wouldn't know." When I didn't respond right away, she pressed. "What's your favorite game?"

"Solitaire."

The lines around her mouth deepened, and she lifted one hand to cover a laugh. "Forgive me, Werner. I don't mean to be rude. It's just—that's what I'd expect."

Anna probably thought I liked solitaire because it's played alone. True, that was part of it. But I also liked how each card played presented new options, new opportunities. And my favorite thing about solitaire was this—I'd never lost a game. If I reached an impasse, I'd shuffle the cards and start over. No one was the wiser.

Perhaps she'd learn that in years to come.

Anna continued to pry. "What games did you play with your family? When you were a child, I mean. When your father was alive."

"My father didn't play games." The words flew from my mouth before I considered them. In all the time I'd known Anna, I'd barely mentioned my father. I could feel the wall rising inside me. Wasn't certain if I wanted it up or down.

"He must have played ball with you. Or checkers. Something."

I offered a painful truth. "My father only played with Renate." Anything she wanted, in fact.

"Not with you? His only son?"

"His way of toughening me up."

Anna hesitated, then said in a near whisper, "He thought you were soft?"

Someday I might reveal how my father treated me. Someday I might trust her with my fragile pieces.

My silence must have spoken volumes because she squeezed my hand. "What was it like when your father died? Is that when your mother took a job?"

I drew a hard breath, then forced my face and tone to reveal little. "Ja. I was fourteen; Renate was ten. We needed food and clothing."

"Didn't your godfather help?"

"Onkel Edmund wouldn't let us starve, but he had his own family to care for." Anna nodded, so I continued. "Mutter took cleaning jobs, mostly in offices on weekends and evenings. She'd get home after midnight, wake in time to see us off to school, then go back to sleep. Then she'd do her own cleaning and cooking and shopping before she left for work. After a few months, she was ready to collapse."

Anna leaned closer to me and flashed an uncertain smile. "So, you helped her. A good son would do so."

Her statement brought such relief! I could almost touch it, this unfamiliar, welcome sense of being understood. "As I said, Mutter knew I like order, so she gave me the job of cleaning our house before school. I learned to make a few basic meals."

Anna pressed her soft lips against my cheek. "If we have a son, I hope he's like you."

I smiled. She lifted her chin, a silent urge for me to continue, so I did. "I couldn't help in the evening for long though. I'd already pledged to the Youth, so I had meetings to attend and duties to perform. Renate took over the cooking. She still does it. Shopping too."

"And the cleaning?" Anna's expression told her amusement. I didn't need to answer.

Her acceptance comforted me. I thought perhaps the wall could stay down. Perhaps being known was not as frightening as it seemed.

Until it was.

Chapter Nine
Rennie

Nuremberg, Germany
10 September 1938

At breakfast, Werner greeted me with a thin smile. "You enjoyed the torchlight parade?"

I warmed at the memory. "It was indescribable. I understand what you and Onkel Edmund always said."

Any further discussion stopped when Anna slid onto a chair beside Werner, a plate of jam-slathered toast in her hand. She was cleaned and pressed, dressed in her nurse's whites. She and Werner exchanged a polite smile and nod as was proper for sweethearts at that time of day. "Off to the clinic this morning, I see," Werner said to her.

Anna spoke in a rush. "It will be ever so busy. All these people in town. The hospitals are overwhelmed." She bit the toast and tore it away, leaving specks of strawberry at one corner of her mouth. "Our clinic will take walk-ins."

Since Mutter was a stickler for table manners, I'd never seen a person chew with an open mouth. Anna's tongue moved in a most extraordinary way, flicking bits of food from her lips and pulling them in so they joined the wet blob of tan mush in her mouth. She must have mistaken my staring for interest because she clarified. "For folks who need care for small problems, a turned ankle, or stomach trouble."

Werner didn't look at Anna while she ate; he stared at his coffee instead. Now he turned a slow smile to me. "You were saying, Renate."

"I'll take whatever assignment I'm given." The guilty knot in my gut had gone, and I never wanted it back. "And I'll do extra. Stuff envelopes, raise money. I promise."

My brother nodded, but his expression showed caution. "Because of, shall we say, past transgressions"—I flinched—"you will start small." He pulled a folded paper from an inside jacket pocket. It was a list of two or three dozen names. "These Munich boys are at the encampment. Find them. Tell them to be at the Frankischer Hotel at eleven Uhr. They are to be in uniform and ready to be interviewed by the international press corps."

I glanced at the clock. I was due to meet other BDM members at half past eleven to distribute food at the Luitpold Arena. "I'll have to leave now."

Werner waved his long fingers. "Then do so." As I rose, he spoke again, his voice filled with warning. "If any of the boys on this list are missing from the press conference, you will be responsible."

I raced out the door to catch the streetcar.

Despite the crowds I'd seen, I wasn't prepared for the size of the encampment. Spread before me were acres of tents, rows upon rows of them. Scores—no hundreds, maybe thousands—of boys filled the area. I had no idea where to start looking for those on my list.

A cluster of boys washing at a long water trough glanced up at me. One, a tall, good-looking Youth, draped a towel about his neck. "Looking for someone?" he asked. His gaze slid to my feet then lifted and lingered too long on other parts.

In my rush to leave Sabine's house, I hadn't changed into my BDM uniform. I knew what kind of girls wore street clothes into a group of thousands of male Youth. I straightened and tried to look official. "I'm here on Youth business. Where are the troops from Munich?"

He gestured to the rear of the encampment. "That way. If you don't find them," he said, winking, "come on back. Us boys from Heidelberg might suit you fine."

I hurried away.

Past long rows of tents, I tried to look as if I knew where I was going. Stares, catcalls, and whistles assaulted me any number of times. Twice, I asked for directions, each time choosing a boy sitting with a book or a cooking pot. After a quarter hour, I spied Klaus, Sophie's stepbrother, at a water pump. I rushed to him, grabbing his arm to reassure myself of his reality. "I'm so glad to see you," I blurted out. I tugged him out of earshot of any eavesdroppers, then whispered, "I've been so worried."

He stepped back enough to let my grip on his arm loosen. "Hello, Rennie. Good to see you."

I was near to bursting, but couldn't mention Sophie's name or inquire about his mother or stepfather. Couldn't take the chance. "We have to catch up soon."

He glanced around before he answered, his voice soft and even. "Soon, yes… Stop at the bakery when you get home."

"But…"

"Next week. What brings you to the camp?"

I'd almost forgotten. I pulled the list from my skirt pocket. "These boys need to be at the Frankischer Hof at eleven Uhr. Interviews with the international press corps."

As Klaus scanned the list of names, I took him in. Even out of uniform and smeared with dirt, Klaus was a good-looking fellow. Like Erich, he'd grown taller and more muscular since I'd seen him last. Wanted to be a boxer, from what I remembered. "Most of the boys are nearby. A few are wandering, but I can round them up." He folded the paper and nodded. "I'll take care of this."

"But Werner said…" I straightened. "It's my responsibility."

Mischief sparkled in his robin's-egg blue eyes, the familiar Klaus I'd always known. "I won't allow the Scharführer's little sister to get in trouble. She might tangle me in one of her schemes." His sauciness, appealing to girls everywhere, was intact. His tone changed to a more serious one. "I'm teasing, Rennie. I'll track them down. If you'd like, I mean."

He'd said it with a small hesitation, as if he wasn't fully in control. Unusual for him. Must be his family's troubles weighing him down. "Thanks for the offer," I said, retrieving the list, "but I'll take care of it."

In thirty minutes I'd found each boy and delivered the message. Even when I found dear, sweet Erich with an armload of firewood, all I did was give him the same information I'd given the other boys. All business. Werner would be pleased.

To avoid walking past the boy from Heidelberg, I hurried down another of the endless rows of tents in a direction I hoped would take me near the streetcar stop. In minutes I was lost and asked directions of someone hunched over a book.

When the figure looked up, I realized it was a grown man in uniform. SA, as Vater had been. My breath caught.

"Are you quite well?" he asked, scanning my face with concern.

I nodded. "I'm surprised to see an adult. I thought the camp was for Youth."

He smiled, but there was no warmth behind it. "Shows how far we've fallen."

"I beg your pardon?"

"What do you need?"

I explained my problem, and he pointed me in the right direction. I thanked him and was ready to leave when I stopped. For reasons I'll never understand, I blurted out, "My father was SA too. He's gone four years now."

The man lowered his gaze a moment, a gesture of respect. "I'm sorry." Then he looked up. "Four years, you say? So, he died in '34?"

"Yes. June 30th."

"June 30th." We spoke the date at the same time, but his voice tense and sad. "Ah. The Purge. We lost a lot of men that night."

The Purge?

Another man, an officer I assume, barked orders nearby. The man I'd been speaking with folded his book and rose. "Best be on your way, fatherless girl."

When I climbed onto the streetcar, I was grateful to rest my pounding head against the window's cool glass. Werner knew what happened to Vater the night he died—he'd been with him! If Mutter wouldn't tell me, I'd ask Werner. Once we were home.

The rest of the day passed in a blur of activity. With BDM members from around the country, I made sandwiches for the mass of people attending the day's events. I raced to the Frankischer Hotel before eleven Uhr to make sure the boys all showed up for the interviews. They did, thankfully. Then I ran back to help BDM hand the food out to spectators. Hundreds of us even cleaned up the stadium afterward, bagging the trash so the venue would be ready for the next event.

When I met Werner and Anna for dinner, I told them I was quite satisfied with my day's work. "How did the boys' interviews go?" I asked.

My brother lifted his chin as he spoke. "The international press was impressed with our Youth. They are disciplined and intelligent, a shining example of our nation's great future. And tomorrow's Day of Hitler Youth will be covered in newspapers worldwide." He leaned back in his chair and tugged his uniform smooth. His voice rose in pitch, the familiar nasal whine he used for grand announcements. "The world waits to hear our Führer's speech."

I smiled. My Germany had a leader admired worldwide. "What will he talk about?"

Anna spoke up, her voice filled with disdain. "Those Czechs, no doubt."

In a recent newsreel, I'd learned that the Czech president refused to take a stand against the oppression of Germans who lived there. That upset the Führer.

"It's a shame the Führer has to waste his time fighting for basic rights of ethnic Germans," Werner said. "We're a cultured people. We know our rights." He snorted. "Those Czechs. Such a petty race."

Anna agreed, head bobbing. "Ridiculous."

My gut tightened, and I excused myself. In the cluttered attic room, I closed my eyes and recalled the songs and waves of energy that had lifted me just twenty-four hours earlier. I focused on the sense of unity I'd felt, the pride that had surged within me and around me and carried me along so buoyantly. Beam by incredible beam, I recreated the glorious cathedral of light in my mind—its wonder, its spectacle. In a few minutes time, I was able to loosen the unwelcome tightness in my belly and push it aside. If only it were gone for good.

Again, Anna and Werner were at Sabine's table when I came down for breakfast. This time, my brother stood behind a chair, hands gripping its curved wooden back. "Ah, you're in uniform, Renate. Good. Be at the stadium's east entrance at nine Uhr. I have a special job for you." He strode out.

Anna focused on scraping a butter knife along a burnt piece of toast. "Do you know what he wants me to do?" I asked her.

She sighed. "I guess you'll find out when you get there. Honestly, Renate. You can't expect me to figure out your assignment." As she spoke, she waved the knife in exaggerated exasperation, causing black specks to fly off and land on her white uniform. "Now look what you made me do!" she shouted, bolting upright and racing from the room. The knife and its debris clattered to the floor.

Anna was a more dramatic actress than I'd ever be. I cleaned up her mess.

My BDM uniform freshly pressed, my shoes polished, my short curls as neat as I could make them, I stood at the massive stadium's east entrance at nine Uhr sharp. I wasn't surprised to see Werner approach with a dozen or more Youth trailing behind him, his usual Pied Piper self. I'd always said it in a derogatory way, making fun of the Youth's unthinking loyalty to my wiry brother. Now I saw the sense in it. Someone had to lead, someone with a clear vision of the future. For many Youth, my brother was that person.

Werner stopped in front of me and saluted, then handed me a stack of flyers. "Normally, our Youth members hand out the programs." He gestured to the pile in my hands. "But today the Youth *are* the program." I nodded my understanding and straightened, ready for the task. He started toward the stadium, then turned to me, causing the boys at his heels to stumble and almost bump into him. "When the international press arrives, tell them the finale will be quite special. The best place to photograph it will be the top tier of the stadium."

I began my assignment. Greet with a pleasant word while offering a program, dozens of times every minute. A girl in a Jungmädel uniform came alongside me dragging a wagon filled with hundreds or maybe a thousand programs. After the busy blur of the next thirty minutes, only a handful remained.

Six or seven men sporting press corps badges approached. Each wore a large camera on a neck strap as if it were a clunky piece of jewelry, a small notebook and pen sticking from a hand or a pocket. I glanced at a few of their tags: they were from Japan, Italy, England, America. Our Youth event must be quite important to draw this kind of worldwide attention.

"Welcome," I said, handing them programs. "I have a message."

One man, a rather lopsided man with an English-style bowler hat, seemed taken aback. "For me?"

"Not for you in particular"—I looked at his name badge—"Herr Massey. For all of you, the whole press corps. The Scharführer suggests you photograph the finale from the top tier of the stands. Something special is planned, and that's your best vantage point."

Most of the men nodded and filed into the stadium, but Herr Massey lingered a moment. "And how did you end up with this job, young lady?" he asked. His German was good, but his English accent was evident. "*Fräulein…*"

"Müller. Renate Müller. My friends call me Rennie."

For a second, his brows quivered, and his face registered recognition. "From Munich?"

"Um, yes. Have we met, Herr Massey?" I asked, keeping my tone polite.

He mumbled something in English.

I tried again. "I'm afraid you have the advantage. Do I know you?"

He tipped his head, an expression of curiosity. "We have a mutual friend."

"Oh? Who is that?"

Without answering me, he continued. "And you are handing out flyers for the Rally because…"

During this exchange, people kept filing past with hands outstretched for programs. Not being able to greet them and do my job as I'd been instructed irritated me, but my conduct in front of the international press was important. My job was to show the best side of the Youth and of Germany. "I'm happy to help however I can," I recited. "Anything to support the Movement."

Herr Massey regarded me through narrowed eyes. "Is that so?" He tipped his hat. "Then good day, *Fräulein* Müller." He took a flyer and moved on, his odd, lurching stride easily lost in the crowd.

Well after the start of the events, I slipped into a seat. Hundreds of flag bearers stood at attention around the stadium's perimeter. For the next two or three hours, various sports groups presented precision programs, each quite entertaining. Costumed girls from dozens of BDM troops performed folk dances. A number of Hitler Youth demonstrated push-ups and march formations while their drummers marked time. Other troops engaged in rifle drills and navigated obstacle courses. In all, it was an outstanding demonstration by our nation's young people. I was proud.

The Youth then gathered at the center of the field to prepare for the finale. At first, their positions seemed random, chaotic. But half a minute later, the final design was clear. They had aligned their bodies to spell out two words on the giant field: **Adolf Hitler**.

My small role helped ensure the press snapped good photos. Those photos would affect how the world saw our Youth, our Führer, and the whole Movement.

Photos have power. Sophie taught me that.

Chapter Ten
Werner

By early '45, it was clear we wouldn't win. Not yet. The Allies closed in—Americans and Brits from the west, Russians from the east.

In a stupor, I stumbled through what was left of the Großdeutsches Reich. All was ash and death. Disgusting. I tore a strip of cloth from my tattered uniform jacket and wrapped my nose and mouth against the stench.

I had information for the Allies. In exchange for safety, I'd strike a deal with the Americans or Brits. They had a reputation for fairness. And cleanliness.

As I approached the Fatherland from the east, the Russians were not even thirty kilometers behind me. Allies or no, I wouldn't talk to them. Rumor was they were cruel to SS prisoners of war. No filthy, lice-infested POW camp for me. Never. I kept walking west.

I wept as I removed what was left of my uniform. Burned everything except my boots and gloves. My SS tattoo remained. Proof of my identity when I approached the Allies.

Dressed in rags like everyone else, I blended with the masses who shuffled through ruined towns and villages. They sought food and shelter. I headed home. Munich, under American control.

When I reached Altstadt, my old neighborhood, I stopped cold. While some buildings stood unscathed, others were hollow shells, windowless with dark, unblinking stares. Grit and dust billowed above heaps of debris, the pitiful remnants of homes, businesses, and centuries-old churches. I tottered down the once familiar streets, stunned by the foreignness of the landscape.

Then I was there. My block. My home, or what remained of it. Shredding what was left of my gloves as I did so, I scrabbled through the ruins. I tossed aside bricks and scorched boards, desperate to find something of my previous life. Nothing.

I tried the next pile of rubble, what had been the Knox's house, hoping against hope I'd find something—anything—to tell me what had happened to everyone. All I found was Willi Knox's shirt hanging on a peg in the basement air-raid shelter. Willi's identification papers poked from a shirt pocket.

And a new plan was born.

I wouldn't turn myself over to the Allies and beg for mercy. I'd get out. I'd find a country that would welcome me, a country with German-speaking communities and a sympathetic government. A country that would benefit from my experience. All I had to do was get there. Now, with Willi's papers, I could.

I'd heard other SS traveled under their own names, but that was months before the Allied noose tightened. More recently, SS traveled with forged papers and fake IDs. I didn't need either.

My identity as Werner Müller, son of a loser and brother of a traitor, former Scharführer and SS member who once called on his Gestapo godfather to keep his head—that identity could be history. If need be, I could be the scrawny, sniffling boy who'd lived next door, the very one I'd despised for his weakness and avoided for his contagion. If need be, I'd become Willi Knox.

Shuffle the cards and start over.

Only problem was my tattoo, the mark of my service within the SS. It was small, a few centimeters square near my left armpit. Never having been in the service, Willi wouldn't have one. For the time being, I'd keep it. Might come in handy.

I hid in plain sight among thousands of refugees, this time walking to the chaos of post-Mussolini Italy. There I found plenty of SS members, all loyal to the cause, in a lovely Alpine village. I mentioned my meticulous record-keeping skills to Vincenzo and his wife Lorena, German-speaking Party sympathizers who owned a local *Brauhaus.* In full understanding of both my real identity and my need to lay low, they offered me a job and a room. I accepted both and dove into the work of straightening out their books.

Evenings, I often met with other SS and Party loyalists in the Brauhaus' private room. We ate sausages and drank beer and exchanged war news, what we'd heard on the wireless, what we'd read in the newspaper. Face to face, we bolstered each other and kept our enthusiasm high. At night, I often awoke short of breath with a raging headache. Lorena said it was altitude sickness.

I knew better.

The Allies continued to advance; their victory seemed sure. Rumors flew. The war would be over before summer.

My head pounded.

The leader of Hitler Youth, Baldur von Schirach, ordered all Youth, even children as young as ten, to defend the Fatherland against the enemy. Ten-year-olds. Pah. At that age, some of my Youth had cried for their mothers during overnight camp.

I could only sleep once I was certain Willi's papers were still tucked in my wool socks. I checked each night.

One evening in March, I arrived early for dinner. As I entered the private room, two fellow officers glanced up at me and stopped their conversation. Assuming their talk involved the war, I asked, "What has happened?"

They exchanged a look. "Several of the men are moving on," one said.

"Moving on? Where?"

"Argentina."

"Are we to reassemble there?"

"Reassemble?" His laugh was throaty and bitter. "No, Werner. They're running away. The cowards."

The other officer chimed in. "Vincenzo and Lorena have connections in Argentina, arranged it all. Visas, work permits, everything. Eight of them are going. Peron's government is sympathetic, and immigration officials there don't ask questions." He shook his head. "Makes me wish I hadn't spent so much money here. Thought Vincenzo and Lorena were loyalists." He spit in his beer mug. "Cowards and traitors." The second man did the same. They both left.

Lorena bustled in, a stack of menus in one hand. She took in the table with its empty seats and dirty mugs, then sighed. "What can I get you, Werner?"

"Weisswurst and a beer. And information." She raised one eyebrow but remained silent. "About Argentina."

"You too? Just when our accountant is happy with the ledgers." With a crook of her finger, she led me to the kitchen where two elderly German brothers, Alfons and Horst, worked. "Talk with them."

Alfons was elbows deep in soapy water while Horst minced onions on a wooden board. Both turned to regard me but continued with their work. I hesitated. I'd met the two men before, but we'd spoken of weather and war news, never anything personal. "I understand you know about travel," I began.

Alfons laughed and wiped his reddened, dripping hands on a stained apron. "Ja."

"What kind of travel?" Horst asked.

"International."

Horst raised an eyebrow.

I took a deep breath. "I hear the others are going…" I hesitated and finished softly. "To Argentina."

Both men stopped their tasks and came closer. Horst's thick neck was ringed with sweat, and the onion-soaked knife dangled from his hand. Coarse hairs sprang from Alfons' ears and nose like gangly saplings.

"We're going too," Horst said, "as soon as our paperwork goes through channels. Before the Allies interrogate us."

The Allies were questioning cooks? What would they do to me?

Alfons must have read my panic because he picked up the conversation. "We cooked for officers, served them. Overheard…" he hesitated. A look passed between the brothers, a shared understanding. Alfons continued, "Why do you want to go?"

"I've got to get out of here," I said. Even as I spoke, I unbuttoned my collar and ran a finger around its circumference.

Both men stared at me, then burst into laughter. Alfons tousled my hair as if I were a child. "Not to worry, Werner. We'll help," he said. "Do you have an alias?"

I spent the next few weeks under the wing of these two men. Their appearance and manner were coarse, but they were true to their word. For a slim roll of bills, they told me who to contact at the consulate, how to get a visa, and what paperwork I'd need to sail and emigrate. Providing all was in order, Alfons, Horst, and six others from our group were due to sail from Genoa in late May. I'd sail a few weeks later. I'd be far away before the Allies came looking for Werner Müller.

I hoped.

Vincenzo and Lorena were good to us, even preparing us for the language of Argentina. Since Spanish and Italian are similar, they began speaking only in Italian, both in the office and in the restaurant. Within a few weeks, I understood much of the Italian wireless newscast.

I was working through a column of accounts receivable when Alfons burst into the restaurant office with the news. Our Führer was dead.

The moment is etched on my heart—the breathless report, my hands pressed to my desk for support, heart and head pounding, my stomach churning with anguish, Alfons' frame filling the doorway, eyebrows furrowed as his gaze moved across the faces of me and the others in the office. Lorena sobbed into her hands, and Vincenzo wrapped an arm about her heaving shoulders. He closed the Brauhaus for the day.

Reports were sketchy and conflicting. German authorities released a statement: our leader had killed himself in an underground bunker in Berlin. International reports said nothing could be confirmed. No body had been identified. It might be several days until the Allies could get inside the destroyed bunker and confirm for themselves.

We agreed—the Führer would not have taken the coward's way out. He would not have killed himself. If he was dead, those dirty Russians shot him.

By evening, Alfons and Horst's flat was filled with my fellow Germans, twenty or more from neighboring towns. Many shared stories of how they'd participated in the dream, how high they'd risen, which noted officials they'd worked under. I listened but shared nothing. The less anyone knew about me, the better.

An hour or so into the evening, Alfons waved in three men in dress SS uniforms. The ashen-faced officers still sported their full complement of pins and honors, each with a slim-waisted, bejeweled woman on his arm. Reflexively, every one of us stood and saluted, "Heil, Hitler!"

The men returned the greeting and gestured for us all to sit. "Tell us the truth," Alfons said as he arranged chairs and cushions for the guests. "Is our Führer really"—he paused—"gone?"

The shorter of the two men, Hans Becker, his nametag read, answered. "Unclear. But know this: for some time, a plan has been in place to move our entire Party's administration to safety. The plan may be underway right now. Our beloved leader may be traveling under an alias."

"But can he get out of Germany?" someone asked. "The Allies are everywhere."

A small, tired smile raised one side of Becker's mouth. "We are everywhere too. The Party faithful await his arrival in Argentina."

Wonderful news indeed! I'd soon be among that group of the faithful.

The following day, more bad news from the Fatherland—our propaganda minister, Joseph Goebbels, was confirmed dead, along with his wife and six children. Their bodies had been identified by both German and Allied sources.

Then we heard a report that shook me to the core. *Reichsführer* Heinrich Himmler, the leader of the SS and the drive behind our *Lebensborn* program, had approached the Swedish Red Cross and offered to surrender the entire western front to the Allies. The Führer had been enraged and ordered Himmler's arrest and execution.

Made me glad I hadn't talked with the Allies.

With Himmler hunted by both the Allies and what was left of the Party, I wondered—when our Führer surfaced and returned to power, what would happen to him? What would happen to SS members who had been under Himmler, officers like me? Would Himmler's blame be shared by all of us? Might it lead to another purge, like the one in '34 that killed my father? I reached into my wool sock and rubbed Willi Knox's papers until I calmed.

As days stretched on, the Führer's fate remained unclear. The body of a man with a small mustache had been found but not identified. A soft shallow trench was discovered to hold the burned bodies of a man and a woman, perhaps our Führer and Eva Braun. Perhaps not. Nothing was certain.

Alfons repeated Becker's assertion—the Führer was on his way to safety right now. A U-boat to Argentina was the most likely scenario, especially since we'd heard of several U-boats landing on unguarded stretches of Argentine coastline. I stayed calm, picturing the Führer's grand arrival there. I'd be loyal to him and him alone. When our Reich was re-established in South America, I could show my tattoo and resume my work.

A week later, Germany surrendered.

That evening, we ate the food of our homeland, drank to the vision, and renewed our individual and collective promises to keep the Movement alive.

When we learned of Himmler's death a few weeks later, I was torn. Should I mourn the loss of another Party leader, my former boss? Or as the Führer would have done, should I celebrate his death as that of a traitor?

And what of Onkel Edmund, the Gestapo officer? News broadcasts hadn't mentioned him by name. Not that he'd help me again. But if he was alive, and I displeased him by fleeing Germany…

When the others got together, I begged off due to illness. It wasn't a lie.

Alfons and Horst sailed under their own names in late June. The six SS who sailed with them traveled under aliases. As the only German still working for Vincenzo and Lorena then, I ate my evening meals alone.

News on the wireless grew more worrisome. In front of the worldwide press, a large trial with an international panel of judges would soon start in Nuremberg. By the dozen, then by the hundred, prominent Nazis and collaborators from occupied nations were charged, with many arrested and scheduled for trial. Even more alarming, the Allies gained approval to arrest under the charge "crimes against humanity," punishable by death.

My headaches worsened.

To emigrate, a resident of Argentina had to vouch for me. Correction. A resident of Argentina had to vouch for Willi Knox. Lorena mentioned a cousin near Buenos Aires in need of a bookkeeper, so I begged her—no, I bribed her—to write him. This cousin came through with the promise of a job for a German war refugee named Willi Knox. My papers were approved twelve days later. I was to sail in four weeks.

Those last weeks in Italy were endless. With every new face, each knock on the office door, my insides liquefied. I couldn't concentrate by day, tossed in fitful sleep at night. Willi's papers stayed with me around the clock.

At long last, I left Werner Müller and my beloved, wounded Europe behind. As Willi Knox, I boarded a ship heading west, then south.

The first night on board ship, I overheard other refugees. They said the Reich was indeed re-forming deep within the Andes. We would arrive in time to see the South American continent transformed into the Reich of our dreams. It would be the land of *Lebensraum*, room for our people. I hoped they were right.

When we docked three weeks later, immigration officials accepted my roll of bills and Willi Knox's paperwork. Argentina was my new home.

Carrying all my possessions in a single valise, I arrived at the address in a small town outside Buenos Aires. Lorena's insight was remarkable. The business her cousin Tomas owned was perfect for me.

Tomas was a quiet man, a German immigrant himself, who bred galgos, Spanish greyhounds. His dogs had champion bloodlines, prized by hunters for their skill chasing down rabbits on the rugged South American terrain. Tomas never asked about my life in Germany, just accepted the referral from Lorena and took me on to keep his books. In exchange, he offered me a furnished room plus a stipend for food. I was surprised but pleased to see Alfons and Horst worked there also. They prepared a daily meal for the kennel workers and made specialized food for the dogs.

Tomas had kept his own books before I arrived—a year's worth of crumpled receipts and check stubs in an aged cigar box. His ledger was peppered with cross-outs and smeared entries. Unbearable. I copied the entirety into a fresh book, complete with ruled columns and figure tallies at bottom and top of each page. At closing time the first day, Tomas peered at my work. He grunted his approval, then invited me to join him at the kennels.

The man was an encyclopedia of information regarding galgos—their breeding, their traits, their habits. He was proud of his animals and knew each by name. "See that fawn-colored wirehair?" he'd say. "He's Jocko, the sire of…" and then rattle off name, color, and type of coat of Jocko's progeny, first in German, then in Spanish.

Over time, I learned to document details of each dog for Tomas and prospective buyers: lineage, speed, agility, visual acuity, endurance. The galgos raised on Tomas' land were second to none, bred over many generations to be the best.

His dogs' bloodlines were purified by mating only the best sires and bitches. Deformed and sickly puppies were drowned.

No need to burden the kennel with useless eaters.

News from the Fatherland was bleak. Many Party leaders were found guilty at the Nuremberg trials, some in absentia. Of those who stood trial, only a few were acquitted. Most received long prison sentences. Twelve were hanged.

Onkel Edmund was not among them. When I thought of how he would react if he found me here, hiding in a foreign land under an assumed name, my headaches worsened.

I blocked him from my mind.

Within a few weeks, I'd sorted out Tomas' books. With my usual efficiency, I developed and implemented a more thorough record-keeping system. I grew comfortable with the business and was able to converse in both German and Spanish with customers, dealers, vendors, and kennel workers. Tomas gained confidence in me. I relaxed.

And still the Führer did not arrive.

Sometime in January '46, Tomas and I were doing a routine check on a newborn litter. I jotted notes about the pups—size, color, coat, vigor. Tomas turned to me. "Did you live on a farm in Germany?" I shook my head. "Work on one?"

"No. Why?"

"You're not bothered when we drown the weaklings. Bothers most men the first few times they see it. So, I figured you understood why."

As bookkeeper, I'd never done the actual drowning, but I did indeed understand the purpose. After months of half-truths, I longed to tell Tomas everything, about why I understood. I trusted him. But I'd been burned by trust before.

He continued, "If I were a betting man, Willi Knox—if that's even your real name…" My heart jumped, but I kept my expression even. "I'd bet you understood specimen selection prior to coming here. How to breed the best with the best. How to destroy the imperfect." He searched my face for a reaction.

"Good thing you're not a betting man," I managed to say. He continued to scrutinize me. "I was not part of the Reich. Unable to serve. Too sickly."

He squeezed the bulk of muscle in my upper arm. "Sickly, huh?" He laughed, an easy laugh. "Don't worry. Authorities here don't care." He took the clipboard from my hand. "Someday I hope you trust me enough to tell me your story. Your real story."

I hoped so too. Living someone else's life was a lonely business.

Chapter Eleven
Rennie

Munich, Germany
11 September 1938

Home.

I hummed as I unpacked my trunk, shaking out and refolding the stale clothes, then tucking them into drawers beside sprigs of fresh lavender. Near the trunk's bottom, I pulled out a sweater and felt the solid rectangular object wrapped within. I'd almost forgotten. I tossed the sweater aside and held in my hands the beloved picture of Sophie and me, undamaged by travel, intact within the Romany woman's frame. There we were, my best friend and me in silhouette, pointing and laughing. I touched a finger to my lips and then to the glass fronting Sophie's image. "Tomorrow morning, I'll start where I last saw you—at the polio hospital. I'll find out where you are and come to visit. I promise."

I squinted at the photo. Sophie and I had been standing together when it was taken, of that I was certain. And yet the image showed distance between our figures. In fact, we stood at nearly opposite sides of the photo! How could that be?

What's more, each of my feet was planted on a line. These parallel lines stretched toward Sophie's figure a short distance, then faded away.

Sophie's feet were side by side, grounded on a single short line. Sophie had one path; I had two.

A memory sparked, something the Romany woman said about choosing my path. I slipped the photo from its frame and examined it more closely. No, I was wrong. The photo was as it had always been—Sophie and me side by side, pointing and laughing at the lunch-stealing bird. Feet together. No paths in front of us.

Clearly, I was exhausted. I laid the unframed photo on my nightstand, finished unpacking, and went to bed.

Mutter leaned her elbows on our kitchen table, arms crossed. "Renate," she began, her voice tight, "your help is needed here." She hesitated as if searching for the right words. "I clean offices five nights a week now. We need the money." Her hands, a working woman's hands, were webbed with angry red cracks. Her fisherman father had taught her to use nightly Vaseline treatments on chapped skin, but it didn't seem to be enough. "I need you to shop and cook. Someone else can stuff envelopes."

All this my first morning home after three months away, just because I told her of my plan to help with the Youth after my daytime theater classes. "It's not like I'm in school anymore," I told her. Like many of my former classmates, my schooling ended after I turned fourteen. A few acting classes and some roles in a local theater company were the only plans I'd made. "Werner and I can do without cooked meals," I insisted. "We'll figure out…"

Her hesitation was now gone. "No. I will not have my children live as if I can't provide for them. My children will eat cooked dinners. Since your father died…" She hesitated, then cleared her throat before starting over. "You'll prepare the evening meal for yourself and your brother. As you've done before."

"But Mutter, I want…"

Her palm slapped the table, sloshing the contents of her coffee cup into the saucer. "Enough. What any of us want is unimportant."

I was a bit more subdued when I said, "I'm trying to bring about the greater good."

Her expression shifted, and her brows furrowed in thought. She placed her cracked hand on top of mine and whispered, "Remember the fish."

"I beg your pardon?"

"A fish swimming alone is easy prey. But hide that fish among the thousands in a school, and he probably won't be a shark's dinner."

I pulled my hand from beneath hers and sat back. Strain and exhaustion lined my mother's face. She'd aged quite a bit in the months I'd been away. "Why don't you rest before work? We'll talk tomorrow."

She reached forward and squeezed my hand, her rough skin scraping against mine. "Please understand." Her whisper was tight and strained. "Blending in, being part of it all is fine. But sometimes the shark snaps at the whole school." She made a guttural sound and ran a finger across her neck.

I drew a sharp breath.

Mutter's gazed fixed on something over my shoulder. She bolted upright and fled the room.

A thin figure stepped around the kitchen doorframe, and I startled. "Werner! When did you get home from Nuremberg?"

He didn't enter the room but leaned against the doorframe and stared down at me. "Just in time, I see. Interesting conversation."

I gasped. "You eavesdropped? On Mutter and me?"

He poured a cup of coffee and mumbled, "Mutter, Mutter." He turned to me. "I'll have your weekday assignment arranged tomorrow. Regardless of what she says"—he lifted his chin toward our mother's room—"if you want extra work to help the Reich, I'll arrange it."

Sometime later, Mutter poked her head around my door. "I'm leaving for work." Her critical eye scanned my almost straightened room and nodded approval.

She glanced over her shoulder before continuing in a whisper. "When it's just us girls, you'll have to tell me about your time at the farm, your work and the people you met." Her expression showed nervous curiosity. "Now that you're home, you'll look up Sophie?"

I matched her whisper. "First thing tomorrow."

She nodded and mouthed, "Be careful." Then she returned to her normal tone, all business. "Make *käesespätzle* tonight. The cheese is in the icebox. I'll be home by midnight."

As she closed the door, I marveled at a new insight. My mother kept secrets from Werner.

A polite receptionist at the polio hospital led me to a door with an engraved brass plaque: Herr Doktor Georg Albrecht.

Inside, his prim secretary stood to greet me. "I'm trying to find a friend of mine. She was a patient here," I said, smiling. Since I wasn't sure how much they knew of the charges filed against Sophie, I'd hold off giving her name until needed.

"Visitation is on Saturdays," the woman said. "Fifteen Uhr. Come back then." She strode to the outer office door and opened it.

I didn't move. "I know about visitation."

"Saturday."

I crossed my arms. "Why should I come back? Tell me if my friend is here or not." When the woman didn't respond, I raised my voice. "If she's here, I'll come back Saturday."

An inner office door opened, and a middle-aged man stepped through. The secretary addressed him, her tone flustered. "I'm sorry we disturbed you, Herr Doktor. I'm trying to tell this young lady…"

The doctor ran a thumb and forefinger along his silver handlebar mustache and said, "And who might you be?"

"Pardon the intrusion, Herr Doktor. I'm Renate Müller."

Recognition lit the man's face. "You're Werner's sister."

"You know him?"

As if in answer to my question, a woman in nursing whites stepped from the inner office. Anna. I should have realized she'd be here—this hospital was her assignment as a student nurse. "Of course he knows Werner," she said. "Herr Doktor Albrecht is my father."

If Sophie had mentioned that tidbit to me, I'd forgotten. So many people near Sophie were connected. A regular web. I shuddered.

"Anna was telling me about the Rally," he said. "Sounds as if you both had a marvelous time."

The man's repeated stroking of his waxed mustache was distracting, but I recalled the high energy of the town, the wonder and magic of the torchlight parade. "It was wonderful," I said honestly.

"Good, good," the doctor said, bobbing his head. He placed a hand at the small of my back and steered me to the outer door. "Nice meeting you, Renate."

"You too, Herr Doktor." I turned to go, then stopped. I'd almost forgotten the purpose of my visit. I faced him again and dared to speak my friend's name "Is Sophie Adler still a patient here?"

His eyebrows shot up. "Adler? As I told the Gestapo, she left a few weeks after I arrived. Mid-July or so."

"When she hurt her arm?"

"I don't remember any arm injury." He turned to the secretary and to his daughter. "Did young Adler hurt her arm while she was a patient here?"

The secretary glanced up from her typewriter and shrugged. Anna's attention darted from one of us to the other before she focused on me. "As I said before, Sophie's arm injury was tended at University Hospital. She did not return here."

"Are there patients who might be in touch with her? She was friends with…" I struggled to recall. "Elisabeth, Marla, a little boy named Fritz, a tall man, what was his name…"

Anna shrugged. The doctor continued to tug on his mustache and said, "You've heard about the charges, nicht? I doubt anyone will speak with you about her, but you can try. Visitation is Saturday at fifteen Uhr." As he and Anna returned to the inner office, the secretary bolted to her feet and opened the outer door. I took the cue and left.

At University Hospital, a pinch-faced woman in Medical Records consulted her files. After telling me the Gestapo had also been there inquiring after Sophie, she pulled out the hospital's discharge ledger. An entry on 13 July, three days after the *Tag der Deutschen Kunst*, showed Sophie had been discharged. The person who signed her out scrawled their name, with only a curvaceous B and E of the initials readable—a woman's signature, to be sure. No address was listed.

I then spoke with Luana Weber, the nurse who wrote the note on Sophie's behalf and mailed it to me. She remembered Sophie fondly but knew nothing more than what she'd already written in her cover letter.

I did visit the polio hospital that Saturday. I inquired of patients I remembered meeting—Elisabeth, little Fritz, Herr Franken—but they'd all been discharged. I was getting ready to leave when a teenage girl with straight brown hair wheeled up to me. "I know you," she said. "You're a friend of that girl. The one who caused trouble."

I kept calm. "I'm Rennie. And you are?"

"Marla."

I remembered her now. Sophie didn't trust her.

"The Gestapo has been here a couple times," Marla continued, "getting information from us. Since you're looking for her, I guess you don't know where she is either."

I was back to square one.

Werner tucked his napkin in his collar as a rap came at the door. "*Willkommen!*" he called.

Sophie's stepbrother Klaus entered, his shoes and trouser cuffs muddy, his normally slicked hair mussed and flecked with flour. He plopped something wrapped in a checkered towel on the kitchen counter, then sniffed the air like an animal on the hunt.

"Ah, Klaus," my brother said, gesturing. "Shoes outside the door, please. Then wash up. Dinner's on the table."

Obediently, Klaus slipped into the washroom and closed the door behind him.

"I didn't know you invited a guest," I whispered to my brother. "There's not enough food."

He jerked a thumb to the towel-covered bundle on the counter. As I folded back the cloth, a rich waft of goodness rose. Inside sat a rounded loaf of dark bread speckled with oats and seeds, the specialty of Bäckerei Adler. Judging from the warm, familiar scent, Klaus was following his stepfather's recipe. "See?" Werner said as I brought slices of the delicious bread to the table. "There's plenty for three of us."

Klaus settled himself at the head of the table in Mutter's chair. As he speared a wurst and heaped red cabbage onto his plate, I turned to him. "Thank you for the bread. Reminds me of your stepfather. I…I'm so sorry to hear what happened."

Werner's head snapped up. Klaus drew a sharp breath. His cabbage-loaded fork clattered to the table, spraying wet red bits on the tablecloth. He bolted to his feet and returned with a rag. "Clumsy of me." His cheeks were crimson.

Werner turned to me, his mouth drawn tight. "Loyal Reich members aren't sorry to be rid of a traitor." Klaus' expression was part discomfort, part gratitude.

When Werner finished eating, he turned to Klaus. "Perhaps you'd like to tell Renate her new assignment."

"You'll work with me."

I was surprised. "At the bakery?" The Adler's thriving bakery had been a family operation in the truest sense of the word. Herr Adler had done the baking; Frau Adler had manned the storefront and kept the books. Both Klaus and Sophie had daily duties as well.

"I'll do the actual baking, keep track of inventory, order supplies. You'll be my assistant." Klaus sounded more comfortable than he had at the Rally, more his usual confident self. "Wait on customers, stock the display cases."

I recalled some of Sophie's tasks. "Who will go to the Viktualienmarkt for fresh fruit and eggs? Oh, and milk and cream? Balance the register and make the bank deposits?"

"You. I won't have time."

"And deliveries? Opening and closing the storefront? Cleaning?"

Klaus smiled, smearing butter on a hunk of bread. "You."

I hadn't touched my food. "It's too much for one person." I turned to my brother. "Werner, aren't there two or three more Youth who can help? Ones who…"

Werner interrupted me. "…ones who need an assignment to keep them out of trouble? Who need to be close so Klaus and I can keep an eye on them?" He pursed his lips. "No, Renate. This assignment is yours and yours alone. Klaus needs the help. You'll start this Wednesday."

"But my theater classes…"

Klaus seemed almost apologetic. "I really do need the help, Rennie. For a few months anyway."

"Why a few months?"

Klaus shrugged. "By the first of the year, I'll be in the Wehrmacht. The bakery will probably close."

Werner nodded. "See? You can take theater classes this winter. Until then, you need to be kept busy."

Busy was an understatement.

Late that night, voices woke me. Werner's high whine. "You never told her?"

My mother's voice, catching. "No. It's too, too…"

"Then I'll tell her."

I crept to my bedroom door and opened it a crack.

"Her reaction may be different from yours, Werner. You were there. She was not."

I pushed the door open and slid into a kitchen chair across from them. "This is about Vater, right? Tell me. I'm not a child anymore." With my knees to my chest, I tugged my nightgown around my bare feet and waited.

Mutter protested. I was too young. I might misunderstand. I should remember my father the way he was, not the way he died. Over each of these objections, I insisted on my own readiness to know. "All right, Renate. All right." The ache in her voice made her pain and exhaustion clear. "I suppose it's time." She patted my hand. "Your father died in the line of duty."

'Died in the line of duty' was all I'd ever been told. "Then he's a hero," I said, my voice catching. Werner rose and turned his back on us to wash his hands at the sink. "Why don't we talk about it?"

Mutter covered her face, her shoulders shaking. She spoke into her hands. "You shouldn't have to know such things."

Werner whirled from the sink. "If you can't tell her without blubbering, Mutter, then I'll tell her."

My mother, face blotchy and eyes streaming, waved my brother away. "This is my job," she said, then covered my hands with hers. In silence, she stared at Werner so long that he huffed and stomped out, closing his bedroom door behind him. She stayed silent a while longer, now and then straining toward his door. When she heard the squeak of his bedsprings, she exhaled and motioned for me to follow her. In our living room, she pulled the drapes and lit four candles on a sideboard. We settled into adjacent wooden rockers as far from Werner's bedroom as our small home allowed. Between the flickering yellowed light and our hushed words, the room might have been a morgue.

She began. "Vater was an SA officer assigned to Party headquarters here in Munich."

I remembered Vater being proud of the SA—his brown shirts, he called them. "What does the SA do, exactly? I know they police the streets and act as event security. But the ones I've met lately seem…" I searched for the words. "Beaten down."

"Insightful, Renate. The brown shirts were once a proud organization," my mother began. "They helped bring the Führer to power. They were there with him from the very beginning of the Movement.

"There was to be a big meeting of SA leaders at the resort in Bad Wiessee late in June that year, '34. Your father was disappointed not to be invited. He'd hoped to work himself into higher administration, but…" Mutter sighed and looked at her hands. "Ah, well." She glanced at Werner's bedroom door. "Either way, the end was the same. The men at the resort met the same fate."

I stared at my mother. "Those men were killed in the line of duty too?"

She hesitated. "Most of them were in uniform when they were killed, so yes, I suppose you could say that."

"I hope the killers were caught and punished."

"My sweet Renate. Always looking for justice. There's no justice when rumors are taken for truth."

"Rumors?"

"That the SA men were different. That they—how to say this… That they liked other men."

I gasped. "Vater? Was he…"

"No, no," she hurried to say, color rising to her pale cheeks. "I, um, I never saw evidence. But as is the case everywhere, some of the men were indeed that way, including their leader Ernst Röhm." Her lips pressed together. "Plus, there was a rumor that the SA wanted to overthrow the army, wanted to become the army. Wanted to grab the power right from the Führer's hands."

"Was that true?"

She shrugged. "What's the difference? When a rumor is repeated often enough, people believe it to be true. The Führer himself believed it." An unchecked tear clung to her lashes. "He believed the SA had to be cut down to size." She formed words with her mouth but barely made a sound. "Officers were killed. Family members too. Spouses, siblings."

I froze. "And children?"

She raised an upturned palm. "That I don't know." She rose and shuffled into the kitchen, returning with a cold glass of water for each of us. "I checked. He's asleep."

I pressed the wet glass to my hot cheeks, bracing for what might be next.

Mutter settled her glass on a doily and folded her hands. "This is so hard." I waited until she composed herself. "Your father joined the SA in '31 before the Führer even became chancellor. A year or so later, he began grumbling about the job. Seems the SA was taking part in roughing people up, bullying shopkeepers, acting as strong-arms during rallies. That sort of thing."

My gaze drifted to a nearby end table, home to two photos in plain wooden frames. One photo was my parents on their wedding day, my handsome father with his eyes full of hope. Those eyes once scanned my report card and winked as he slipped a one-mark note into my pocket. That forehead creased in wonder when I beat him at checkers. Those hands tied the tails on my kite, and that mouth scolded me for letting out too much string and getting the whole mess tangled in the trees.

The second photo was a younger version of Werner and me in front of our home. We're holding hands, common for us at the time. We look comfortable together. Gosh, I missed that. Around the time Vater died, Werner changed, and not for the better.

My mother interrupted my thoughts. "Your father took a desk job. Got him off the street and away from…" She hesitated. "The more distasteful roles. But he had never cared for paperwork, and the desk job was all paperwork."

"So why did he stay? Couldn't he find a different job?"

Her eyebrows furrowed. "The job gave him access to files at the Party headquarters. Confidential files. No doubt he overheard conversations. He was part of the"—she searched for the word—"the Party's school of fish for a couple years. If he moved away from the school, he'd be"—she glanced at Werner's closed door again—"vulnerable."

I squinted at her. "So, he kept working there because…"

She finished it for me. "Because he knew too much. As I told you yesterday, once you swim away from the rest of the fish, you're likely to"—her words caught—"be eaten by a shark."

"If Vater quit to take another job…"

"There would have been immediate consequences. Yes."

"So, he stayed."

"And did whatever they asked." She huffed. "For all the good it did. He was killed anyway. Dozens of others too."

My vision blurred. "Who would do such a thing?"

Was I supposed to know the answer? Did I know?

And then I did. I'd been hiding the answer from myself, shoving it away from my own awareness. "The Party," I said aloud, a hand pressed to my mouth. "The Party ordered Vater's killing." I needed a moment to catch up to my own words. "To keep the SA from taking too much power." Tears started anew. "Did the Führer know?"

My mother nodded, scrutinizing my reaction. "The SS did the actual killing, but I understand the Führer gave his blessing."

I'd been a fool. I allowed myself to be caught up in the Rally's excitement and pulled into the Party's fervor. "Werner knows this, right?" When my mother answered in the affirmative, I asked, "So how can he be such a devotee?"

Mutter waved a hand. "Ask him yourself. I'm done in." She kissed the top of my head and left me alone in the quivering candlelight. Distorted shadows trembled on the walls long after her bedsprings were silent.

Chapter Twelve
Werner

Munich, Germany
30 June 1934

When I was fourteen, a single day split my life in half. Before and after.

Vater clapped me on the shoulder. "I sent your mother and sister on ahead with our luggage. We'll meet them at the cabin." The next day began Vater's month-long vacation, and to my delight, he'd arranged for our family to spend time in the mountains. Other friends and relatives would be in neighboring cabins, so days and nights full of outdoor fun were promised. "I have to work this afternoon, Werner." Vater's smile seemed to approve of me. "Special meetings at headquarters. If you're to be an SA officer someday, you should come with me. See what we do, how we work, what makes the Reich tick."

Ever since I pledged to Hitler Youth and told him of my goal to join the SA like him, Vater had changed. Sure, he disapproved when I helped Mutter with household chores. Unmanly. When I offered to teach neighborhood children basic arithmetic or reading, he scoffed. Woman's work. He continued to scowl at my lack of athletic skill and my love of order. I was a weakling, too fussy for my own good. He never did play games with me or laugh at my stories. But he'd begun to talk to me, telling me of a newspaper article he'd read or a speech he'd heard. It was a start.

"I'm glad for the chance to speak with you alone, Werner," he said as I hurried to keep pace with his strides that day. "I need you to do something."

"Of course, Vater. Name it."

"If I am away, look after Renate."

"Look after her? As her babysitter?"

He glanced my way, his expression pure disapproval, then whipped his attention forward. "Of course not. Her mother and grandmother do that. If anything should…" He hesitated, then arranged his expression into one of pure authority. "When I'm away, you need to be the man of the house. You're to look after Renate, do for her what I would do if I were there."

I didn't want to be difficult. Or maybe I did. "Like what?" I asked.

"Protect her. She's only ten years old. You must be her protector if, um, when I am not here."

Later, I wondered if he had a premonition, or maybe some inside information. But at the time, I stonewalled. "What does she need protection from?"

He stopped dead and faced me, eyes narrowed. "Do as I ask. Protect your little sister. Always. Promise me."

What could that entail? Walking her home from school? Approving her little friends? Simple. So, I promised.

That promise has haunted me for decades.

We resumed walking, Vater and me, the smack of his boot heels on cobblestone setting our rhythm. Unspoken tension hung between us. As we neared Headquarters, I tried to engage him again. "What's so special about these meetings?"

His attention snapped to me, then forward. "SA business. Confidential. You'll wait in my office."

"Will we be there all afternoon?"

"You have something better to do?"

"Oh, no, sir. I mean, if you'll be busy at meetings…"

"Afraid you'll be bored?"

"No, sir. I'm sure I won't."

Silent moments passed, then Vater asked, "What's the problem?" I had little experience talking to my father and didn't know how to ask him what I could do while he worked. So, I said nothing. He made a sound of disgust in the back of his throat and quickened his pace.

I followed a few beats behind as we entered Headquarters. We climbed two flights of stairs, our footfalls echoing through the cavernous space. We passed down a bright corridor with offices on either side. Being a Saturday, most offices were dark and closed, but light, voices, and the clatter of typewriters spilled from others. A rather robust man in uniform moved into the hall, saluted us, and greeted Vater by name. We saluted and squeezed past him. At one open office door, a secretary looked up from her work, nodded at Vater, and resumed typing. Neither seemed curious about me, the short, skinny Youth trailing behind the stocky officer. Vater did not introduce me.

At one office—his, I presume—my father announced he had work to do and disappeared behind a great wooden desk cluttered with mounds of paper and folders. As he sifted through the piles, scribbling on this paper, filing that folder, I sat in the stuffy room in a straight-backed wooden chair, quiet, watching the second hand tick. I scanned the file cabinets, the bookshelves, the window overlooking the Königsplatz. I didn't dare move or ask questions. Just sat. Obedient. Dutiful. Waiting.

I must have dozed off because the jangle of the desk phone made me jump. Vater scowled at me. "Your afternoon nap?" He lifted the handset. "Ja?" His eyebrows furrowed. "Where?" A pause. "My boy is here. We'll go now." He hung up, then rose and tucked a single folder under his arm. One finger tapped the holster strapped to his leg as he strode to the door and clicked off the light. "Let's go."

"I can join you at the meeting?"

He started down the hall. "Quiet."

We hurried past the other offices, now dark and silent. A rumble echoed up from the lower floor, men's voices, dozens of them, loud and agitated. "Who's down there?" I asked my father. His answer was to hurry into a rear stairwell, away from the rising voices. I braved a second question. "Where's your meeting?" Vater whipped toward me, face pale, lips tight, eyes blazing. I swallowed bile as well as further inquiries.

Without seeing another soul, we pushed out the building's heavy back door into an alley baking in the late afternoon sun. At the first street corner, a cluster of SS eyed pedestrians and peered into car windows. My father ducked into an alley. I followed. A second intersection was likewise dotted with SS men in full black uniforms, each watching traffic from a different direction. My father hurried down a side street. I scurried after him.

With both my father and me in uniform, we ought to be safe in front of the SS. They were Party members like us. But

Vater's stealth told me—we were hiding from them. From our own people! I almost ran to keep up.

At the Hauptbahnhof ticket booth, we learned our train wasn't due for fifty minutes. Vater's attention flitted around the station, his expression one I'd never seen on him.

Fear.

Someone was after him. And there I was, by his side.

Any person within fifty meters of us—anyone in the station—might be the person Vater was trying to get away from. My armpits dampened.

My father settled into an empty corner of the station's waiting room and lifted his chin to the neighboring seat. Heart pounding, I sat beside him and accepted his offer of half a discarded newspaper. Without a word, he opened the paper and held it so it hid his face. I did the same, the outstretched page trembling in front of me. After several minutes of an uncomprehending stare at the printed words, I whispered, "Why are we hiding?"

His eyes cut to me, then to his page, but he did not answer. I kept my face to the sheet of newsprint while we waited, not daring to speak again, not moving a muscle.

As the minutes ticked away, the sharpness of my fear waned. The SS were our Führer's personal guard. If they were after Vater, he must have done something terribly wrong. Perhaps against the Party administration. Or maybe against the Führer himself!

My breath caught. If that were so, he deserved to be arrested. And punished.

Then I'd be the man of the house. No longer would my so-called soft interests face Vater's scrutiny and judgment. No longer would I be mocked for what I loved, reminded how I didn't meet his ideal of a son.

I smiled behind the newspaper. *Schadenfreude.* I was taking pleasure in my father's pain. Even so, I kept half an eye on passersby. That caution was for my own sake, not for my father's.

When at last our train was called, Vater rose and tucked his folder and the newspaper under one arm. Without a word or a backward glance, he moved to the platform. I followed, but not too close. Just in case.

Near the rear of the train, we boarded an almost empty car. I stood in the aisle and feigned stretching for a couple minutes. Once we were underway and it was apparent no one in the car meant to arrest Vater, I slid into the seat next to him. We rode in silence with newspapers covering our faces for the next hour or so. As dusk approached, we were the only passengers who disembarked at a small rural station.

Vater peered in the station's empty ticket booth, rattled the doorknob, glanced up and down the platform, and strode to the dusty street. All was deserted.

I stretched out on the station's only bench to watch his agitation. "Was someone supposed to pick us up?" I asked, keeping the smile from my voice. No answer. "What's in the folder, Vater?" He tossed it to me. Our ticket stubs and the address of our mountain cabin. And he'd carried it as if it was important. Pah.

He continued to pace the small platform, searching the horizon in both directions in vain. After several minutes of this, I rose and said, "Looks like we have to walk."

Without a word, he threw the newspaper in the trash and set off on the grassy berm of the rutted dirt road. He strode uphill toward the setting sun, glancing ahead and behind every few steps. Whether he hoped to see someone or dreaded the idea, I couldn't tell.

After a few dozen paces, he left the grass and moved farther from the road. Now against the tree line, his head whipped constantly, first across the road to the right then to the woods on his left. Dusk moved quickly to semidarkness as he hurried up the hill. His right hand never left his holster.

The arrogance I'd felt earlier disappeared with the daylight. Shadows deepened. Twigs snapped. My feet slipped on the damp grass. My stomach knotted. Breath came quick and shallow.

Vater rushed on. Soon his shadowy form was almost invisible at the crest of the hill. He never turned to check on my well-being.

My fear was displaced by anger. Hadn't I tried to please him? To be uncomplaining even though I hadn't eaten since thirteen Uhr? Hadn't I been obedient and quiet, both in his office and since we left? He didn't appreciate me. He didn't understand how loyal I was to him and his authoritative demands.

Silhouetted against the fading light, a figure emerged from the tree line. It approached Vater, who startled and stepped back. The figure pressed close to Vater's side. Their shadows merged.

Three sharp blasts deafened me. Vater crumpled sideways and fell.

Endless moments passed.

Neither figure moved, not the one standing, not the one on the ground. Then the standing figure pulled back one leg and kicked the figure on the ground. The thump echoed through my chest.

A sound must have escaped my mouth because the standing figure turned. "Who's there?" he demanded. "Show yourself." He marched down the tree line toward me. The dim rising moon glinted off the item he held in his hand. A gun.

I was silent, frozen with my hands in the air, still holding Vater's ridiculous folder between my thumb and forefinger. Even in the pale light, I could tell the shooter had a handsome face, chiseled and strong. Maybe midtwenties. Black uniform. SS. I refused to look at the gun in his hand or the dark wetness that I knew splattered the front of his uniform.

A few paces from me, the man spoke again. "Huh. Just a boy, a scrawny one. What are you doing here, boy?" I didn't answer, couldn't answer. Stood there with my hands in the air. "I said, what are you doing here?"

I couldn't think straight for the ringing in my ears and the pounding of my heart.

"I won't hurt a kid," he continued. "Not one who's pledged to the Führer. You have pledged loyalty, haven't you?"

I nodded, more grateful than ever for my Youth uniform.

He hooked a thumb to my father's resting place. "Men like that, the SA. They're not loyal. They are traitors to our great leader, traitors to the Reich."

Pulse crashed in my ears.

"You know that, right, boy? SA"—again he indicated my father's fallen body—"they planned a takeover. Want to get rid of our Führer."

I was stunned.

"I ask you again. What are you doing here?"

I flicked my attention to the SS man, then back to the motionless form up the hill.

"Answer me, boy."

Time to be the man of the house. "Delivery," I said, waving the folder in my hand. I gestured to my Youth uniform. "I…from Party headquarters."

"Come here."

I took a few halting steps, then stopped.

"If you're loyal to the Führer, you have nothing to fear from me. I want to see you. Come here." His tone held authority. I obeyed. He scanned my uniform, wrinkled and unkempt after a long day of travel. "You're on foot," he stated. "No messenger bikes at the rail station?"

Words wouldn't come. I shook my head.

He huffed. "Probably stolen. Jews. No doubt sold it." He snatched the folder from my upraised hand and scanned its contents. With a bored "humph," he tossed it to the ground. And then he was gone, his shadow dissolving into the tree line. When I could no longer hear his footfalls, I collapsed.

When my head cleared, I was surrounded by the sounds of deep night—crickets, owl calls. Thick cloud cover hid whatever moonlight there had been, so I was in near dark. Instinct shouted two things: stay safe and find Vater.

Heart pounding, I started forward. I tripped over a tree root and sprawled flat. I fumbled along another dozen steps and tripped, landing hard on one knee. On that second contact with the ground, I smelled it. Metallic. Sickly. Sour.

I didn't have strength to rise. Using the dim light, I crept forward on hands and knees. The stench grew stronger, clawed at my throat. Wetness squelched between my fingers. It was sticky, this wetness. I shuddered and leaned a bit closer, hoping against hope it wasn't…

Vater. His normally ruddy face was chalky in death. His midsection from ribs to pelvis was scorched lumps of innards.

Blobs of something squishy.
Blood.
Excrement.
On my hands, on my uniform…

I was in a white room, sterile and unfamiliar. The harsh smell of bleach burned my nostrils. Another smell was beneath the bleach, a foul one. A man was saying, "You have much to bear right now, Frau Müller. But your son needs to remain a few days. He is in shock. Almost catatonic when he arrived."

Mutter's moonlike face hovered over me, swollen and pale with dark red encircling her eyes. I tried to speak, but she interrupted. "Not now, Son. Rest. We'll talk later." She stroked my forehead, her palm cool, then settled her hands on the bedrail.

I reached toward her and froze. My knuckle creases, the half-moons at the base of my fingernails were stained and dark. Fouled.

I scrubbed. Coarse brown soap and a bristle brush. Several times a day. Many times a day. As often as I could. The dark stains disappeared as my skin grew pink, then red, then raw.

But I couldn't rid myself of the stench. It was in my nose, in my skin. My pores oozed it. I snuck to the hospital kitchen for a bottle of vinegar and washed my entire body with it. The stench remained. Next was hydrogen peroxide from the nurses' supply cabinet. No good. Then back to the kitchen for a salt shaker. Pouring it on the bristle brush, I scoured until I bled.

They confined me to my room. That lasted a while.

Which gave me lots of time to read news reports. The SS man was right. Vater's beloved SA had overreached. They'd become greedy. They'd wanted the Führer to give them more authority, a larger role in the Reich. They'd wanted to take over the army! For all we know, they might have tried to overthrow the Führer!

Traitors!

Eliminating more than ninety members of the SA leadership, including my father, had cut the organization down to size. The Night of Long Knives, the Führer called it. And as I pondered this purge of the SA leadership, I came to understand a hard truth: if our Führer's closest allies could be targeted for assassination, anyone could be.

I would never let that happen to me.

The day I was to be discharged from the hospital, a full week after Vater's funeral, I locked myself in the bathroom and used a hand mirror to examine every inch of my healing skin. I sniffed the air, sniffed my hands, my knees, every part of me once contaminated with the horror. Assured I was free of foulness, I dressed in crisp clothes and sat on the clean white sheets to await my mother.

I was to be man of the house, a different man than Vater had been. Shuffle the cards and start over.

Right there, on the edge of the hospital bed, I made a short list of promises that I've kept ever since.

Number one: I will support whoever is in power. I will back them with everything I have.

Number two: I will always back the winning side. Never will I be caught on the side of the losers. Never.

Vater chose poorly. He got what he deserved.

Chapter Thirteen
Rennie

Munich, Germany
21 September 1938

Tante Gerde, Mutter's last surviving sister, was gravely ill. Hours after receiving the news by telegram, Mutter was packed and ready to go to her side in Hamburg. "You and your brother will be fine while I'm gone," she said. "Any problems, Onkel Edmund will help you."

I tensed. Onkel Edmund never smiled, never laughed, never seemed to relax. Plus, he was Gestapo. And since the Gestapo took orders from the SS, and I now knew the SS carried out Vater's murder…

I'd only been home a few days, and she was leaving. "When will you be back, Mutter?"

"When I'm no longer needed." I must have looked puzzled because she added with typical frankness, "When Gerde is either well or dead."

I kissed my mother goodbye and sent along my wishes for my aunt's speedy recovery. The sooner my mother came home, the better.

Mornings at the bakery started early, so Werner was sleeping when I left for work at five Uhr. I wasn't surprised to find Klaus rolling biscuit dough in the bakery's work area when I arrived. "What do you want me to do?" I asked, bleary-eyed, tying an apron around my middle.

He gestured to a cooling rack stacked with goods. "Those go in the display case. They need signs and prices. And wash those pans for me." He lifted his chin toward a haphazard heap of loaf pans and baking tins. "We open at six." A timer chimed. He tossed me a towel. "And take those out of the oven."

Between customers, I restocked the display case and washed pans and bowls. The morning flew, and about thirteen Uhr, Klaus pushed through the curtain separating the work area from the storefront. He flipped the sign on the front door to **Closed** and stretched his long arms overhead, grunting.

I looked around. "Now what?"

He handed me a list. "Deliveries, the address of each and their order. They pay cash." I scanned the list and nodded. Only five or six stops, all right here in Altstadt. Doable in an hour with a wagon hitched onto my bike. From a pocket, Klaus pulled another list. "From the Viktualienmarkt." Dozens of fresh eggs, plus milk, butter, a half bushel of plums…

I looked up at Klaus. "How am I to carry all this?"

He jerked a thumb over his shoulder. "There's a pushcart out in the alley. My mother used it too."

As he turned to reenter his curtained work area, I called, "Before you go…" No customers. No eavesdroppers. No interruptions. This was my chance. "You promised to tell me about Sophie." I propped an elbow against the display case and tried to appear relaxed and casual. My insides churned.

Klaus lifted a finger, the silent signal to wait, and slipped through the curtain into the baking and storage areas. A metallic thunk told me he'd locked the store's back door. The curtain lifted, and he beckoned me to join him in the food prep area. He offered me the only chair, and I accepted. "Before we begin, you need to understand something. I've earned my own reputation, made a name for myself despite the weakness in my family."

Weakness?

Klaus lifted a finger. "First, the man who fathered me. His weakness was revealed by the Great War. Gassed. I was in diapers when he died, a broken shell of a man." He raised a second finger. "Then my mother married Hans, the former owner of this bakery."

A wave of sadness passed over me at the mention of Sophie's Papa. "But Herr Adler isn't weak. He's quite passionate, dedicated to his family."

Klaus' eyebrows shot up. "You speak of him as if—didn't you hear? The sentence has been carried out."

It took a moment until his words registered. "He's…Herr Adler is dead?"

Klaus' face was stone. "Executed as a traitor. Hung by the neck."

My hands flew to my mouth. It could not be!

Klaus nodded. "Did you see the sign?" I sat frozen, uncomprehending, so he grabbed me under one arm and lifted me to my feet. Then he dragged me out the front door of the bakery, spun me to face the building, and pointed. Where a weathered wooden sign had once announced the Bäckerei Adler, a crude placard identified **die Bäckerei des Volkes**, The People's Bakery.

Back inside, Klaus leaned his muscular frame against the display case. His tone was confident, defiant. "The name change was needed for two reasons. First, it reflects my more modern view. The Volk, the People, are more important than an individual, more important than family."

I wiped my eyes but found my voice. "This was your stepfather's business, one he started. And your mother's too, and yours and Sophie's. You all worked so hard."

"A new business with a new name. A name without the connection to a convicted and executed traitor."

"And your mother—is she…"

Klaus huffed. "Last I knew, she was headed for a re-education camp for political prisoners. It's not far from here, in Dachau." He straightened. "And I know nothing of Sophie or her whereabouts, so don't ask me again. In fact, don't mention my sister by name at all. Not to the customers. Not in the neighborhood. It will only bring trouble for you. For this business and me as well."

The following afternoon, I rode into the park, struggling with the horrible news about Sophie's parents, hoping beyond hope Sophie herself was all right. I was more determined than ever to find her, to let her know what I'd learned. I'd gotten no leads to her whereabouts from the polio hospital or University Hospital, from her brother, or from eavesdropping on customer conversations. But there was one more place I could look.

Because of pedestrian traffic, I pedaled past the pickle jar several times, peeking beneath the scruffy pine tree to see if the earth had been disturbed. It had. Once the area was free of visitors, I jumped off my bike and hurried to the spot. Using a spoon I'd stashed in my pocket, I unearthed the lid, then lifted the jar free. The torn scrap of paper inside was written in Sophie's hand. Her penmanship was sloppy, as if hurried.

R,

By the time you read this, I will be far away. Don't tell K or W. Don't try to find me. It's better this way.

S

My best friend. The one I'd searched for, the one I'd prayed for, the one I stole for and betrayed my own brother to help. Now she was gone. Without a goodbye, without a hug. Without acknowledgment of our friendship. How could she be so indifferent? I tore the note into bits and threw it in the trash.

Hours later, my hurt and anger cleared. Her note began to make sense. Sophie must know about the charges against her. If found, those who knew her whereabouts and didn't tell the authorities would be charged along with her. Leaving town without saying goodbye was her way of keeping me safe. In fact, it was the act of a true friend.

Even without her request, I wouldn't have told Klaus or Werner anything. But there was one person who ought to know she'd gone away.

I couldn't write Erich to say I'd heard from Sophie. The Gestapo read private mail, often letters from people like Erich and me who were associated with criminals. My letter would have to set the stage for Erich's understanding. Subtle, yet crystal clear.

For a few minutes, I let myself consider a selfish idea. With Sophie gone to parts unknown for an undetermined length of time, maybe, just maybe, I had a chance with Erich.

But my loyalty to Sophie won out. I wouldn't betray her by seeking Erich's affections. At the end of a long, newsy letter to him, I added,

The artist we spoke of is far away now, on holiday. She requests anonymity while she works out her next masterpiece.

As always,

Rennie

I sealed the letter with a kiss and dropped it in the postbox.

His response came in a few days, lacking any comment of the local news I'd shared. It read only,

Rennie,

Thank you for letting me know. I hope to get tickets to the opening night gala when my favorite artist returns to Munich.

Erich

Message received. Sophie was the only girl for him, even though she was a wanted criminal and hiding who knows where.

Just before six one morning, I stepped out front to sweep the walk. A thin figure was crouched below the bakery's window, huddled against the morning chill. It was a young boy who sprang to his feet, tugging at the back of his pants. Recognition struck us both at the same time.

"Bruno!"

"Rennie!"

I approached the grinning Romany boy. "How have you been? How's your mother? Still selling her potions?"

He nodded. "She is well but very big now." His arms stretched in front of him.

"Your mother is with child?" She must have been expecting when I saw her last summer. I hadn't realized. I leaned against my broom and smiled at the boy. "You're going to be a big brother."

He nodded, bouncing on his toes. "I'll be Dya's helper, at least until my father gets back."

Funny, until that moment, I hadn't considered the existence of Herr Lunka. "He's away?"

Bruno nodded. "Touring with his band. He plays the accordion."

How wonderful. A tour. Maybe someday I'd be on tour too. I'd step onstage in a foreign theater, deliver my lines in an elegant costume…

Bruno's words brought me from my reverie. "…and Herr Adler used to give me bread."

"I'm sorry. What?"

"Dya and I are travelers. We don't have a mailbox, so father can't send money while he's on tour. Sometimes Dya and I run short. Herr Adler was generous, often gave us bread. Thought I'd see if the new owner would do the same. It's his son, right? Like father, like son?"

"Stepson. And no, I don't think the new owner will give you bread. But you can ask." I opened the front door and ushered the boy inside. He smiled as if nourished by the amazing aromas alone. "Klaus?" I called. "Can you come here a moment?"

Klaus poked his head around the curtain. "I've got two timers running. What do you need?"

"This young friend of mine has a question."

Klaus took in the skinny, dirty boy. His judgment was quick. "No handouts."

Bruno's winning smile never faltered. "Your stepfather was kind to me and my mother. Gave us bread sometimes. Thought you might do the same."

Klaus scoffed and gestured to the front door. "If you could read, boy, you'd see this bakery is no longer associated with the Adlers. It's my bakery now. Runs by my rules. My number one rule is this: No handouts." He strode to the front door and pushed it open, stepping to one side to allow Bruno to get past. Once the boy was on the sidewalk, Klaus locked the door. Scowling, he disappeared behind his curtain.

Quiet as I could, I unlocked the door and stepped outside. I hurried to reach Bruno, already a dozen paces away and said, "Meet me in the back alley tomorrow, same time." With a nod and a smile, he took off running.

So, I made it a habit to set aside a few rolls or biscuits or even a small loaf as the bakery closed each day. Next morning, I'd pretend to take the trash out to the alley. There, I'd meet the boy with my gift of day-old goods. It wasn't much, but it was the best I could do. Many times, he conveyed his mother's appreciation too. Once, Frau Lunka even sent me a gift—a lovely journal bound with red leather.

To my delight, Bruno often brought news from the Hubers' farm. It seems he and his mother were frequent visitors there. I hoped Frau Huber was able to spare a portion of the farm's fall harvest for a pregnant Romany woman and her too-thin son.

If she did, I hoped Uta didn't find out.

There was a great fuss in Munich late in September. The Führer was in town to meet with foreign dignitaries, a big diplomatic event. Flag-waving Germans lined the streets to welcome the dignitaries, but Klaus and I had to hear about it on the radio. All we did was work.

A couple weeks later, I was stocking display cases when the tinkling bell behind me announced a customer's arrival. Anna stood in front of me in her nursing whites, hands on hips, surveying the bakery with her judgmental eye. I forced a smile. "Anna. What brings you in today?"

She sashayed around the storefront, wiped a finger along the top of the cash register, and slapped her hands together. "Is Klaus in the back?"

"Yes, he's…"

She yanked aside the curtain to his work area and marched in.

I followed, protesting. "Customers aren't allowed here." When Klaus looked up, elbows deep in a bowl of dough, I said, "I'm sorry, Klaus. She barged in."

"No problem, Rennie. Go back to what you were doing."

"But…"

"Really, it's fine." He wiped his hands on his apron and said to me, "Instead of going to the Viktualienmarkt after we close, why not go now?" He jotted a few words on a slip of paper and handed it to me.

I stared at him. "You want me to close the storefront?" I glanced at the list. "For apples, eggs, and cream you won't need until tomorrow?"

"If a customer comes in, I'll take care of them." Klaus had often told me how much he disliked waiting on customers, how he'd rather bake for twelve hours in the summer heat than try to satisfy one persnickety hausfrau. "Take ten mark from the register."

Anna scraped a fingernail against a spot on the wooden worktable.

I closed the work area curtain behind me, opened the cash register, and slammed the drawer shut. Then I stomped to the bakery's front door, opening and closing it so the bell tinkled. On tiptoe, I returned to the closed curtain and listened in.

"Just questions, as we expected," Klaus said.

"About what?"

"About Sophie. What happened the day she hurt her arm."

"Has she been in contact?"

I couldn't hear Klaus' mumbled reply.

"And her belongings?"

"Still in her room."

"And you'll let me know…"

Klaus sounded frustrated. "Yes, yes, I'll let you know…"

"…if you hear anything, if her room is disturbed…"

"…or if Renate spills the beans. Yes. I'll be sure to tell him."

Him? My blood boiled. Werner and Klaus didn't scheme up this work assignment to keep me busy. They designed it to use me to find Sophie!

"Despite what your family has done, Klaus, he gave you this chance."

"I've played my part as he told me I must. He better keep his end of the bargain."

There was a pause. When Anna spoke again, her voice was deep, each word enunciated for effect. "Was that a threat, Klaus? Are you threatening the Gestapo?"

Wait. They weren't talking about Werner.

Onkel Edmund was behind this. He's the one who arranged my work assignment at the bakery. Onkel Edmund thought I'd lead the Gestapo to Sophie.

Once again, a line from *Julius Caesar* seemed to say it all: *Alas! Thou hast misconstrued everything!*

Without tinkling the bell, I slipped out the bakery door.

Chapter Fourteen
Werner

Argentina
Late 1940s

Months turned into years. Hundreds, maybe thousands, of Party refugees settled into safe lives in Argentina and Chile. But not the Führer. And not my godfather, Onkel Edmund the Gestapo. Dead or vanished underground, I didn't know. My headaches disappeared with him.

Countless Party refugees made their way to the United States under their own names. There they'd help in a different kind of war, a new one called the Cold War. It was an international battle using spies and finances against a common enemy: Communism.

I was content in Argentina, protected by Peron's regime, surrounded by like-minded men and yet saved from the fate of other Nazis in the ruins of the Reich. Although our Führer never arrived as we'd all hoped, we kept the dream alive, among ourselves at least.

In '49, Peron's government passed a law allowing foreign nationals to live in Argentina under their own names without fear of prosecution or extradition. I did what many other SS did—I changed back to my true name. Got checks, legal documents, everything in my birth name. At long last. To mark the occasion, Horst baked a chocolate cake. In creamy white icing, he wrote across the top, *Welcome to Argentina, Werner Müller.*

That night in a haze of camaraderie and drink, I told Tomas my whole story, including my involvement in Lebensborn. No doubt it confirmed what he already knew, but he never told a soul. He was good to me, Tomas. Closest thing I ever had to a friend. Even set up a date with his wife's sister. But women wanted personal details of my past, promises for the future. Pah.

And I kept Willi's papers. Just in case.

"Visitors from Ireland will arrive late this morning," Tomas told me one day in 1950. "Two men with a translator."

Other South American breeders sometimes toured our kennels, but I didn't remember any breeders from overseas. "What do they want?" I asked.

"They raise greyhounds. Want to see our kennel set-up, our breeding system. I'll show them your record-keeping."

Tomas often bragged to other breeders about my meticulous books. Said it set his business above the rest.

Several hours later, Tomas escorted three men into the office. Tomas spoke to them in Spanish, and a translator interpreted his words for the Irishmen. "Werner Müller, our bookkeeper. He can explain his record-keeping system."

One of the men, a fellow with a scraggly beard, narrowed his gaze and spoke in my native tongue. "Werner Müller? From Munich?" His tone and expression unsettled me.

All business, I stuck out my hand and answered in German. "And you are?"

He did not take my hand. "Erich Fischer. From Munich. From Altstadt, to be exact."

My old neighborhood. My quick intake of breath gave me away.

Erich nodded, scanning me up and down. "It's you, all right. My old Scharführer, here in the flesh."

I searched my memory for details, for a younger version of this strapping man. If I remembered right, my sister and her little friends had swooned over him. He was near Renate's age.

Tomas smiled and looked from one of us to the other. "You two know one another. Imagine that."

Erich flashed a quick smile at Tomas. His smile disappeared when he turned to me. "And here I thought you were dead like everyone else." His voice held no pleasure.

I did not reply. He'd grown tall with defined muscles and a weathered face, a desperate expression. Waves of dark hair fell below his collar. The beard made him look grizzled, unkempt. Could pass for an Argentine. Pah. Wouldn't pass muster in the Youth or the Wehrmacht now.

Erich and I stared at each other a few moments. Tomas read the strain and said, "Let's get this tour underway, shall we?" He led Erich and the others out of the office and toward the kennels.

When they returned to examine my books, I avoided eye contact with Erich. A short time later, the others stepped outside for a smoke, and Erich cornered me. "Where's Sophie?" he asked.

"Sophie who?"

He grunted his disgust. "Sophie Adler. Your sister's best friend."

Ah. The useless eater. I'd tried to bucket Sophie, so to speak—to get rid of her like Tomas got rid of deformed pups. My efforts led to my sister's first betrayal. Her second betrayal too, come to think of it. My life ruined. All because of that crippled friend of hers.

Erich tugged my arm. "Tell me where Sophie is."

I didn't know, so I shrugged.

"Then tell me how to contact Rennie. She'll tell me."

I remained silent.

"If you don't, I'll tell Tomas what you did during the war."

I laughed. "Tomas knows."

Silence fell between us as Erich waited for me to continue. When I didn't, he leaned against the wall and filled the void with his own words. "After the war, Altstadt was..." He shook his head. "Almost everyone I ever knew, everyone I ever cared for, was dead. Or missing. Or gone, just gone, who knows where. I couldn't find Sophie. She and I were, well..." He hesitated. "I needed a new start. Somewhere I could work with animals, but a place with fresh air, far from the destruction." He fell silent again. "First, I moved to Belgium, worked with horses. Then to Norway and the sheep. Ended up in Ireland. Gentle people. Dogs. Rolling hills." He paused and smiled. "Lovely place, Ireland."

When he resumed his tale, he seemed disappointed to be standing in my office. "Anyway, I took to raising greyhounds. They're beautiful. Sleek and fast." He tipped his head and waited.

This was where I was supposed to tell him what I'd been doing. But I kept silent.

Erich raised his eyebrows, expectant, then settled into my chair. When he put his feet up on my desk, I knew I had to tell him something. "I've been here since '45," I said. "Got this position through a former employer." I turned to walk away, but he jumped to his feet and spun me around.

"But why are you here?" he growled, his face too close to mine. "Word is war criminals escaped here, to Argentina."

I cleared my throat to cover the catch in my voice. "War criminals? Like who?"

He studied my face. I tried to appear relaxed and confident, but even before he spoke I could tell he didn't believe it. "Criminals like Edmund Koch, for one. Is he here too?" Before I could respond, Erich continued. "Haven't you heard, Werner? Nazi hunters never sleep. They won't give up until every last Nazi has been tracked down and brought to justice." He must have read the alarm on my face. "There's word of a new breed of Nazi hunters too, the Mossad they call themselves, straight out of Israel. Not worried about diplomatic channels, liable to send out a sniper. They know Nazis are in South America. They'll track you all down, wait and see."

I said, "Pah," but inside, I was frozen.

"Don't want me to tell them you're here? Then tell me where Sophie is."

Not an idle threat. I chose my words with care. "I don't know where she is."

His voice rose, shrill. "Is she even alive?" He scanned me, top to bottom, bottom to top. As if I hid information there. "I know you were responsible for her disappearance, Werner. That day at the parade. You sent us on a wild-goose chase while you got rid of sweet, defenseless…"

Were those tears? After all the pain and destruction and death we'd seen, after the ruin of our dreams and the loss of our Führer, after years and continents separated us from those times, he was crying over a little cripple he hadn't seen in a dozen years? Pah. Weak, annoying little man.

"I know about Sophie's parents," he continued. "Her Papa in '38 and her mother in Ravensbrück in '41."

Served them right. Traitors, both of them.

"And her brother Klaus in Leningrad in '42."

News to me, but not a surprise. Sent to the Russian front, no doubt because his family betrayed the Fatherland. *Sippenhaft.* A decent man doomed by his own flesh and blood. Only rolls of money and a godfather in high places saved me from the same fate.

"Then where's Rennie? No doubt she and Sophie kept in touch. Tell me, or I'll name names. Yours. Lots of others."

I had to give him something, so I spit out a small piece of truth. "The last time I saw Renate was early January of '39." Erich flinched in obvious shock. I smiled. "Yes. Eleven years ago, at the Hauptbahnhof in Munich."

I took advantage of his stunned silence to regain control of the conversation. "When the new Reich is built, I'll recommend you for a good position, Erich. A man with your talent, you could go far." I lifted my chin and straightened, my SS posture and bearing recalled in an instant.

Erich's eyebrows shot up. "The new Reich?" He chuckled, then began to laugh. His laugh grew louder and larger until he had to press his hands against his knees for support, his breath and words coming in great heaves. "Don't be an idiot, Werner," he said, gasping. "The Reich died when the Führer killed himself. Took the coward's way out. As you did."

"I didn't kill myself."

"You ran."

I had no response.

"I can't let it go," he said, straightening and wiping his eyes. "I need to know what happened to Sophie after that day in the park." I opened my office door and stood beside it until he left.

By the time Erich joined the others for dinner that night, Tomas had written me a glowing letter of reference. On my behalf, he promised to contact friends who owned greyhound racetracks in the United States. I was to telephone Tomas every three or four weeks to learn about possible job offers.

I wrote Erich a note, sharing a nugget of information that would send him on another wild-goose chase. One that would keep him occupied for years.

But as I walked to the guesthouse with the note in my hand, I had to admit that his presence had brought Renate in the front of my mind. I recalled a time when Renate asked me why Vater's death had changed me so completely. "I like the old you," she'd said. "You were the big brother who watched out for me, for all the kids in the neighborhood. You wanted to be a primary school teacher, remember? What happened?"

At the memory, something inside me wanted to soften.

"I'm certain you still have a tender heart," she'd said back then. "The real you is in there somewhere. I'll figure out how to remind you of it. How to bring it back."

Pah. That tender heart made me vulnerable. Never again. I slipped the note under the guesthouse door and left.

Correction. Willi Knox left.

Shuffle the cards and start over.

By morning I was well across Uruguay. Disembarked in a small town near the border with Brazil. As good a place as any.

A man can scrape out a decent living if he presents himself as clean and intelligent. As Willi Knox, I picked up odd jobs, tracking inventory for a wood export company, keeping books for a salesman. I didn't question business practices; employers didn't question my background. If I showed up on time, worked well, and minded my own business, they were content. So was I.

Other than basic food and shelter, my needs were few. I interacted with people as little as possible, even my fellow countrymen.

Now and then I'd bump into someone known to me from wartime operations. When recognition flashed and was acknowledged with a curt nod, by unspoken agreement our heads would duck and turn away. No conversation, no public declaration of identity, familiarity, or knowledge of our former jobs. With Nazi hunters on the trail, we trusted no one. Not even one another.

After every recognition, even a fleeting one, I got a letter of reference, packed my bags, and moved on. No ties; no chance of revelation.

Tomas was my sole contact—and then only by public telephone every few weeks. I couldn't risk more. A good man, Tomas. He used his connections to find me work in the United States. The larger country with fewer Nazi hunters would help me sleep at night.

Over time, I solidified my identity as Willi Knox, bookkeeper and record keeper extraordinaire. When Tomas confirmed my job opportunity, I filed the paperwork for emigration.

Nazi hunters. Forcing me to yet another continent. Pah.

For decades, I lived my American life as Willi Knox, bookkeeper at a greyhound breeding kennel and racetrack near Palm Beach, Florida. When my health started to fail, I moved into one of those retirement communities Florida is famous for. It's been peaceful here.

Then that woman and her damned book showed up.

Chapter Fifteen
Rennie

Munich, Germany
'31 or '32

I can picture it all as if it were yesterday.

From my position on the floor in front of my dollhouse, I see a young Werner, maybe twelve or thirteen years old. His skinny frame is folded on itself, dwarfed by Vater's armchair. Our schnauzer Emmett lies in his usual position at Werner's feet, waiting for a walk, a treat, or a scratch behind the ears.

Now and then, Werner calls to me and holds up the oversized book he's reading. It is filled with diagrams and sketches, and he tells me about the ones he finds interesting. How zeppelins fly, the way bridges are designed, how telescopes bring distant planets into view. "The world is changing fast," he says. "I'm going to be a teacher. I'll show children how much there is to learn!" He picks up a notebook and jots something down.

"What are you writing?"

"An idea for my students. To track the constellations, chart how they change during the year."

I have no idea what he's talking about, but I smile at him anyway.

Emmett trots alongside Werner when he answers a knock at our door. It's Frau Keller from down the street. "You're a miracle worker, Werner. She got an A on her homework. Can you come tonight? Nineteen Uhr?"

"Of course," he says with a smile.

I peer over my dollhouse roof as Werner scratches sweet Emmett, then climbs back into the chair. "What does she want?" I asked.

He curls up. "Help for her daughter. Arithmetic."

I am in awe of my big brother. I want to be just like him.

It was one of the last times I saw the gentle Werner, the real Werner before, well, before everything. I hold the memory close and try to keep it clean and untainted by all that followed.

When Vater came home that evening, Mutter scrambled around the kitchen getting his meal prepared. Werner was readying to leave, and Vater asked where he was going. "To the Keller's," he answered.

Our father huffed. "Addition and subtraction again. Is that all you can do, play with children? Now geometry, trigonometry, calculus—that is mathematics for a *real* man."

"I like teaching young children, Vater. Now if you'll excuse me, I must go. I gave my word."

Vater's face flushed, and one cheek quivered.

Mutter ventured a few words. "The boy must keep his word, Pieter."

Vater glared at my mother, then waggled his fingers in dismissal. "Go then. But this is the last time. I'll not have a sissy-pants for a son." Werner ducked out the door.

Vater grabbed the newspaper and started to his armchair, then stopped short. Werner's notebook full of teaching ideas lay sprawled nearby, its spine facing the ceiling. Vater flipped through the pages, muttered about basic arithmetic and weakling sons, then strode out the back door.

Moments later, I heard the definite thunk of the metal trash can in the alley. Vater reentered and strode to the kitchen, slapping his hands together. "That's that," he announced to Mutter. Then he turned from her and marched past me to the bookshelf, where he selected a volume and settled it, spine up, on the arm where Werner's notebook had been. *Mein Kampf.*

Within a year, Vater was dead and a new Werner had been born.

I still wanted the old Werner back.

8 November 1938

What an unusual morning. Customers who usually left the bakery right after buying their goods lingered in whispering groups. While I stocked display cases and rang up sales, I eavesdropped. Couldn't make heads or tails of what was being said. One woman must have noticed my confused expression because she asked, "Haven't you seen today's headline?"

I told her I hadn't. Since I got to the bakery each morning at five Uhr, I seldom read the paper until evening. As she started to fill me in, Klaus peered around the curtain to listen. "One of our diplomats was shot in Paris," the woman told us. "Name of vom Rath. The assassin is a Polish Jew. Authorities got him." She reached out a folded newspaper. Several conversations stopped, and folks faced Klaus as if waiting for his reaction.

Klaus pushed past me and grabbed the paper, flipped it open, and leaned against a wall, his face lost from view behind the printed words. I busied myself with the tasks at hand, glancing over at him now and then. Several minutes passed. He folded the paper and returned it to the woman with a polite nod. "Perhaps we will have another martyr for the cause."

Heads bobbed at this assessment. The woman added, "Today of all days. The fifteenth anniversary." More nods from the group.

During this exchange, the bell over the door tinkled and a man with a walking stick entered. "Today is the fifteenth anniversary of your bakery?" he asked. Both his accent and his appearance were familiar to me. Klaus turned to him and stared in a most impolite manner. The man responded with a tip of his hat and a slight bow. "Peter Massey of His Majesty's British Empire."

Klaus' expression changed to one of amusement. "Surely even you Brits know the date, why the Reich's leadership is in Munich today."

"To lay wreaths at the Feldernhalle," Herr Massey said. "For those killed during the putsch." So, this Brit knew what every German knew. In '23, our Führer and some of his colleagues tried to remove foreign interference from our government, tried to give us control back over our own country. In a battle with police right here in Munich, sixteen Party members had been killed. Each year, the Party commemorated the uprising with ceremonial wreath laying, reenactments, and speeches.

The woman with the newspaper turned to Klaus. "What do you think will happen?"

"Justice," he announced.

All chatter in the bakery stopped. Everyone seemed to wait for Klaus to continue, everyone except Herr Massey. He focused on the chalkboard list of goods and prices.

Klaus looked from his attentive customers to the distracted Brit. "Those in authority will decide what justice is, how it's meted out," he said before disappearing through the curtain into the work area. In ones and twos, customers left, some talking in excited tones, others tense and hushed.

That left me alone with the familiar British man. His walking stick clacked on the tile floor as he made his way to the counter. I asked, "Have you decided then, sir?"

His gaze slid to my name tag, and a smile lit his face. "Ah, just the young lady I was looking for. I have an order, Fräulein Müller."

As he said my name, I remembered. "You took photographs at the Nuremberg Rally, nicht?"

"Yes, indeed." He handed me a slip of paper. "Please deliver my order to this address after fifteen Uhr today." As I prepared to jot down the particulars, he paused. In a softer voice, he asked, "It will be you making the delivery, yes? Not…" he lifted his chin to the curtain and the workroom behind it.

"Klaus bakes. I deliver."

"And you do everything else, I expect."

I smiled but didn't tell him how right he was.

The order Herr Massey placed was larger than any we'd had in the weeks I'd worked there, and I assured him of on-time delivery. After he paid and left, I rushed into the work area and handed the list to Klaus. He gave a low whistle. "If he's satisfied, maybe he'll tell other foreigners. Good for business." He looked up at me. "I'll take everything to the address myself."

"He asked me to deliver it."

Klaus winked. "Wants to look at a young girl again."

I shrugged him off. "Since when do you deliver?"

"Since we have a customer with a huge order."

"He wants it delivered at fifteen Uhr."

Klaus groaned. "Never mind then. By fifteen Uhr, I need to be in uniform. Practice for the commemoration ceremony."

Just as well.

As I expected, the streets were busy that afternoon, what with all the Party dignitaries and the Führer himself in town for the activities. What I didn't expect was my stomach's nervous flutter as I rode my bicycle, laden delivery wagon attached, through the crowded streets. Brown-shirted SA men and SS in their intimidating inky black clustered in small groups on corners and outside stores, eyeing pedestrians as if daring them to cross a barrier or enter a banned place of business. I did as many people did—I avoided eye contact and sped past.

The address the Brit gave me was in an unfamiliar neighborhood. The homes were small and close together there, the streets narrow. As I parked the bike in front of the address, a flat-fronted row house, I greeted a woman walking her dog. She looked down and hurried away. In the upstairs windows, shadows moved. The draperies snapped shut.

Having Klaus deliver may have been better.

A small metal tube engraved with Hebrew letters was nailed alongside the front door. This was the home of a Jew. I glanced up and down the street. Would there be trouble if I were caught delivering to a Jew's house?

A thin girl about my age answered my knock, half her face peeking around the doorframe. "Delivery from die Bäckerei des Volkes for"—I pulled out the calling card—"Herr Kauffman. Is he at home?"

The girl's eyebrows furrowed. "No, he's working. My father ordered baked goods?"

"Herr Peter Massey placed the order."

The girl moved to allow her full self to be seen. Both her expression and her unruly black hair were familiar somehow. She flushed. "Herr Massey is so kind to us."

I nodded. "May I bring the order inside for you, Fräulein…"

"Kauffman. Esther Kauffman."

"Esther Kauffman," I repeated.

"And you are Renate Müller."

A memory swirled. "You lived on Reichenbachstraße a few years ago."

"Come in, come in, Rennie." As I followed her, I wondered—would stepping inside a Jew's home get me in trouble?

Esther gestured for me to sit in one of two threadbare chairs in the tiny room. I declined and remained standing, my hands gripping the chair's back. Her brows furrowed, then she mimicked my position by standing behind the other chair. "You're a friend of Sophie Adler's, nicht?"

She spoke my friend's name! Tears formed in an instant. "Ja. Haven't seen Sophie for months." To use her name myself was a delight. "She told me how you two used to exchange notes in a pickle jar."

Esther bit her lip and looked at the floor, so I changed the subject. "Well, the baked goods are from the Adler family's bakery. I'll bring in the order."

"I'll help."

In minutes, Esther and I had emptied the cart's contents onto a small wobbly table in the galley kitchen. She smiled and chatted as we unpacked bread and rolls, several pies, and a dozen tarts. Her oohs and aahs floated into the flat's stale air along with the heady aroma of fresh baked goods. I wondered, not for the first time, why everyone complained so much about Jews. If Esther was an example, they weren't hateful at all. "This is a lot of food. Are you expecting company?" I asked.

She shrugged. "When Herr Massey is so generous, we share with our neighbors."

As I turned to go, a glint of metal caught my eye. A length of pipe fashioned into a crutch was propped in a corner of the room. A gasp caught in my throat. I pointed to the crutch. "Is that… Who does it belong to?"

Alarm flashed across Esther's face, then she softened. "It's Herr Massey's. He left it here when he visited last."

Herr Massey did use a walking stick, so I suppose it made sense he'd have more than one implement. But still… "Sophie used a crutch like that," I said.

Esther opened the door and stood beside it. I took the hint.

Werner came home full of bluster. "If vom Rath dies, there will be hell to pay."

I dished out our dinner and slid into the chair across from him. "Poor man. He is expected to die then?"

"The Führer sent his own doctors to care for him."

"Sounds like he has a fighting chance."

My brother huffed and concentrated on his potatoes. I'd have to listen to the radio news myself. "Important communications will come in tonight," he announced. "I'll answer the telephone and the door."

"All right."

"You're to stay in your bedroom with the door closed while I speak."

"All right." Werner was itching for a fight. I refused to engage.

As soon as he finished eating, my brother clicked on the radio. Vom Rath's condition was unchanged. Back and forth Werner paced as I cleared the table and washed the dishes. He paced as I took the trash out to the alley, even as I settled beside my sewing box and a pile of mending. Finally, a knock came and he raced to the door. "Klaus. Come in, come in."

Klaus opened his mouth to speak, then noticed me sitting in the living room. "Ah, Rennie. The big delivery went well?" I assured him it had but offered no details. Neither he nor my brother needed to know I delivered to a Jew, especially one I remembered from the neighborhood, one who mentioned Sophie by name.

Without hesitation, Werner announced, "Renate, you will excuse us."

Even through my closed bedroom door, the tension was clear. First, there were only Werner's and Klaus' voices, then they were joined by at least two others I didn't recognize. Later, after the front door opened and closed a few times, the only voice left was Werner's as he spoke on the telephone. The bits and pieces I heard made it clear—if the diplomat died, blame for the shooting would be placed not just on the assassin. All Jews in Germany would be blamed.

I added Esther and her father to my prayers.

Strange as it seemed, I'd accepted the idea that the picture frame had special properties, something to do with its Romany origins. The familiar image of me and Sophie laughing and pointing at the lunch-stealing bird did indeed look different in the frame than out of it. I'd experimented with it a dozen times, and the result was always the same: the original image was present only when the photo was out of the frame.

When placed in the frame, two things happened. First, the figures of me and Sophie separated to the far sides of the photo, and second, those lines beneath our feet appeared. Paths, Frau Lunka had called them.

A couple weeks earlier, I'd had enough of the spooky image. I'd taken the photo out of the frame and tucked it next to my rosary in the nightstand. The frame went in the bottom dresser drawer. The two had been apart ever since.

Before I switched off the light that night, I felt something, an urge to connect the photo with the frame again. I tried to dismiss it, told myself I was rattled by the day's events, that I was reacting to the Kauffmans' imminent danger. But even when I clicked the light off and lay in total darkness, the urge was there.

I tried to push it away. It only grew more insistent, a relentless curiosity. The urge took on substance and became almost tangible, a virtual tap on my shoulder. I rolled over.

The urge lessened.

Ah, peace.

Then there it was, firmer this time, almost a physical nudge. "All right!" I cried. "I'll put you back together!"

When I slid the photo between the glass front and the backboard, I gasped. The figures of Sophie and me had returned to our original positions, side by side. The distance between us was gone! What's more, each of our feet stood on its own line. Our four paths converged at a single point a short distance ahead of us.

But most striking was this: our paths had taken on color. Color! When Sophie snapped the photo, she hadn't used expensive color film. Yet there it was. The paths we stood upon were laid out in glorious color. I struggled to remember what Frau Lunka told me of the meaning of various colors.

Beneath my feet were one red line and one blue line. Red was something strong, like power or maybe blood. Blue meant loyalty, that I remembered. Frau Lunka had told me it was a weakness of mine, although I still didn't see how.

Sophie's feet stood on two different color lines as well, one blue, the other black.

I remembered black. Black meant death.

Sophie's death.

At the point where my paths and Sophie's converged, all color faded away. Three pale lines emerged from the juncture. One traveled straight right, one straight left, and one straight down, all three quite short.

Four lines in. Three lines out.

The frame didn't predict the future. It showed the choices we faced. As Frau Lunka had said, the frame revealed what is possible. Death was a possibility for Sophie.

The thought was unbearable.

Instead, I focused on how my path and Sophie's would come together. Choices we made would affect us both. Our fates were tangled together.

Again.

9 November 1938

News poured in with the morning customers. Vom Rath was still alive, and the day's commemoration activities would go on as planned.

Following afternoon deliveries, I made an unscheduled stop. Esther answered my knock, her face half-hidden behind the door. Her eyebrows furrowed when she recognized me. "Another delivery?"

"Not today. May I come in?"

She scanned the BDM uniform I'd worn because of the day's activities. "What for?"

"Please, Esther. For a moment."

She mumbled something and shut the door. Then a chain rattled, and the door opened fully. After a quick backward glance to ensure I was unseen, I slipped inside.

Esther leaned one hip against a chair, arms folded, her lips tight. I shifted and said, "You've heard of this vom Rath fellow, how he was shot." Eyebrows raised, she nodded. "Well, I came to warn you. There's trouble brewing."

"What kind of trouble?"

"I don't know specifics. But I know if vom Rath dies, Jews will be blamed."

Esther threw up her hands and said what anyone would say—it wasn't fair, the blame for one person's actions shouldn't be spread to everyone.

I stopped her. "You know Party officials are here in Munich. They'll spend today eating and drinking and one-upping each other's ideas. Who knows what they'll come up with. I have a bad feeling and I…I had to tell you. Be careful."

Esther's eyebrows furrowed. "You're a Youth member. Are you trying to scare me?"

"No, not on purpose. But when those men find a scapegoat…I want, well, I thought you should know, just in case."

She took a deep breath and nodded. "I see. Thank you." Her grip on the chair softened a bit.

"Can't you go somewhere?"

"We're trying to leave, believe me." Her hands and her voice lifted in frustration. "We can't just hop a train and go live in another country. Most countries don't want us. They have their quotas for immigrants. Only so many Jews allowed."

Chiding myself on my ignorance, I made sure my tone was respectful. "What are you going to do?"

"My uncle lives in Poland, so maybe we can go there. We'll know in a few months. We also filed papers for Palestine."

"You have choices then."

She huffed. "Choices. Father fills out forms, checks the want ads in other countries. We'll go anywhere that will take us. So far, nothing. I have my hopes set on Palestine."

"Why there?"

"Jews from all over the world have settled there. A Jewish homeland of sorts. Youth Aliyah, the program I applied for, it's all young people providing the labor to build homes and work the farms."

"Like our Youth summer work program."

Esther's eyebrows shot up. "No. Nothing like that."

I hesitated. "At any rate, be careful, Esther." Then a thought. "Do you have relatives you could stay with, maybe visit the mountains for a few days? Until this blows over."

"I'll mention it to"—she scanned the room—"to Father."

On my way home, I did my best to skirt the heart of town where the day's activities were to take place. I knew there would be a reenactment of the march on Feldernhalle, complete with loudspeakers announcing the names of those killed. Wreath laying and speeches would follow, the crowds and officials and torchlight processions. Too many devotees for my comfort.

As I approached Altstadt, uniformed officers and Youth members were everywhere. They cluttered doorways, clogged intersections, congealed on street corners. Some eyed me as I pedaled past, a few laughing and talking in loud voices. A block from home, a group of rowdy Youth catcalled and whistled. I raced home and bolted the door behind me.

Werner wasn't home, no doubt attending some official dinner or other. I should have attended one too. Werner and Onkel Edmund would notice my absence. But I wouldn't go out, not with all those men on the street. I drew the blinds and turned on the radio.

Not five minutes later, the Mozart waltz that accompanied my dinner was interrupted by an announcer's voice. Vom Rath had died. In moments, shouts rose from the street, male voices raised in excited crescendos. I peeped through the blinds and saw a dozen or more Youth, fists raised, walking up the center of the street to join other rowdies at the corner. I abandoned the window.

The telephone jangled. "Renate. Good. You are home." Werner's voice was high, nervous.

"Where are you? There's a crowd at the corner…"

"Draw the blinds. Stay away from the windows."

"Why? What's going on?"

"Keep your uniform on. But don't go outside. Not until morning. No matter what." He hung up.

I turned out the lights, curled into Mutter's wing chair, and huddled under an afghan. Only the yellowed glow of streetlamps lit the room, their beams pushing around the edges of the closed blinds and forming thin golden chains on the carpet.

Loud voices echoed down the street, dozens of them at a time, excited, angry, or a combination of the two. The voices, all men's voices to my hearing, rose and fell as they passed our home. They seemed to converge at one end of the street where the voices united in a low growl. When the growl grew to a roar, I pulled the afghan over my head and prayed. For myself. For Werner. For Esther and her father. For Sophie, wherever she was.

Then I heard running feet and laughter, harsh and cruel. Shattering glass, a crackling whoosh. A woman's voice pierced the night—"No!"—followed by shouts and a splintering crash. I tossed the afghan aside and stared at the orange light which now flickered around the blinds. I crawled to the window and peered out between low slats, the stench of smoke invading my nose. Fire, not too far away. Property destroyed in the name of the Party. The Party to which I pledged loyalty.

The Party whose Rally I attended and loved.

The Party that wanted all Jews to pay for one person's actions.

The Party that accused Sophie and her parents of treason.

That hung Herr Adler.

And murdered my father.

Enough.

I stood, yanked open the blinds, and took in the scene below. Hooligans prowled the street, some carrying torches, others clutching rakes, broom handles, or shovels. The night sky glowed sickly orange as fires raged nearby, somewhere in my own neighborhood and elsewhere in the city as well.

I pulled a chair to the window and sat there cross-legged most of the night. My heart pounded with each burst of raucous laughter, with each shout and scream and crash of glass.

But never again would I look away.

Chapter Sixteen
Rennie

10 November 1938

In the morning, Werner's bed was empty.

Outside, smoke and airborne soot attacked, so I covered my nose and mouth with a handkerchief for my three-block walk to work. Debris from last night's destruction littered my path—broken bottles, scraps of singed cloth, splintered broomsticks. I hurried past, refusing to think about the horror inflicted on my city and its people. Cinders and scorched papers settled around me like burnt confetti as I unlocked the bakery's alley door and stepped inside.

No Klaus. I listened at the base of the stairs leading up to the Adler's flat. Silence. I climbed the stairs and knocked. "Klaus? Klaus, it's Rennie. We open in an hour." No answer. I knocked again and jiggled the doorknob. Locked. "Klaus? Are you all right?" Silence.

Klaus had once shown me where their flat's spare key was hidden, in a cupboard in an otherwise empty coffee sack. Calling his name all the while, I retrieved the key and let myself in.

I hadn't been in the Adler family's flat in months. The change was disorienting. The usual order dictated by Frau Adler, everything scrubbed and tidy, was disrupted. Dirty dishes were piled in the sink. Others, coated with dried food scraps, sat abandoned on the kitchen table. Towels and dirty clothes were strewn about in heaps, and floury footprints spotted the wooden floors. It was obvious—the flat was now home to a single man with no one to clean up after him. "Klaus? Klaus, we open in an hour. Are you baking today?"

I kept calling as I moved through the kitchen toward the bedroom I knew to be his, half-afraid to look but with full knowledge I had to do so. His door was open, his bed empty. Same was true through the rest of the flat. Like Werner, Klaus hadn't come home last night. I locked the flat behind me.

I did the only thing I could do. I swept the soot and grit off the sidewalk in front of the bakery, opened on time at six Uhr, and sold whatever day-old goods we had on hand. Just as well. Customers were few, and those who came in were pale and shaken. After making their purchase in near silence, customers returned to the streets and the remnants of destruction.

By eight Uhr, I flipped the sign to **Closed**, jotted a note to Klaus, and locked up. I hurried home with a handkerchief again across my nose and mouth and crawled into bed.

At midday, I ventured out on my bike. Teams of people swept streets, scrubbed windows, and opened shops.

A pall settled over me as I approached Esther's part of town. The destruction there was much worse, the air still thick with sooty smoke. Several storefront windows had been smashed, and large shards and splinters of glass and debris littered the sidewalk. The scorched carcass of an auto smoldered in front of a place of business. Scrawled in red paint over a home's front door was the word *Jud.* I swallowed against panic.

For safety's sake, I hid my bicycle behind a clump of shrubs and picked my way forward, glass crunching underfoot. I searched for signs of normalcy amid the ruin, hoping and praying Esther and her father had fled.

Then I reached Esther's rowhouse. Tattered curtains blew through shattered holes where windows had been. A flashlight lay on the front steps, its heavy handle splotched with something dark. The metal tube alongside the front door sported several new dents, and a splotch of red paint obscured the Hebrew lettering. Without a top hinge to anchor it, the door itself was askew, half out of its frame.

I entered, managing to croak, "Herr Kauffman? Esther? Are you here?"

Slashed chairs oozed stuffing. Tables lay upside down, plates and glasses smashed beside them. The paper contents of open desk drawers were strewn across the floor. The hulking hull of a dresser sat to one side of a bedroom, its drawers in splinters, clothing dumped into heaps. Heart pounding, I searched the rooms, the closet, under the bed. No one was there.

Shaking, I stepped back outside where a young boy picked through the litter on the street. "Where…where is everyone?" I asked him.

He shrugged. "Gone."

"What about these people?" I gestured. "The Kauffmans."

From down the street, a woman's voice called out, "Dieter? Who are you talking to? Come here right now."

"Coming, Mutter!"

"Where did the Kauffmans go?"

"How would I know?" The boy shrugged again. "Gone is gone."

Even after retrieving my bike, I trembled so violently I could not ride. I walked the bike all the way to Altstadt where the sidewalks had been cleaned and the destruction wasn't as extreme. But I couldn't shake the image of the wrecked apartment from my head or from my heart.

11 November 1938

Klaus was elbows deep in bread dough when I arrived, one cheek sporting a gash and a dark bruise. He said, "Thanks for covering yesterday."

Since I didn't intend to talk about it, I nodded.

"My orders came through," he continued. "I'm to be sworn into the Wehrmacht in ten days' time."

That loosened my tongue. "Any idea where they'll send you?"

He flashed the famous Klaus smile, the one other girls went wild over. "Can't tell you. Big secret assignment." He raised a floury index finger to his lips.

"And this?" I asked, gesturing around me. "The bakery?"

"What about it?"

"Who will run it?"

He shrugged. "Maybe my mother will be released by then."

"Is there news?"

"Your Onkel Edmund said politicals are being released. If she is among them, she'll find her way here. If not"—he shrugged—"the bakery closes."

I'd known the closure was likely, and perhaps I should have been pleased. After all, without the day job at the bakery, I could attend theater classes and audition for roles in local plays. But in truth, I enjoyed the bakery—interacting with customers and sneaking food out to Bruno. Most of all, I loved being part of a place once so integral to Sophie's life. If the bakery closed, I would lose our connection, the only piece of her I had left. I yanked the curtain closed and busied myself in the storefront.

Sales were slow, and what few customers we did have wanted to gossip. When I turned from them to scrub the front window with vinegar and yesterday's newspaper, they took the hint and left. Near midday, I told Klaus I was going to the Viktualienmarkt, turned the sign to **Back in one hour**, and pushed the wheeled cart up the street.

Vendors and customers at the market showed the same varied reactions as the rest of us—stunned silence for some, nervous chatter for others, judgmental swagger for a few. For most, eyes flitted from face to face as if afraid to light somewhere, afraid to see the hidden beast capable of such horrific destruction in our own city. I filled the cart with apples and plums, fresh eggs, cream, and butter and started to the bakery.

A familiar man with a bowler hat and walking stick strode half a block ahead of me. "Herr Massey," I called out. "Herr Massey!" I walked as fast as I dared so as not to bounce the cart on the cobblestones. Breaking all those eggs would be an awful waste. But still…

As the Brit turned a corner, I saw a dark bulge against his chest. He paused, lifting the bulk of a camera to his face. In moments, he started walking again.

I followed half a block behind, block after block, calling out, rushing when and where I could, all in vain. It wasn't until he stopped at the hull of a burned synagogue that I caught up with him.

He lowered his camera and took me in. "Fraülein Müller." He returned to his examination of the ruined building, tipping his head this way and that, lifting the camera and clicking a few times.

I'd heard the synagogue had been burned, but my deliveries hadn't brought me to see it in person. I could barely breathe, and it wasn't only the smoldering stench which scraped at my throat. "Horrible," I croaked.

"Indeed."

I couldn't rest until I knew the answer. I whispered, "Are the Kauffmans all right? Esther and her father? I went to their flat and…"

He nodded. "They are safe for now." I breathed a prayer of thanks. He pulled a card from his pocket, jotted something, and reached the card to me.

"What's this?"

"On Monday, meet me at this address. Say eighteen Uhr?"

"Why?"

His expression did not hint at an answer. "Come alone."

All weekend I thought of Esther and her father, wondering what happened to them and what awaited me Monday evening. The address Herr Massey gave me was not the Kauffmans' wrecked apartment but a different address a kilometer away. Werner must have noticed my distraction because when the butter I was melting started to scorch, he announced, "No one will want you as a hausfrau if you can't cook a simple dinner."

"I don't want to be a hausfrau."

He folded his newspaper and looked down his nose at me. "Nonsense. You are a daughter of the Reich, a pureblood. Our pureblooded women will produce our nation's future."

"I've told you. I'm going to be an actress."

Werner's sigh was outsized. He was an actor in his own right. "Fine. Be an actress for a few years. Then you will be a hausfrau."

I had no intention of arguing with him. The expected womanly duties of *Kinder, Kirche, Küche*, children, church, and kitchen, might be in my future. But not any time soon.

This was as good a chance as any to bring up a touchy subject. I turned off the stove and wiped my hands on a towel. "So, Werner. I was wondering."

His nose was again buried in the newspaper, and he responded with a grunt.

"What do you think of everything that happened this week?"

He lowered the paper and peered at me. "What do I think?"

I steadied myself. "Yes. About the arrests, the fires, the broken windows." He didn't flinch. "The beatings. People died, you know." Still no reaction. I tried for something close to his heart. "The city was a mess."

Eyebrows furrowed, he nodded. "It was indeed. The Volk came together and cleaned up." He folded the newspaper and put it aside. "And you, Renate? What do you *think*?" His tone showed suspicion, as if thinking itself was wrong.

Instead of answering his question, I stated a fact. "You still support them. The Party. You never question whether they're right or wrong, even when…"

Werner rose and lifted a finger to hush me. His voice held warning. "Don't say it, Renate. Don't even think it."

"Here in our own home?"

He strode to the window and pulled aside the curtain. A quick touch on the window latch and a glance to the sidewalk assured him that we had no eavesdroppers. As he returned to his chair, he paused at the two photos on our end table. "Because, Renate," he said slowly, "I promised to keep you safe." With a gentleness that surprised me, he touched the framed photo of our parents on their wedding day. "Even when you make it hard, I keep that promise."

I moved beside him and lifted the photo of us as children. "How old are we here? You're maybe eleven, and I'm seven?"

He smiled. It had been a while since I'd seen him smile. "Something like that."

"About the time you gave me the nickname Rennie."

The smile remained as he gazed at the photo. "Renate seemed too formal for such a little thing."

My voice dropped to a whisper. "You haven't called me Rennie in a long time. Wish you would again." I took his silence as agreement. "Me and all the kids in the neighborhood, we just loved you."

His eyes flew to mine, and their expression hardened. "Young children are woman's work."

"You enjoyed little kids. You were good with them. I remember."

He spun and strode to the window again. His back to me, he pulled aside the curtain and stared out. His shoulders lifted and fell a couple times before he straightened and turned to face me. "We must rise when our country calls us, Renate. Take on the roles we're assigned. Only when we each accept our share of the load will our nation regain its rightful place in the world."

I gestured with our childhood photo and tried to push his tender side to the surface again. "But this, Werner. I miss this person." His postured softened, just a bit. "I miss us, the way we were. You used to be so…"

Quick as a flash, he grabbed the picture from my hand and strode out the back door. The clank of the trash can lid told me where it had gone. He didn't come back inside for the dinner I'd made.

Sometime after midnight, I heard him snoring. I tiptoed into the alley and retrieved the photo, sneaking it back to my room. There I slipped the photo into the Romany woman's frame.

The transformation was almost instantaneous. Stretching before my image were the same red and blue paths I'd seen before, my choices of power and loyalty, although the red line was duller than it had been before. Werner stood with both feet planted on a bright red path, while an adjacent yellow one, joy if I wasn't mistaken, was unused.

He'd chosen power over joy, that much I knew. But the yellow path was still there! Maybe he could still step into a life of joy!

I closed my eyes and basked in the wonder of it. What if I were loyal to my brother, to the person he truly was? If I chose my blue path by being loyal to my brother, would he step onto the path of joy? Maybe all he needed was a nudge. I might be able to give him that nudge.

When I opened my eyes, I was struck by a detail I'd missed before. Near the edge of the photo, my path and

Werner's intersected and knotted together. Emerging from that knot were two lines: one red, the other black.

I yanked the photo out of the frame and shoved it in my nightstand. Now I had two photos that showed possible death.

I don't think I slept that night.

Two days later, a new picture stood beside our parents' wedding photo. In a plain wooden frame was an image of Werner and me in uniform—he as Scharführer, me as a brand-new member of BDM.

Ironic. That photo had been taken the night of my pledge to BDM. The photographer was Sophie.

The address Herr Massey gave me was a large, stately building, its empty window boxes underlining broad windows. In the vestibule, I faced a row of labeled brass mailboxes with a black buzzer above each. As instructed, I pressed the buzzer for **Apartment 4A, Ellende**. A woman's voice came through the speaker. "Ja?"

"Um, yes. I'm looking for Herr Massey. My name is Müller, Renate Müller." The harsh buzz that unlocked the door was the response I got.

The building's interior was the nicest I'd ever seen. Flocked wallpaper graced the walls, and a cut crystal chandelier hung in the entry hall. Wood floors and banisters gleamed. I checked the bottom of my shoes to make sure I wouldn't track dirt up four shiny flights of stairs.

A middle-aged woman in a housedress and apron opened the door. "Fraülein Müller? This way, please." She led me through a formal living area, past a row of bookcases laden with leather-bound volumes and stacks of newspapers. At a heavy paneled door, she knocked as she pushed through and announced me. Then she stepped back and said, "I'll get tea."

Herr Massey looked up from a desk littered with sheets of paper and open folders. "Lovely. Thank you, Beatrice," he said as she closed the door behind her. The Brit moved to a small sitting area with a table and four wing chairs. He took a seat and gestured for me to do the same. "So, you found us."

"Yes, your housekeeper showed me in."

The man laughed. "Beatrice Ellende isn't my housekeeper. She's my sister." I nodded, hoping my flushed cheeks weren't too obvious. "She allows me to stay with her when my work brings me to Munich, as it often does. This lovely room is her late husband's study." I took in the rich paneling, the heavy drapes, the leather chair behind the expansive desk, the thick carpet beneath my feet. The room was warm and deep and comforting. And silent. Street noise—in fact, all sound—was swallowed in the room's plush interior, so much so that when Frau Ellende entered with a laden tea tray, I startled.

She pushed the door closed behind her, settled the service on the small table, and sat beside her brother. "Have you told her yet?" she asked. Herr Massey shook his head.

I looked from one to the other. "Told me what?"

"The reason I asked you here." He studied me a quiet moment or two, then rose and moved to a drapery-covered window. "I believe you to be trustworthy. I hope you will remain so."

Was I about to face one of the paths, one of the choices I'd seen in the picture frame?

He parted the drapes to reveal, not a window, but a paneled wall indistinguishable from the rest of the room. With a practiced hand, he pressed a seam between two panels. They split apart with a distinct pop revealing a deep, dark space within.

"We're ready," he said into the void. A thin man with spectacles and salt-and-pepper hair stepped from the darkness and stood beside Herr Massey. "Renate, please meet Herr Kauffman." Before I could move or speak, another figure stepped between the panels.

I jumped to my feet. "Esther!" I ran over and grasped her hands. "You're all right!"

Esther's wan smile barely reached the corners of her mouth. She squeezed my hands and released them. "We're all right, my papa and me, thanks to these two." She gestured to Herr Massey and Frau Ellende. "And we must thank you too, Rennie. When I told Papa of your warning, it confirmed rumors he'd heard. Then Herr Massey showed up. He'd gotten wind of it too." She smiled at the Brit. "He and his sister made sure we weren't home when the Nazis came calling."

Herr Massey spoke up. "This is Beatrice's home. She deserves the credit." Frau Ellende smiled and raised her teacup in tribute to their praise.

I peered past Esther and her father into the secret space between the panels. Tiny and dark. So closed in. My throat tightened.

Frau Ellende followed my gaze. "An old servant's passage," she explained. "It leads to a small bedroom, not much more than a windowless cupboard. Not suitable for people in this day and age. Except in emergencies."

Herr Kauffman spoke for the first time, his voice thin but filled with gratitude. "We hear nothing—no street noise, no loud tenants."

Frau Ellende added, "And no one hears us. This room seems to absorb sound. My late husband said the previous owner designed it this way to keep secrets from the servants." She gestured to the floor with her chin. "Don't know how trustworthy my downstairs neighbors are. If they hear footfalls, I tell them my brother is in town. They know he uses the room as a work area, meets clients here and such." She winked at her brother. "Newspapermen work such odd hours."

What remarkable luck for the Kauffmans to have found such help. I looked from Frau Ellende to Herr Massey and back. "You already told me Esther and her father were safe. Why did you risk showing me their hiding spot?"

Herr Kauffman gave the answer. "I insisted you come so Esther and I could thank you in person. The warning you gave may have saved our lives."

Esther squeezed my hand. "Sophie was right about you." Every time Sophie's name was mentioned, I teared up, and this time was no exception. "She said you were trustworthy, that if you gave us a warning, we'd better heed it."

I stared at her. "When did she say that?"

Rustling, shuffling sounds drew my attention to the hiding place. Inside it, a bundle of clothing shifted and rose, creating a thin silhouette in the shadowed space. One hand trailing a wall, the figure moved to the paneled door.

Sophie.

Chapter Seventeen
Rennie

I was speechless. I'm quite sure I looked a fool, mouth open, staring at my best friend. Her once long blonde braids were cut square at her shoulders. Her clothing hung from her shoulders and hips as if it belonged to someone much larger. She stepped past the panel door and hesitated, one hand gripping a crutch.

I rushed forward and swept her into an embrace. The force knocked her off balance and I tried to right her, but we tumbled into a heap, both of us breathless and laughing. Wiping my eyes, I helped her up, then grasped her arm and led her to a wing chair. I kept repeating, "Sophie! You're here! You're really here!"

Once I recovered from my shock, I settled beside her. Sophie patted my hand and gestured to the others in the room. "These good people have kept me safe."

All I could do was stammer, "Tell me everything."

"It's a long story, Rennie."

Herr Massey said, "I'm sure Renate has plenty to tell too."

Sophie patted my hand. "You first."

I needed to get the worst off my chest. "You know treason charges have been filed. Against you."

Sophie bit her lip and nodded. "Have they figured out your hand in it?"

"Yes. Werner's too, accidental though his role was." When Sophie gasped, I added, "Onkel Edmund intervened."

"What happened?"

I related the tale. "Of course, Werner's not stupid. He knew I helped you, and he felt betrayed. Sophie, I betrayed my own brother."

Sophie brought her hands to her cheeks. "Oh, Rennie. I'm so sorry." Eyebrows furrowed, she said, "I shouldn't have gotten you involved."

"No need for you to be sorry. What I did, I did of my own free will. I just didn't realize…" Sophie squeezed my hand, and I smiled at her. "Anyway, I felt terrible that Werner took the blame while I got off scot-free. Now he's obligated to take whatever assignment Onkel gives him. 'Your days of keeping your hands clean are over' is what Onkel told him."

Sophie giggled, then pressed a hand to her mouth. "I'm sorry to laugh. Unkind of me."

I giggled too. "One way or the other, he'll have to serve. For his sake, I hope it's not messy work. He'd never make it as a foot soldier."

She nodded. "And what does your uncle know about you?"

"I think he knows what I did, but he has no proof. Since Werner took the fall, I'm making it up to him. That puts me under the nose of a Party loyalist at home and at work."

"Speaking of which, how is my step-brother?"

"He's fine." She must have resented Klaus' apparent lack of concern for her whereabouts, but politeness kept her from saying so. "He leaves for the Wehrmacht soon, and I can't run the bakery alone. It will close soon unless your mother returns from Dachau."

"He's heard from her?"

"He says no, just rumors." I studied her sad expression. "Sorry to be the one to tell you."

Her tears glistened. "The bakery closing is like losing Papa and Mutti a second time."

I grasped her hands. "Oh, Sophie. You know then, about your Papa." She nodded, her silent tears flowing freely. I stayed quiet until she dabbed her eyes and looked up at me. Then I continued, "Klaus hasn't said so, but I think he's nervous about where his Wehrmacht assignment will be. *Sippenhaft*." That medieval German tradition spread the guilt of one person's actions onto other family members, even if they themselves had never been involved in wrongdoing.

Sophie nodded. "He's got a traitor for a sister, a traitor for a stepfather, and a mother in custody for helping a traitor. Poor Klaus." She almost smiled. "I never thought I'd say those words."

While Frau Ellende bustled out to get sweets, the two men settled in chairs across from us and Esther perched on a chair's arm beside her father. There was so much I had to tell Sophie, so much I wanted to know, to understand. "When I came home from the farm," I began, "I looked everywhere for you. The note you left in the pickle jar said you were far away. Why didn't you tell me you were still in Munich?"

"That's my doing, Renate," Herr Massey said. He leaned forward and patted Sophie's hand. I saw a real connection between them, a mutual respect and genuine warmth.

Sophie picked up the story. "Herr Massey tracked me down at University Hospital. I was there after I fell out of the wheelchair. Did you know?" I shook my head. "I'll tell you the whole story another time. Anyway, I had surgery." She touched a spot on her upper arm. "Day after the operation, Frau Ellende showed up and signed me out."

Herr Massey nodded. "What Sophie did by passing me the film was treasonous. Could have been arrested at any time. We weren't taking chances."

Sophie shot him a smile filled with gratitude. "Frau Ellende has been so kind. She cared for me here while I healed."

As if on cue, Frau Ellende pushed into the room carrying a tray laden with shortbreads and chocolates. After placing it on the table, she dragged the desk chair into our midst and settled herself on it. "Sophie stayed with me right here in this room for a couple weeks. The panel room was ready in case it was needed. But this room is so…" She gestured to the muffling softness around her. "The neighbors never heard a thing."

"I stayed pretty quiet anyway. I was in pain," Sophie said as she touched her shoulder again, "and plenty scared. My parents had already been arrested. It was before my father…" She fell silent.

Herr Massey continued for her. "A couple weeks later, I had to return to England for a time. Both of us did." He gestured between his sister and himself. "Sophie couldn't stay here alone. Arrangements had to be made."

Sophie nodded. "I'd mentioned my old friendship with Esther, told them how she'd forgiven me for being so awful when they had to move." She and Esther shared a tender smile. "Herr Massey tracked them down."

He laughed. "Being a newspaperman, I'm good at that."

Frau Ellende chimed in. "I couldn't let the Kauffmans stay here with Sophie. My neighbors knew Peter and I would be away."

"You stayed with the Kauffmans?" I asked Sophie. She nodded.

Herr Kauffman picked up the tale. "Sophie was good company for my Esther. Of course, our home isn't as lovely as this." He shot another grateful look at Frau Ellende.

"Like many folks in their neighborhood, the Kauffmans had too little to eat," Herr Massey said. "And yet there I was, asking them to share what they had with Sophie."

"Plus, they were putting themselves in danger, you know, sheltering me since I'm a traitor," Sophie added. I shuddered to hear her speak the word.

The Brit continued. "Before I left for England, I stocked the Kauffmans' shelves with canned goods, enough so they could share some with their Jewish neighbors. And before I returned to Munich, I contacted a local grocer and placed a large order to be delivered to their flat. So that became our signal—a food delivery meant I'd visit within a day or two."

"So, when I came with the bakery order…"

Esther smiled. "I knew Herr Massey would come by soon, even if just to check on Sophie and me and my papa. And the crutch you saw…"

"It was mine," Sophie said. "I was listening in the next room. I wanted so much…but I waited. We'd all agreed to wait until everyone was sure we could reveal ourselves safely."

"But it doesn't explain the note you left in the pickle jar," I insisted. "You said you'd gone away, Sophie." My gut clenched, and I spoke the horrible truth. "You didn't trust me."

Herr Massey shifted. "That's my doing again, Renate," he confessed. "Sophie was plenty worried about you, as she said. But when I saw you passing out flyers for the Reich, so entranced, appearing so dedicated to their cause…"

Sophie finished. "He told me you'd changed, that the Party won you over. I told him it must be for show, that you were probably acting as a Party loyalist to stay safe. But since I couldn't see you or talk with you myself, I had to trust his judgment. You needed to think I'd gone so you'd stop looking for me. At least until we knew for sure where your loyalties lay."

During this last explanation, shame rose in me. "The Party did win me over, for a few days at least. The Rally—it was so, so powerful. All those people coming together, the music, thousands of people singing, soldiers and Youth parading, the lights…" I recalled the moments. "Hypnotic, you know? As if I were in a trance." I smiled at them. "But the trance didn't last, what with Klaus at work and Werner at home and Anna showing up everywhere and Onkel Edmund watching my every move." I smoothed my hair in an exaggerated flourish. "I may not be taking theater classes, but I sure am practicing my acting skills." Sophie smiled, and the others chuckled. I turned to Herr Massey. "When did you decide to trust me?"

"Ah, that. My travels often take me past Sophie's family bakery. Now and then, I'd peek in and see you hard at work. Early one morning, I saw a street urchin lurking in the alley behind the bakery. You opened the door with a broom in one hand and a trash bag in the other. The urchin rose and faced you. I expected you to chase him off with the broom, but you didn't. You handed him a bag."

I filled them in on my latest efforts on Bruno's behalf. A few days earlier, I'd stepped into the alley ready to hand Bruno a half dozen cinnamon rolls. There was no movement nearby, no grinning boy popping around a doorway to greet me. I waited a few moments, peering this way and that, then kicked the trash can to get his attention. No Bruno. I left the bag of rolls on top of the can and whispered a prayer for his well-being. By the next day, vermin had chewed through the bag and carried the rolls away. I hadn't seen Bruno at the bakery's alley door since. "They're travelers, he and his pregnant mother. I have no way to find them."

Those listening to my story looked concerned. Sophie asked, "Does Klaus know you give the boy food?"

I shook my head. "He thinks I'm taking out the trash. Never figured out the trash goes out at the end of the day, not first thing in the morning." We shared a chuckle at Klaus' expense. I didn't feel bad about it.

Herr Massey nodded. "Anyway, when I told Sophie what I saw, how you gave food to the boy…"

Sophie straightened. "I knew you were who you've always been. A good-hearted person who would help anyone in need." She squeezed my hand.

She still believed in me. I wanted to linger in that happiness, but the hour was late. "So, what now?" I asked. "The Kauffmans can't go back there."

Herr Kauffman said, "Ah, but we must. I'll go tomorrow and clean up. With any luck, I can bring Esther and Sophie back there in a couple days."

"But…but you're not safe there. If the Gestapo comes"—I gestured to Sophie, who sat biting her lip—"she can't run. She'll be arrested." I turned to Herr Kauffman and

Esther. "And you two! You'd be in terrible trouble for hiding her."

Herr Kauffman raised a hand to hush me. "When we took Sophie in, we knew full well what was at stake." He smiled at Esther, then at Sophie. There was genuine affection between these three, and my heart warmed. "But you're right," he continued. "We have a plan for the future. Esther and I expect our papers to come through any day now. Poland perhaps, or Palestine."

"And then…"

"Then we'll go. Leave our home and what's left of our belongings. Start a new life."

"I have connections with immigration," Herr Massey said. "I may be able to hurry their paperwork through. With any luck, they'll be out of the country in a few weeks."

I nodded, almost afraid to ask my burning question. "And Sophie? Can she go too?"

Sophie answered for herself. "No, Rennie. I'm a wanted fugitive, a traitor. My name and my image are everywhere. I must stay hidden."

My heart was broken. I knelt beside her chair and leaned my head against hers. In moments, the others gathered around us, encircled us with their arms and their love. "We'll figure something out," Frau Ellende said. "You have my word."

"And mine," her brother echoed.

Regardless of their good wishes for Sophie, I knew the truth. The picture frame had shown me that one possible outcome for Sophie was death.

All day at the bakery and all evening at home, the radio bombarded us with the Party's version of good news. Our country's enemies were leaving, our men had jobs and could support their families, our country was unified in the effort to regain lands taken from us in the Great War. I'd heard it all before.

Except I'd become savvy enough to read between the lines. Our government harassed, deported, and imprisoned people who didn't fit their mold of perfect. Our government created jobs building roads and bridges so our expanded army and its supplies could push forward. Our government forced its way into countries that were actually independent nations.

When I made deliveries each afternoon, I didn't need to read between the lines. I saw the truth with my own eyes. Take the gray day in late November, for example, when a few dozen ragged men surrounded by SS approached my location. The men wore signs around their necks which said **Out with the Jews** and **I will never again complain to the police.**

I climbed off my bike and joined other gaping pedestrians on the sidewalk as the group passed. Several people near me jeered, calling names and slurs at the shuffling men. I scanned the group for Herr Kauffman or Herr Massey and whispered a prayer of thanks when I did not see them among these poor souls.

I hoped a roundup like this was an isolated incident, but I was wrong. Over the next few weeks, six more such groups, some all men, sometimes both men and women, marched right down our streets. There may have been more. Those were just the ones I saw.

Chapter Eighteen
Werner

Munich, Germany
June 1931

With Mutter's shopping list, a five-mark note, and a clean handkerchief folded in my shirt pocket, I was entrusted with a trip to the Viktualienmarkt. I grabbed Mutter's market basket and set off on a beautiful morning. All of eleven years old, I was.

Before I reached the market, four boys on bicycles surrounded me. I took them in, their scuffed shoes, their filthy trousers and mussed hair, their mocking expressions. "Look who it is. Where are you going, Müller?" one, the apparent ringleader, asked.

I'd seen these boys in the neighborhood but didn't know their names. How did they know mine? Maybe they learned it from the street thugs who'd held me down and threw mud on me a couple years back. Or maybe from the ones last spring who pulled my shirt up over my face and ran off laughing. An uncomfortable prickle started up my neck.

"He's going to the market for his mommy," another said, his voice taunting. They all laughed.

I steadied my voice. "Let me pass." As I started walking, they closed ranks.

"Look at those shoes," the third boy said. "Does mommy shine them for you?" More laughter.

"No, he shines them himself. Wants to impress the ladies at the market." His voice rose in a poor imitation of an elderly woman. "Oh, such a nice little boy." In his normal tone, he added, "Here's what I think of those shoes." A glob of spittle landed on the sidewalk past my toes. The offender wiped his chin and reared back. His next attempt hit its target. The sound of wet slop against leather made my stomach roil. The other boys howled.

"Who runs errands dressed that way?" the fourth boy chimed in, gesturing to my pressed shirt and trousers. His rumpled, torn garb looked as if he hadn't taken it off for days.

"Better yet, what *boy* dresses that way?" the ringleader said. This time, there was no laughter. As if by unspoken agreement, the four dropped their bicycles and encircled me. My breath came quick.

More verbal taunts about my slicked hair, the bleached whiteness of my shirt. The circle tightened. I held my breath against their unwashed stench.

On the sidewalk, an old man approached. I tried to meet his eyes to plead for help. He skirted us and walked on, shaking his head.

"Better clean off your spit, Joachim," one boy said. "You'll ruin pretty boy's shoes."

Joachim scuffed the sole of his shoe across the top of mine, smearing the spittle and marring the shine with a coat of mud. He admired his handiwork, then looked up at me. "Your shoes should match." He repeated the spit and mud process on the other shoe. The boys roared their approval.

On the opposite sidewalk, a woman pushing a pram took in the situation. Without a word, she hurried past.

I was fair game. Filthy hands grabbed and ripped and smeared whatever they could reach. My belt was unbuckled and yanked off. My shirt ripped. Buttons popped. My shirt pocket tore, its contents snatched by greedy fingers. I covered my head and fell to my knees. As the assault continued, I huddled into a ball. Time passed. One minute? Twenty?

Then no hands or feet touched me. Bikes rattled, and mocking laughter moved away.

The tread of boots approached, and a gentle hand on my back roused me. "Are you all right, boy?" a man's voice asked. "Come. Up on your feet."

Dazed and trembling, I rose and faced my rescuers—a group of three men in Party uniforms. The man in the center, the man we called Onkel Edmund, was my father's best friend and my own godfather. He wore an expression of surprise that matched my own. In silence, he took in my tearstained face, my torn shirt, the scrapes and filth on my exposed skin. For several agonizing moments, he focused on the dark, wet triangle between my trouser legs. His nostrils flared. He scowled. Then he turned heel and strode away. The other men followed.

I left the trampled market basket on the sidewalk and stumbled home, where Mutter clucked and fussed and helped me wash. She fed me soup and tucked me into bed.

A few hours later, Vater burst through the door. "Where is he?"

"Resting," Mutter said. "Just bumps and scratches. He's all right."

"He won't be all right for long. Get him out here."

With a gentle rap on my door, Mutter peeked in my room. She needn't have bothered. I was already up and moving to obey my father. His angry tone demanded my immediate response.

In full dress uniform, he paced the living room, hands behind his back. He whirled to face me. "You let those bullies get the better of you. What is this—the third time? The fourth?"

"I'm sorry, sir."

He raised a hand. "Don't speak. Listen." He turned and resumed pacing. "We've been through this before, but still you insist on being the boy everyone picks on." Disgust darkened his face. "Today, I'm at work. My phone rings, and it's Edmund. 'That boy of yours, he's a weakling,' Edmund says to me. 'I found him in the middle of the sidewalk sniveling and crying and wetting his pants,' he tells me." My father glared at me. "Like a baby. Never have I been so ashamed of my own flesh and blood."

Mutter gasped and started to protest. Vater stopped pacing long enough to glare at her, and she fell silent. I gave no response, just stared at my father's boots as they strode across the room countless times. "Edmund rubs elbows with high-ranking officials," my father continued. "People of influence. There I am, working to better myself, to better my wife and children. And there you are, dragging me down in front of the one person who might help me advance." He stopped in front me, jerking my chin up to force eye contact. "Well? What do you have to say for yourself, sissy boy?"

Mutter had always been my savior, ready to defend me at the first sign of trouble. But that day she stared at her shoes, mum.

Vater followed my gaze. He shook a finger at Mutter and spoke through gritted teeth. "This is your fault, woman. You made him soft. From now on, he'll answer to me." He turned to me and bent into my face so close I could smell the sausages he'd eaten for his midday meal. "I will not have a sissy for a son. Is that clear?"

I nodded, resisting the urge to pull away. A small sound caught his attention. He turned to see little Renate standing behind Mutter, her dolly dangling upside down from one small hand. Her bottom lip trembled, an apparent response to the tension in the room. Through clenched teeth, Vater growled at me, "We'll finish this later." Then brightness broke across his face as he bent to pick up my little sister. "Here's my girl," he said, using the gentle tone he reserved for her.

Renate wrapped her arms around his neck and snuggled against his chest. They cooed and murmured sweet things to one another while Mutter and I stood in silence, waiting to be dismissed. Vater settled into a chair with his precious daughter on his lap. Renate's dolly dropped to the floor, forgotten.

I went to my room.

Hours later, Vater opened my door without knocking. His posture and coloring showed less anger, but when he spoke, his tone was resolute. "Here's what will happen. You will tell our neighbors you are available to do chores for them this summer. Whatever they need help with, you *will* do. Mow grass, trim tree branches, carry out the trash, move furniture. Anything. Everything."

"Yes, sir."

"You will not complain that the work is too hard or too dirty."

I swallowed. "No, sir."

"You will not accept payment."

"Of course not, sir."

"And whenever possible, you will work in uniform."

I stopped. As a new pledge to the Hitler Youth's *Pimpf* for boys my age, I'd only worn my uniform a few times. I loved its crisp feel, its pointed collar. Using it for manual labor would ruin that.

Vater saw my hesitation. "All work done in uniform is considered done on behalf of the Movement. It will be reported to your leader. You will be a shining example instead of a laughingstock."

"Yes, sir." I would learn how to starch and iron my uniform.

"Who knows? We might make a good Nazi out of you after all."

Chapter Nineteen
Rennie

Munich, Germany
13 December 1938

I greeted Herr Massey as I would any bakery customer. He gestured to the work area behind the curtain and mouthed the words, "Is Klaus there?" When I nodded yes, he cleared his throat and said, "Two crullers, *bitte*." Among the coins he placed in my open palm was a small folded paper.

I slipped the note in my apron pocket and rang up his purchase. "Danke, come again," I called as he left with his purchase. Then I poked my head around the curtain and said, "Klaus, I need to..." I pointed to the washroom.

"Fine. I'll listen for the bell."

The note was simple: *Nineteen Uhr tonight at my sister's.* Even as I pulled the chain to flush the note, I could barely contain my excitement. I'd see Sophie again.

Herr Massey greeted me at the door of his sister's flat and beckoned me into the study. The good frau was already seated there, but there was no sign of Sophie or of the Kauffmans. I tried not to show my disappointment. Frau Ellende gestured to a chair, which I accepted. After the usual queries regarding my health and job, Herr Massey sat facing me, his expression serious. "We've got a dilemma," he began.

"Good news and bad news, all rolled in one," his sister said. "Good news first. There's a new operation in place to get vulnerable children out of Germany, to take them to England and several other countries. All legal and safe, even endorsed by the Party. They're calling it the *Kindertransport*." She filled me in on the details.

Through social service agencies like the one she worked with, parents could obtain tickets for children under age eighteen. Because of the targeted vandalism of early November, now remembered as *Kristallnacht*, many parents requesting tickets for their children were Jewish. Leaving their homes and parents behind, these children would travel on a westbound train across Germany and then into Holland. There, the children would board a ship and cross to England, where a host family would await them. The host family, usually complete strangers to the child, would then foster the child until their parents could join them.

"Can Esther emigrate that way?"

Frau Ellende nodded. "Indeed. Her father was one of the first in line to secure her a ticket. She is assured a seat on a transport leaving Munich in early January."

"I'm glad to hear that!"

Herr Massey raised a hand. "There's more. I'll travel home to England to spend Christmas with my family. That is if my wife and children remember me!" He shook his head. "This crazy job of mine. Anyway, I leave December twenty-first."

Frau Ellende chimed in. "And I leave next week." She gestured to the pile of boxes along one wall of the study. Moving boxes, already packed and sealed. I hadn't noticed them when I arrived. "I'm heading home to England too. For good this time. I've been thinking about it for quite a while, what with my husband gone and all. Nothing but my job to hold me here. And Germany, well, I don't care for much of what I see." She straightened. "I'm approved to be Esther's guardian in England until her father arrives."

Such a kind woman. "And Herr Kauffman, he can emigrate soon?" I asked.

She tipped her head. "That remains to be seen. He filed paperwork. Now we wait."

Herr Massey chimed in. "His papers will take several weeks to come through. He'll act as Sophie's guardian until then."

"Once Herr Kauffman leaves, what then? Who will watch out for Sophie?" Herr Massey raised his shoulders and let them drop; Frau Ellende looked to the floor.

I picked up on what the woman said earlier. "This Kindertransport is for vulnerable children, right? Well, if anyone is vulnerable, it's Sophie! Get her a ticket so she can go to England on the same train as Esther. You could be her guardian too!"

Frau Ellende laid a hand atop mine and furrowed her brows. "Sophie has been charged with treason. She cannot leave the country under those circumstances." She straightened and continued, "Today, we learned of a change in plans. It seems Esther's ticket to Palestine has come through. The Youth Aliyah program. Palestine is where she really wanted to go, so she leaves January second."

I was confused. "She's not going to England then? You won't be her guardian?"

"No."

"Then why are you leaving? You could stay, keep Sophie here with you!"

Her expression showed regret. "No, I cannot. I already gave notice at my job. I'm all packed." She gestured at the stacked boxes. "My heart hasn't been in Germany since my husband died. No, I must go home to England."

I turned to Herr Massey. Lint on his shirtsleeve had his full attention.

"Let me get this straight," I said, ticking off the facts on my fingers. "Esther has been approved to leave the country. She has two valid tickets to two different destinations. Both leave the country within a twenty-four-hour time frame. She's using the ticket to Palestine, which means her ticket to England won't be used."

Frau Ellende regarded me. "I'll turn it into the registration office."

I clapped my hands. "But think about it! By the time Esther's name is registered at Party headquarters as having boarded the Youth Aliyah transport…" I paused, hoping they'd pick up my line of reasoning. When they didn't, I finished, "…the Kindertransport will be across the border."

Both adults looked confused, so I clarified. "Sophie will be the Kindertransport's Esther Kauffman! It will take some doing—a blonde-haired, blue-eyed girl with a leg brace passing for a dark-haired, dark-eyed girl who walks fine. But this could work!" I looked from one adult to the other. They looked skeptical.

Herr Massey spoke first. "It's a terrible risk, Renate, both for Sophie and for Esther. What if the deception is discovered?"

But I continued to make plans. "She'll need shoe black in her hair, maybe a plaster cast over her weak leg so it'll look as if it's broken…"

Frau Ellende raised a hand. "Not so fast. Peter is right. This plan puts both girls at risk. Herr Kauffman too."

"And you, Beatrice," her brother chimed in.

She waved it away. "I'll be in England by then." She hesitated, her brows furrowed in thought. "We would need the approval of all parties before we even consider this."

We ironed out a few preliminaries. Herr Massey would talk the plan through with Sophie and the Kauffmans. From my contacts in local theater, I would assemble the disguise Sophie needed and have it ready if the plan was a go.

Then Frau Ellende added, "There's one thing we forgot. When Esther travels, she'll have her identification papers with her. Sophie, well, she can't use her own papers."

I deflated, and I think Herr Massey did too. After a few silent moments, the woman continued. "But I know a forger…"

Herr Massey stared at his sister, then threw his head back and laughed. "Beatrice, you are full of surprises!"

She shrugged. "In my job, you meet all sorts of people."

When I was done grinning, I added, "Make sure the forger records Esther's,—I mean Sophie's—eye color as blue." No theater makeup could change a person's eye color.

Frau Ellende nodded. "Will do. And I'll have him draw up two copies, just in case."

Two copies of forged papers seemed a bit excessive to me. Regardless, I was delighted with the plan.

A week later, Herr Massey bought an entire *Schwarzwälder Kirschtorte* and whispered that the plan was a go.

Within days, I loaded up my rucksack and bicycled to the Kauffmans'. Esther met me at the door, her dark eyes darting up and down the street. When I slipped inside, she bolted it behind me. "Has there been trouble?" I asked.

She wrapped her arms around her stomach. "I just can't wait to leave." My heart broke for her.

Using the wall for support, Sophie entered from an inner room. Her hair had been cut into a shoulder-length bob, no doubt in preparation for her disguise. As I hugged her, I touched it and whispered, "Your hair looks nice." Her eyes glistened, so I pulled back and asked, "Where's your crutch?"

She gave a rueful huff. "Gone. My brace too." She stuck out her slippered foot and lifted her skirt to reveal her withered right leg. "Herr Massey thought it best to take them apart and throw them in the trash a couple pieces at a time."

"How are you getting around then?"

"I have the underarm crutches he brought me. It's just hard to hop in here." She gestured around the small flat. My heart broke for her too.

I tossed my rucksack on a chair and started to unpack it. "Well, everything is falling into place." I pulled out rolled strips of soft cloth and a sack of plaster of Paris powder. "These are for your leg cast."

Esther nodded. "My father will take care of that a day or two before."

A tin of shoe polish was next. "Black. For your hair."

Esther lifted her own hair. "Yep. Same color as mine. That'll help you look more like me, Sophie." She squeezed Sophie's arm, then turned to me. "I'm giving her the dress I wore for the photo. That'll help too."

Sophie shot Esther a grateful look, but she couldn't disguise her fear. "Between the hair and the clothes, I should pass…"

I finished for her. "For a Jewish girl named Esther Kauffman. Yes." I hoped my tone gave her confidence. My own confidence in our flimsy plan had waned in recent days.

Without further ado, I said my goodbyes to Esther, wishing her well in her new life in Palestine. To Sophie, I said, "I could come to the station to see you off."

Sophie shook her head, her blue eyes pooled with tears. "That would just draw attention to me. We should say goodbye now, Rennie."

We fell together and hugged, then wept and hugged some more. I wondered if I'd ever see her again.

3 January 1939

In the next twenty-four hours, either all would be well, or all would be lost. Such an important day had to start with church.

I scrounged together a few *pfennige,* dropped the coins in the offering box, and knelt in front of the candle array. "Dear God, by now Esther should be safely out of the country. But my friend Sophie needs your help. Please keep your hand upon her and guide her to England. Amen." I blessed myself and started to rise when I remembered—my friend wasn't the only one in need of prayer. I lit another candle and knelt back down.

"I'm afraid for my brother, Lord. He's lost. I want to lead him to his path of joy, but I can't. He doesn't want to take that path. Not yet anyway. So, if I'm not, um, nearby, can you please remind him of who he used to be? Of who he still is deep down? Return him to his true self. If he won't choose joy, then please guide him away from the Party to a place of safety.

"And me. If the authorities find out what I've done, oh, Lord, give me strength. Amen."

Werner wasn't home when I returned from church, so I had a few moments to myself. From beneath my folded clothes, I pulled out the journal Frau Lunka had given me. In that beautiful leather-bound book, I wrote a note to vindicate those who might be blamed if something went wrong that night. The rest of the journal I left empty. I'd use the pages for a play based on my experiences. Provided all went well.

With trembling hands, I slipped the photo of Sophie and me into the frame. The change was instantaneous. Before me were the two familiar paths, and I still had a single foot on each. My blue path of loyalty remained, but the second path, once red, had changed to palest green. Green meant safety. At least I had a chance.

Sophie's feet were still on two separate paths as well. As before, one of her paths was black, but the path beneath her other foot was the bright green of summer fields. Yes, Sophie faced either a safe haven or certain death.

Ahead of our images, our four paths merged. They didn't meet at a single distinct point as they had earlier. Instead, their junction was a tangle of color with three short paths exiting the jumble. One blue, one green, and one black. Loyalty, safety, and death.

Since the blue path of loyalty had been beneath me in the photo with Werner, I was confused. How could I possibly be loyal to both my best friend and my brother? If I chose one over the other, would I push them onto the black path toward their death?

As I reached the frame toward my nightstand, a door slammed hard enough to shake the house. I jumped. The frame fell from my hand and crashed against the metal edge of my bedframe and onto the wood floor.

Werner's footsteps pounded up the stairs, and he burst into my room. "*Was ist los?*"

I tried to look contrite despite my trembling hands. "Startled by the slamming."

Werner huffed. "Such an actress you are." He closed the door behind him as he left.

By some miracle of Romany magic, the glass hadn't shattered, but the bottom of the frame itself had snapped off. Only three sides of the frame surrounded the photo.

The photo, well, it had returned to its original form—Sophie and me at the castle a year earlier. Gone were the changes, the colored paths. We were side by side as we'd once been, two laughing friends enjoying a carefree day.

Before.

I lifted the frame's bottom and snapped it into place, eyeing the photo for telltale changes. It worked—the paths were visible again. I experimented, first removing the glass pane. The photo returned to its original form. Glass pane on, the lines were visible. The same held true when the backboard or any of the sides were removed. Each piece of the frame was needed for its magic to work.

This frame was precious, every single bit of it. My room—our home—was no hiding place for a magical device. There was only one person I trusted with the frame. There was only one place to hide it where she might find it at some future date.

I snapped apart the frame's sides. Then I wrapped them, the glass pane, and the backboard in handkerchiefs and stuffed them in my coat's deep pocket.

Despite the damp chill, it seemed half of Munich was in the English Garden Park. In an open area, groups of children threw snowballs at one another, ducking behind makeshift walls of white, laughing and shouting. Three girls lay on their backs, wiping arms and legs through the snow, rising to admire their snow angels as I passed. Nearby, two young boys shoved stick arms into a lopsided snowman. All happiness and friendship, people enjoying time together. I wiped a tear from my icy cheek and pedaled on.

I rode past the crowds into a quieter part of the park, stopping a few meters from the familiar scruffy pine tree. After a quick look up and down the path to ensure I was alone, I stepped into the snow.

With last summer's landmarks under a blanket of white, I circled the tree, desperate to remember the exact position of the buried pickle jar. I used my now sodden shoes to push loose snow aside and noticed a mound of dirt. The mound gave way beneath my heel.

Seeing neither pedestrians nor spies, I squatted and pulled a segment of the frame from my pocket. I pushed the sharp end into the loosened dirt and dug. A metallic clunk told me I'd struck the jar's lid. My fingertips outlined the lid, then worked downward until I cleared a handhold. Using the bottom of my wet skirt to grip the jar's lid, I unscrewed it and reached inside. A slip of paper held a familiar scrawl.

S,

I leave soon and haven't found you to say goodbye. Now we'll be farther apart than ever. Oh, how I wish it weren't so.

Maybe we can start anew once this is over.

Please remember me. I will never forget you.

Always,

E

I thumped onto my bottom. Erich still cared for Sophie. I pressed the note to my cheek, hoping to catch his scent, wishing I could absorb his essence through this precious item. All I felt was the cold; all I smelled was damp earth.

I'm not sure how long I sat there—one minute, maybe ten or twenty, but the wet cold roused me. I wanted to be happy for my friend. The boy she was crazy about was crazy about her too. After all she'd been through, she deserved happiness.

Me? I was empty and frozen as the pickle jar.

But my mind was made up. My feelings would not dictate my actions, not when loyalty to my friend was at stake. I shook myself and got to work.

Silly me. I hadn't brought a pencil. I couldn't write an explanation for the items I was leaving. I had to trust that Sophie would return to Munich when all was safe, whenever that was. I had to trust she'd dig up the jar and make sense of the contents. Until that very moment, I hadn't considered—maybe the frame pieces wouldn't even fit in the jar.

A woman's voice from behind startled me. "Are you all right?"

I whirled. Anna and her father, Herr Doktor Albrecht, stood on the path. Recognition crossed her face, and her tone changed from concern to suspicion. "Renate. What are you doing?" She picked her way toward me, placing her feet where mine had already flattened the snow.

I shoved Erich's note into my pocket beside the disassembled frame. I rose and said, "*Gutes neues Jahr*, Anna, Herr Doktor."

Neither of them returned my New Year's greeting. Anna took in my wet, dirty glove and the jar lid at my feet. "The famous pickle jar," she said, her tone full of scorn. "I wondered where it was. Werner said the Adler girl was involved in mischief here before she disappeared." Her gaze narrowed. "And your involvement is?"

With a deep breath, I stepped on stage for an unrehearsed performance. "Sophie and I often exchanged notes here. I thought she'd remember our tradition of sharing dreams for the New Year." I added a bit of drama by peering down into the empty jar and arranging my face in a sincere frown. "But no."

Anna stepped close enough to look into the empty jar herself, then trained her gaze on my face. Searching for sincerity, I knew. Anna's belief in my loyalty to the Reich was essential. "She has forgotten me, forgotten our friendship," I said. "The dirty little traitor." The horrible words coming from my own mouth made me shudder.

For a moment, Anna didn't respond but kept up her scrutiny of me, the overturned pile of snow and dirt, the lidless jar, the entire ridiculous situation. She hissed, "Renate, do not cross me."

My heart pounded its response, but I think my sincere expression held fast.

Her father spoke from his position on the park's path. "Is there a problem?"

Her attention shifted to him, and the spell broke. "*Nein*, Vater," she said. "Renate was hoping to catch a traitor." Anna started toward him across the crushed snow. "The Adler girl."

The doctor nodded. "Like her mother and father, that one. A shame."

When Anna reached her father's side, she turned to me. "Are you coming, Renate?"

"Of course." I returned the lid to the jar, covered the hole with soil and snow, and retraced my steps to my waiting bicycle.

Since Anna knew the location of the pickle jar, nothing could be hidden there. I had to find another way to get both the frame and Erich's note to Sophie. During my bike ride home, I considered my options. I could package the items and mail them to Herr Massey in England. But mail was often searched, overseas packages in particular. If the frame's magic fell into the hands of the Gestapo… I shuddered.

The most logical way to get the items to Sophie was to give them to her myself before she left on the transport at midnight. To do that, I'd have to sneak out of the house and down to the Hauptbahnhof after Werner went to sleep. I had no idea what excuse I could make for being on the streets alone at such an hour.

Chapter Twenty
Rennie

As I unlocked the door to our house, familiar voices called out. Otto and Conrad, my old charges from the farm, walked down the sidewalk wearing big smiles and lugging a large round basket between them. Their grandfather stopped a few paces behind and crossed his arms, waiting and silent.

"We brought you a holiday gift." Conrad gestured to the gingham cloth-covered basket. "Apples!"

Otto added, "Late-season apples. They've been in the cellar a while, so they're kind of soft." He shrugged. "Can't sell them for eating, but they're good for baking. Mother thought you could use them in strudel."

"Five or six dozen."

"How thoughtful," I said. "Please thank her and send her my regards."

Conrad added, "The apples must go to the bakery. Tonight."

"Well, aren't you the bossy one," I said, laughing. "Let me change out of these wet clothes. You can help me take them there."

Otto looked at his watch, then at his waiting grandfather. "No time to help, I'm afraid." Lips tight, he whispered, "Lots going on. There's a spy at the farm."

Before I could respond, Conrad tugged my arm and hunkered down beside me to tie his shoe. Pretending to scratch my knee, I bent close enough to hear him. "The contents are for you, Rennie. No one else may see."

"No one," Otto echoed through clenched teeth. "Unpack the basket at the bakery. Tonight, in an hour or so." Conrad rose, and the two boys joined their grandfather on the sidewalk. With a small wave, they were gone.

Odd. I lifted a corner of the gingham and peeked underneath. Apples, lots of them. I'd have to lug the heavy basket to the bakery three blocks away. Since Werner would be home in a couple hours demanding his evening meal, moving the basket soon made sense. I shoved the basket into the shadow of a hedge and raced in the house to change into dry clothes.

In minutes, I returned to reclaim the oversized basket. When I grabbed its handles and lifted, the awkward bulk pulled me off-balance. I readjusted and lifted again, leaning the basket's weight against my stomach. After a dozen steps, I stopped. I needed the cart. The basket went back under the shrubs while I hurried the three blocks to the bakery.

When I returned with the old wooden pushcart, Werner was just arriving too. "Why do you need that?" he asked.

With what I hoped was a serene expression, I smiled at him. "The Huber boys brought a basket of apples for strudel. They'll spoil in the cold, so I need to take them to the bakery."

"When will my dinner be ready?"

"Not for a while. I have to do this first."

"Then give me something to tide me over. Apples, you say? Where are they?"

I gestured to the spot where the basket sat, half in shadow. Werner reached beneath the cloth cover and grabbed an apple. Instantly, he gasped and dropped it, juicy bits splattering my legs. He fumbled in his pocket for a handkerchief and scrubbed at his hand. "Are they all that way? Rotten? Are there bugs or…" He straightened and took several deep breaths in an obvious fight against revulsion.

I stifled a giggle, then repeated what the boys had told me—these were late-season apples, best for baking. My heart pounded, pushing the boys' other words through my veins. *For your eyes only, Rennie.*

My brother dragged the basket into full view. With one hand over his nose and mouth, he removed the gingham cover. Even in the fading sunlight, it was easy to see why Frau Huber sent these apples for baking. Some were shriveled and dotted with dark spots. The skin had split on others, exposing pale flesh to sluggish grazing bees. Werner drew back. "They're spoiled!"

"They're not spoiled, Werner. We use soft fruit all the time. I cut out the bruised bits and…"

"You would sell goods baked from this…this animal feed? Not suitable for members of the Reich."

I waved him off. "What do you know about produce or about baking? You don't shop. You don't cook." Then I pressed my lips closed. Dangerous. I'd slipped out of role play and had revealed my own thoughts.

Werner ignored my outburst and gestured to the apples. "Take those away. They'll attract bugs. I won't have bugs at our door."

Grunting, I lifted the huge basket into the cart and pushed it down to the bakery. Alone.

In the alley behind the bakery, movement in the deepening shadows stopped me. “Frau Lunka!” I held a hand to my chest. “You startled me.”

A finger to her lips and a nod at the door told me what she needed. I obeyed and unlocked the bakery’s alley door. When I reached inside and flicked on the overhead lights, the Romany woman whirled and flipped them off.

“What? Why…”

“We cannot be seen, Renate Müller.”

“Fine, but the apples come inside. Can’t let animals get them.” I lifted the cart and its contents over the threshold and pushed into the storage room. She followed and closed the door behind us, trapping me in the dark with her scent of outdoors and woodsmoke. I reached behind me and flipped on the light again, ignoring the woman’s protests as we blinked against the sudden brightness. “No one will see us.” I gestured around the windowless storage room.

But we might still be heard. “Wait here,” I commanded, before retrieving the hidden key and climbing the stairs. I knocked on the door of the upstairs flat. “Klaus? Are you home? It’s me, Rennie.” No response. With his departure to the Wehrmacht imminent, he was probably out cavorting with friends. I let myself in, checked through the empty rooms, and with relief, locked up behind me.

Frau Lunka hadn’t moved but stood peering at the cart with its laden basket on board. “Conrad and his brother, they brought you that?”

Had I said anything about the Huber boys? “The cart belongs to the bakery. The boys brought the apples in the basket.”

“Ah. So. That’s what you need.”

"Excuse me?"

"The basket. The basket is what you need. There are instructions inside for you, nicht?"

When I pulled off the basket's gingham cloth, no paper was visible, just a dozen sluggish insects that rose toward the overhead lights. Careful not to bruise the apples even more, I tipped the basket sideways. Dozens of apples rolled into the cart, bumping along the cart's wooden slats until stopped by its half-meter-high sides.

Deep in the now empty basket, a juice-splattered envelope was indeed visible. On the single sheet of paper inside was:

Dear Renate,

I hoped to keep the unexpected harvest at the farm until spring, but our cellars are already full. Then I thought of you. Once prepared, please deliver the goods to your overseas customer.

Visit the farm when you can.

Fondly,

Frau Huber

What overseas customer? I turned the note over, checked inside the envelope. Nothing else.

A small sound drew my attention. Frau Lunka scrutinized my face but otherwise seemed her usual self—layers of clothes, the dirty kerchief tied around unruly hair, thick-soled shoes encircled by puddling snowmelt. The small sound came again, and I zeroed in on its source.

I lifted the corner of a lumpy cloth in the Romany woman's arms. The sleeping baby was perfect—round cheeks, long dark lashes, soft lips that moved rhythmically as if nursing. I whispered, "This is yours?"

Frau Lunka nodded, her focus on the infant. "She is Petra. Born at the last full moon."

Just a few weeks old then. I marveled at the sweet infant a few moments, then turned my gaze to her mother. "How did you know about the letter?"

"She told me. The farm woman."

"Frau Huber?" The Romany woman nodded. "Do you know what her letter says?"

"That's why I'm here."

I reread the note. "She doesn't mention you by name. Only a customer." I lifted my head. "An overseas customer."

The woman didn't respond and instead dipped her attention to the sleeping infant. She began to sway and hum.

"The customer who wants the apples, that's you?"

She stopped swaying and lifted her eyes to mine. The pain I saw there almost took my breath away. "I have no need of apples."

"Then why are you here?"

"The basket."

"Oh, you want the basket." I lifted it by one handle. "I'll just wipe it out and…"

Frau Lunka raised a hand to stop me. "The basket is for you. You need it for what is ahead."

"I'm sorry?"

"The farm woman hoped to keep the baby safe for me, but she cannot. Too many already, too much harvest. The noose tightens."

"The noose?"

"Conrad and my Bruno, they talked," she said, stroking the infant's black hair.

"About a noose?"

"No, about the basket. The false bottom."

I squinted at the basket. Now that she mentioned it, the basket was familiar. "Well, I'll be." I reached deep inside, sticking a finger into a hole at what appeared to be the bottom of the basket. With a little wiggling, the "bottom" lifted clean away, revealing the true bottom almost half a meter below. It was the same basket Conrad used last summer to hide the snake. That boy.

Frau Lunka's tight voice pulled me from my musings. "The roundups. Not just men and boys anymore. All of us now, us Roma. Whole families, whole communities, women, even babies." With a shrill whistle, she jerked her thumb backward. "Gone. *Kaputt.* Bruno and me, we must flee deep into the woods. We must travel far, hundreds of kilometers. I cannot take Petra. Winter. Too dangerous for her." She reached the sleeping bundle toward me. "This is better."

I stared at her. "You can't leave a baby in a bakery! Who will feed her, take care of her?"

"Bruno has made arrangements."

"With whom?"

"With the Englishman, the reporter who takes photos. He told me if Petra comes on the train, he or his sister will take her in."

"On the train, the transport leaving tonight? Herr Massey said so?"

She nodded. "They will care for her until we arrive."

For a few moments, I was speechless. "All right," I managed. "Petra has a guarantor in England. Her travel papers are in order? She's on the approved passenger list?"

Frau Lunka didn't answer but started to sway again, clucking in response to the infant's sighs.

Panic beat its way into my chest. "Passengers on the Kindertransport need certain papers. There will be officers there, SS, police." She didn't react, which only raised my anxiety. "These people are not stupid. They'll be on the lookout for stowaways."

"I have watched other boardings. The officers look for valuables, jewels, money. Not infants." She reached under the swaddling blanket and pulled out a small amber vial. She thrust it forward. The handwritten label read: **One dose. Twenty-two Uhr.** "For tonight." Then she withdrew a good-sized satchel from a voluminous sleeve and shook it. "Give this to the girl," she commanded, still rocking Petra.

"What girl?"

"Your friend. The one in the photo."

"Sophie?" Reflexively, my eyes flew to the alley door. "She knows about this?" Her nod was my answer.

Long moments passed before I could speak, but in that time, I softened. It was just like Sophie to offer help when she had so much at stake herself. Even with all she'd been through, she still thought of others first. My chest swelled with love for my friend.

I peeked inside the satchel. Several diapers, some infant-sized clothes, three milk-filled baby bottles, and an amber vial identical to the first. That label instructed: **One dose. One hour before crossing.** I held both amber vials up to the light. "Is this medicine? The baby is sick?"

The woman's eyebrows drew together as she scrutinized my face. "Petra must be quiet until Holland. Nazis at the border crossing. Until then, only the girl can know."

"Her name is Sophie. Since you want her to care for your baby, call her by name." I placed the vials and the satchel on a low shelf and faced the woman. "And how do you expect to get a baby onto the train? No papers." Instead of answering, she chucked the infant's soft chin. "Frau Lunka? Frau Lunka?

Please! Talk to me! Why are you here at a bakery with the baby and the satchel and all the talk about the basket?" Then I gasped. "You want me to…you expect me to place the basket on the train with your baby in it?"

She looked up at me then, those dark eyes of hers desperate. "Bruno and I must flee. Maybe we stay together; maybe we split up. Either way, we cannot take a newborn. It is winter." Her voice broke. "This must be." With that, she let loose the mournful howl of a wounded animal, all her longing and passion and desperation tossed into the storeroom's air.

Afraid neighbors would soon pound on the alley door, I tried to shush her. When she settled into a whimper, I broached the topic again. "So, the vials hold a sleeping draught. You want Petra to sleep on the way to England in the false bottom of the basket." She nodded. I continued, my voice soft but urgent. "The Nazis allow one suitcase per passenger. There are limits to its size and type. A round woven basket isn't allowed. It's not luggage."

"You will find a way."

My face grew hot. "Find a way? To what? To put Sophie, the baby, me, all of us in danger? Why would I do that?"

Frau Lunka stopped rocking and stated the truth. "Because you're not one of them. Your path divided from theirs some time ago." Her eyes narrowed, she studied my face. "I see the possibility of redemption tonight." She nodded. "Yes, redemption by helping my Petra." From a deep fold in her clothing, the woman pulled several official-looking papers. "In case they are needed."

Identification papers and a Kindertransport ticket for Esther Kauffman, a dark-haired, blue-eyed Jew. The duplicate set of forged papers Frau Ellende had mentioned.

I didn't ask how Frau Lunka had gotten them or why I might need them. Nothing that woman did surprised me anymore. "I'll keep these safe." I tucked them in the inside pocket of my coat.

Frau Lunka bent and kissed the infant's soft cheeks, the tiny fists, the dimpled knees. Ever so gently, she placed the still-sleeping baby on an apple-free spot on the wooden bed of the cart, whispering blessings all the while. When she straightened, she wiped an eye. Her anguish was clear. "Bruno and I will watch tonight. If there is danger, he will help." She kissed both my cheeks. "From the day I met you, Renate Müller, I knew you would help my children." In a whoosh of cloth and woodsmoke, she was out the door.

I raced after her and into the darkening alley, but she was already gone. For several long moments, I stood there, listening to her misery-filled howl echo down the alley. A couple neighborhood dogs responded by barking. Other dogs joined in.

"What a racket!"

I whirled to Werner's voice as he marched down the alley toward me. He'd come from the other direction. For that, I was thankful.

The baby. I couldn't let him see or hear the baby. I stepped back to block the bakery's alley door. "One dog barks, they all bark," I said, louder than necessary. "I…I came out to see what the trouble was."

He stopped in front me. "I expected you home already. Came to check, make sure hooligans didn't steal those wonderful apples." His tone was sarcastic.

I kept still in the doorway, my mind spinning. "Danke, but no need for concern. I'll be home soon."

"Now, Renate."

"I need to finish here and…"

"I want dinner. Come." I knew the tone. He wouldn't take no for an answer.

My throat was tight and my heart pounded as I flicked off the light and locked the bakery door behind me. I was leaving an infant behind, unprotected. Before the night was out, I would try to send that same infant past the clutches of those who wished her harm. I'd put her on a train bound for a foreign land.

At the bottom of a basket.

With the help of an escaping traitor.

What was I doing?

On our silent walk home, I struggled to come up with a plan. How could I return to the bakery and prepare Petra for her journey? What details did Sophie know about the baby and where she'd be hidden? And how on earth was I to give Sophie the frame pieces and the note from Erich, plus smuggle a basket holding a hidden baby onto the train while the platform crawled with Gestapo and police?

After the dinner dishes were washed and put away, I excused myself to my room. Even though the crumpled paper I found in the pickle jar was meant for Sophie, I traced my fingertip along Erich's handwritten words.

And stopped myself. I couldn't waste time on longing. Much needed to be done. Below Erich's words, I jotted my own note.

Once you're over the border, you and your fellow passengers should enjoy the apples, all the way to the bottom of the basket.

I folded the paper into a small rectangle and pressed it flat, leaving an unmarked section of paper visible. That's where I wrote **Property of Esther Kauffman** and handstitched the paper rectangle into the lining of a wool hat. At a quick glance, it would pass as the required clothing label.

As I came downstairs, I heard Werner's end of a telephone conversation. "No, I didn't plan to go." A pause. "What is it, jewelry? Money?" Pause. "Ah, so. Name?" A pen scratched on paper. "Spell it." Another pause. "Ja. I will go. I will handle it personally, Onkel Edmund." A longer pause. "Midnight, right. No one will slip past me. Heil Hitler."

My brother would be at the Hauptbahnhof when Sophie tried to board the Kindertransport at midnight. I slunk to my room and collapsed on my bed.

Over the next thirty minutes, I came up with a desperate, last-ditch effort plan. I hoped and prayed I wouldn't need it.

Chapter Twenty-one
Werner

West Palm Beach, Florida
2005

When I open my eyes, that Susanna woman sits across the room, looking out the window. "Still here?" I croak.

She turns to me and smiles. "Nowhere else I'd rather be."

Pah. I let my heavy lids close. At some point, she says, "Ah. There she is," and soft footfalls move across the room. The door clicks shut.

Good riddance.

Next thing I know, a new voice pulls me from my rest. "You're sure it's him?"

"Trust me." That's the Docken woman speaking.

There's movement at my bedside, and someone leans over me. The other voice. "Hmm. The nose is right. Hard to be certain after all these years."

I'll admit nothing. My papers are in order. They say I am Willi Knox.

Now let me die in peace.

One of those annoying nurses comes in and announces, "Time for meds, Mr. Knox. Up and at 'em." The head of my bed starts to rise. I don't have the strength to protest. I turn to the nurse's voice and dry swallow her pills. When I close my eyes, she clucks her tongue. "Don't be that way, Mr. Knox. You have company. These ladies have come a long way to see you."

In German, the unfamiliar woman's voice speaks again. "Across a great distance. And many years." A hand presses my shoulder. "There are things we must discuss."

My eyes fly open. The hand belongs to a gray-haired woman. She is not over-tanned and leathery like Florida women. Appropriately wrinkled for a woman near my own age. Thick, wire-rimmed spectacles hide her light eyes. Perhaps she's one of my Lebensborn. Better appreciate that I saved her from a squalid life in a second-rate country.

But it's old news. I focus on my heart and command it to stop beating. I am determined to succeed.

"Aren't you curious?" she asks.

I tune her out and focus on the irregular thumping in my chest. Why doesn't my heart obey my will?

"Even a little curious? Susanna has done years of research to find you. And I've traveled thousands of miles to see you one more time. To talk with you. To make sure you got the journal, the letters. To make sure you understand. I need to thank you, to tell you what happened to me, to Anna…"

I take a sharp breath.

The stranger raises one eyebrow to regard me. "Still you think of her? All right. We start there."

I dread what I'm about to hear, but I long to hear it anyway. I scan this woman's face and drink in her every word.

"Sometime after you left Munich, Anna began her work as a nurse at Hadamar."

Hadamar. A hospital, one of the centers that carried out orders. Eliminated useless eaters. I remember the place.

"Both Anna and her father, Herr Doktor Albrecht, worked there during the war. He was convicted of murdering thousands of children and adults, the T4 pogrom, it was called…"

I search for more in this woman's face, this stranger who says she knows me. A glimmer of familiarity, but it's fleeting. I can't gather air to ask her name.

"…for murdering defenseless people. Genocide. Mass murder. Call it what you will. People killed because they were deemed unworthy of life. Because they were disabled."

I draw a breath and utter the longest sentence I can manage. "What…Anna?"

Susanna Docken rises and moves to the window, leaving me to hear the news alone. The wrinkled woman pats my shoulder. "Died in '46. Her father was convicted of war crimes at the Nuremberg Trials, executed. When Anna's trial date approached, she killed herself."

Somehow, it's not news. A piece of me knew she'd been dead all these years. All these empty years. Leave it to Anna to force death to her beck and call. If only I could do the same. "Knew…her?" I ask. My voice is weak.

The stranger nods. "Oh, yes. I knew Anna. Quite well."

Before I can learn how she and Anna were acquainted, I fade. Whispers wake me sometime later. The stranger and Susanna Docken sit close together, heads bent. They are studying the object in Susanna's hand—the framed photo of Renate and me. They look up when I stir. The stranger says, "Good. You're awake."

Not by choice.

"I'm sure you want to know what happened to your sister."

Without my permission, Susanna slides the hospital tray in front of me and centers a framed photo on it.

Gone is the simple black and white of me and Renate as children. It's been damaged. Someone has drawn lines on it with crayon.

The stranger must notice my reaction because she nods. "We'd never seen anything like it either. But the marks are not on the photo." The older woman taps the dull silver frame. "Romany-made. Has its own special powers, shall we say."

Susanna adds, "The frame doesn't just hold the photo. It shows choices."

I gather air to say, "Colors."

Susanna points to a forked line in front of my image and the splotch of green beneath Renate's feet. "Watch." She slides out the photo and presents it to me.

Incredible. The image is ordinary again, the familiar sepia tones of a faded black-and white-photo. No paths, no color. I study the empty frame—the glass is clear. No markings. I look from Susanna to the older woman, waiting for an explanation.

Susanna obliges me. "Any photo is a snippet of time, a single moment. But when we slip a photo in this frame"—she lifts it from my fingers and slides it in the frame—"we see more. We see what is possible." Again, a line appears before my feet, starting slate gray then splitting in two. One fork brightens to the same green as Renate stands upon. The second fork is quite different. Its gray origin darkens to black. Stays black. And both forks are short. Very short.

Her voice drops. "We also see what cannot be changed." She indicates the green spot on which my sister's image stands. There is no path in front of her.

So, she is dead. My little sister is dead.

I didn't protect her. I broke my promise to Vater, to myself. Something rises in me, an emotion I've held in check far too long. It rises, presses against my chest. I cannot breathe.

It's my fault.

Here, at the end of my life, I see the cascade of events I set in motion.

I am a thief.

I stole photos from the crippled friend of Renate's, that Sophie girl. I made sure they were made into propaganda posters that mocked cripples.

Renate found the photos and passed them back to Sophie. She sent them to England.

When Sophie went into hiding, Renate sought her out, schemed a way for Sophie to escape. Renate made that happen. It wouldn't have been necessary if I hadn't stolen the photos.

My theft started it all. My sister's arrest, her eyes rolling in terror as Onkel Edmund pushed her into the black sedan.

My assignment to Lebensborn. Hundreds of wailing children. Ripped them from their parents' grasp by my own hands.

The older woman brings me back by saying, "Looks like you have a choice before you—and soon. We brought you this"— she indicates the framed photo—"and these other items"—she gestures to papers and that old book in her lap—"to help you understand your options."

Questions flood me. I don't want to know the answers.

But I must know.

These women must go away.

They must never leave.

I followed orders.

I am a monster.

I don't want to hear another word.

They must tell me everything.

I point to the still-unnamed older woman sitting beside Susanna Docken. "You?" She smiles, and that's when I recognize her. My sister's childhood friend, the cripple, Sophie Adler. "Traitor…"

Susanna starts to protest, but Sophie waves her away. "It's all right, Suze. Werner has attached that label to me for a long time."

Susanna chimes in. "History views you as a patriot, someone who told the truth about a moral wrong."

Sophie gives her a soft smile and turns to me. "Yes, I am Sophie Adler, Sophie Fischer now. And you are Werner Müller."

No point anymore. I nod.

Susanna lets out a sigh and says, "So I was right."

I moisten my lips, and say, "Renate."

The two women exchange smiles. "Thought you'd never ask," Sophie says. From her purse, she pulls out an envelope, yellowed and crinkled with age, and from it, a brittle sheet of paper which she unfolds with great care. "This was delivered a week after I arrived in England. Rennie posted it in January of '39, the day I left Munich." She hands me the paper, but I shake my head. She slides her spectacles down her nose and reads:

Dear S,

I'm writing this letter and sending it off before our performance tonight. Even with your low-budget costume, I am sure you will convince your audience. I have faith in you. As for me, I admit to stage fright. I'm afraid I'll flub my lines, miss my cues.

Sophie stops reading and peers at me over her glasses. "She sure did love the theater, your sister. Think of her every time I go to a show."

I stopped going to shows decades ago.

She continues.

By the time you read this, the play will be over, and the audience will have moved on. Since it may be some time before we work together again, there are a few things of a personal nature you need to know.

Again, she stops reading. "This next piece refers to my late husband. Erich Fischer—remember him? You bumped into one another in South America years back." I nod and wave for her to continue.

About E. He is crazy about you. He longs to hear from you. We've written several times, and each communication is centered around you. Always you. When possible, let him know you care. He's waiting for you.

She takes her specs off and looks to the ceiling. "See, *mein Schatz*? We found him." She turns her gaze to me. "Forty-three wonderful years we had together, Erich and me." Her cool, dry hand grasps one of mine. "Erich tracked me down, found me in England. Because of your help." I was confused, then remembered—I'd slipped a note under Erich's door before I left Argentina. Told him Sophie had gone to England. "So thank you, Werner, from the bottom of my heart. Your small kindness allowed Erich and me to find one another again." Her eyes are moist.

I didn't act out of kindness. I did it to send him on a wild-goose chase in a country teeming with refugees.

Didn't I?

This Sophie, she doesn't understand. My actions were the reason she was accused as a traitor! The reason she had to flee Germany in the first place! Why is she thanking me?

She releases my hand and clears her throat. Susanna Docken rubs a small circle on her back. Sophie seems to gather herself. She readjusts the specs and says, "This next part is about you, Werner."

I brace myself to hear my sister's words.

About W. I hope he will understand the role I play tonight. If he acts from his true self, my actions will make sense to him. If he does not, I pray he will eventually forgive me. I act tonight to be loyal to myself, to my friend, and to the person W truly is deep down.

She'd used the same phrase a long time ago. Haunted me, it did.

He protected me the best he could for a long, long time, and I will always love him for it. If you see him, let him know I forgive him for being so cold and calculating during our production last summer. And I forgive him in advance for his role in whatever happens tonight.

All I did was protect myself. Back the winning side.

I cannot shuffle these cards. There is no starting over. Not for me. Not for Renate. Not for any of us.

She's dead. It's my fault.

Something tightens my chest, presses upward. My eyes leak. The Something has a name. Shame. Capital S. Decades of it.

Shame thickens my throat. A great wall of it marches upward until I cannot swallow, cannot breathe. And still it advances, gathering compatriots unseen for years: guilt, regret, anguish, loneliness, loss, longing, despair, bitterness, pain, disappointment. Together, these unacknowledged emotions create an invasion force. Unwelcome. Unstoppable. Their weight conquers me.

In a great, heaving sob, I push them out. The bed quakes beneath me. I relinquish all control of my body, my mind. I tremble and cower, I flinch and rage, I am vexed and heartbroken. I weep for Anna, for my dead sister, for the anguished parents who begged me to leave their precious child alone.

I committed so much evil in this one, dreadful life. My Catholic upbringing tells me the truth—the black path in the frame is the one I deserve.

I sob until I am empty. I am blackness itself.

Take me now.

Chapter Twenty-two
Rennie

Munich, Germany
3 January 1939

Werner sat reading the newspaper when I came downstairs thirty minutes later. I draped Mutter's oldest winter coat over the stairs' newel post. Keeping my steps and tone light, I closed the living room drapes. Time for my dramatic role. "So, I was thinking about those apples, the ones the boys brought from the farm."

Werner grunted and spoke into the newspaper. "The animal feed."

"What if I brought them to the train tonight? For the Jews."

He placed the newspaper on his lap. I had his attention. Good.

I continued, moving out of sight to close the dining room drapes. "Since those *Kinder*, those Jews, leave at midnight, it'll be dark on the platform, nicht? I can bring the basket of apples there, hand them out. Bad fruit for…" The rest of my planned monologue stuck in the tension in my throat.

My brother straightened and his fingers worked the newspaper into crisp folds. "Rotting fruit for those greedy Jews," he said. "That's what they deserve, after all they've taken from the rest of us. Ja." He nodded and licked his lips, tasting his idea. "Better yet, keep the basket covered. Place the whole thing on board as the train is about to leave. Let them smell the fruit. When they're hungry, they'll find it spoiled." He'd taken my suggestion and pushed it further. The way I'd learned to manipulate him frightened me.

As he reveled in "his idea," I returned to the living room and inched toward the telephone's notepad.

"You'll bring the apples to the Hauptbahnhof before midnight," he said.

"I have to go to the bakery to pick them up." Almost close enough to read the note.

"I'll be at the station tonight too. My help is needed with some, with details."

"Oh?" I tried to sound casual. "Details at this late date?"

"I'm to double-check papers at the train doors."

At last, I was able to read the name scribbled on the pad. *Kauffman.*

A gasp caught in my throat, and I faked a coughing spell. They knew. Somehow my uncle's Gestapo office had learned of a possible stowaway on that night's transport. I had to warn Sophie. Grabbing Mutter's coat, I started for the door.

Werner called after me. "And Renate?" I turned. "You have a bright future in the Reich. Vater would be proud." I lifted my chin to acknowledge his words and closed the door behind me.

Leaning against the door to compose myself, I took a few deep breaths to stifle a sob. Kept from my brother's view by the drawn draperies, I circled to the side of the house. There I picked up the bulging rucksack I'd tossed from my bedroom window and raced to the bakery.

Lying in the wooden cart right where I left her was Petra, awake and cooing softly. As I had earlier, I checked Klaus' flat and was relieved to find it still empty.

"Hello, sweet one." I cradled the baby against me, rocking a bit. "Big night for us." I ran the tip of my finger along the downy hairs of her cheek and across the small curve of her nose. As my finger moved closer to her mouth, her bow-shaped lips opened in search of a nipple. "You're hungry?" I reread the instructions on the two vials and checked my watch. "You have to wait a bit."

I laid clean towels on a worktable, then placed her on top and loosened her swaddle. Her little legs kicked, and her tiny fists waved in their newfound freedom. I giggled.

While she was content, I sorted through the apples in the cart. Sure, they were imperfect and a bit bruised and misshapen, but they were quite edible. Werner must have gotten the only rotten one. "There's justice in that," I said aloud, chuckling. But in case an official at the train platform checked… I grabbed a rolling pin and smacked an apple with it, sending juice and apple bits flying. With a bit of practice, I was able to strike an apple with the right amount of force so its skin split and softness leaked out. About two dozen met my rolling pin's handiwork.

I took a few minutes to clean up my mess and wipe the inside of the basket. Along the very bottom of the basket where little Petra would lay, I placed several layers of the bakery's linen towels to pad the baby's back against the hard wicker surface. I curled the towels a bit and tucked them in along the edge of the basket bottom to make a little nest.

I remembered Conrad telling me the basket's weave let in enough air for the snake, but this was no snake. This was a living, breathing infant. So, with the lid of the false bottom snugged in place, I shone a flashlight at the basket's side. Its bright beams appeared on the bakery's far wall. Light passed through. Air would too. Good.

Near twenty-two Uhr, I removed Petra's soiled diaper, placed Frau Huber's apple-splattered note inside it, and tossed it in the trash. As I pinned a clean diaper in place, I whispered a prayer for the baby's safety. Then I emptied one vial's contents into a milk-filled bottle.

By then, Petra was starting to squawk. Grateful for the infant care I'd done at the Hubers', I cradled the baby girl, kissed her soft forehead, and placed the bottle to her lips. She winced at first, whether at the false nipple or the medicine-altered taste, I didn't know. When I didn't withdraw the nipple, she explored it again, then sucked eagerly.

In minutes, the bottle was empty, so I nestled her upright against my shoulder and patted her back. A loud belch was my reward. "Well now," I said, smiling as I lowered her into view. Her eyes were already closing, a combination of a full belly, the late hour, and the sleeping draught in her milk. "Rest easy. And please stay quiet," I whispered. Then I laid her swaddled form in the makeshift nest at the very bottom of the basket.

Before I fit the false bottom into place two handsbreadth above her, I peeked at the tiny child through the weave in the basket's sidewall. So small and vulnerable, so dependent on the kindness of others. Relative strangers, at that. With another prayer and a shudder, I shut her inside the wicker prison.

Above the false bottom, I packed the best edible apples. The frame's segments wrapped in linen bakery towels were tucked in between the fruit. Atop that, I laid the partially squashed apples, then covered the whole thing with the gingham cloth. If officials at the Hauptbahnhof questioned Werner's judgment about giving away fruit, they had only to look under the cloth. They'd see spoiled goods and be satisfied.

Or would they dig through the whole basket? Turn it upside down?

I couldn't think about it.

I double-checked the contents of the rucksack I'd packed at home. Most valuable to me were my two favorite photos: the one of Werner and me as children and the laughing one of me and Sophie. Those I stuck inside the red leather book with its note of vindication for those I love. I anchored the book in my skirt's waistband and pulled the bulk of my sweater over top.

Theater accessories like clothing pads, face make-up, a tin of putty, and a wig all stayed in the rucksack in case I needed them. The satchel from Frau Lunka was stuffed in there too. Near the top, I tucked the forged travel papers and topped it off with a few stale bakery rolls in case an official took a quick look.

All set. I slipped the bulging rucksack over my shoulder and plopped the wool hat with its 'label' on my head. This really was happening.

As I stepped out of the bakery, it occurred to me—people associated with this place, this bakery, had a history of treason. I was about to become part of that legacy. An odd combination of pride and terror filled me. I clutched the basket's handles to steel myself, then loaded the basket into the cart and pushed it out the door.

A couple blocks before I reached the Hauptbahnhof, I paused, bringing the cart to rest. From my inside coat pocket, I retrieved an addressed envelope, its entire top edge lined with stamps. After a quick kiss and a "Get to England safely" prayer, I dropped it in the mail slot.

From nowhere, a slight figure appeared. I squinted and moved closer. "Bruno?"

He stepped closer, his furrowed brows speaking volumes. "And? You have her?"

I nodded and tapped the basket.

Bruno's smile was tight. "You will not see us, but we will be nearby, me and Dya. If there's trouble, I will help."

I nodded. "Thank you." He stepped back as if to leave, so I said, "Before you go—the frame. Am I the only one who can see…?"

He kissed my cheek. "Dya and I cannot thank you enough." Before I could blink, he faded into the shadows.

Chapter Twenty-three
Werner

On that horrible morning in January '39, two rough-handed henchmen tossed me into Onkel Edmund's office, then turned and left. In full Gestapo uniform, my godfather paced the length of the room, hands clenched behind his back. I stayed silent. Anything I may have said would only highlight my own confusion, anxiety, and yes, rage about what had just happened at the Hauptbahnhof. I was facing the Gestapo because my sister had compromised me. Again!

Onkel Edmund whirled, his voice a snarl. "This is what becomes of children when they're coddled." He pointed a finger at me. "A pushover instead of a man." He jerked a thumb toward a window, at the imagined form of my sister. "And a criminal instead of a loyal daughter of the Reich. Pah!"

My insides twisted, and my underarms grew damp.

I was supposed to protect my little sister, and she'd been hauled away as a common criminal…

…which she was. She duped me! How had she done it? How long had she been planning her little farce, stringing me along? Her and her nonsense about service and loyalty and being a good citizen. The girl was an actress! Nothing but a phony.

My godfather was saying. "I told your mother I'd keep an eye on you two while she's away. Now this!" He waved a hand in dismissal. "And after I gave you a second chance last summer."

"I am most grateful."

"What am I to think? You and Renate conspired right under my nose tonight."

My mouth dropped open. "Me? I didn't know anything about her scheme!"

"You expect me to believe that?"

I stammered. "Well, yes! It's the truth!"

He tipped his head. Whether curious or doubtful, I didn't know. He said, "So I'm to believe Renate acted alone."

"Yes."

"That she engaged in this activity without your knowledge or consent, right under your nose?"

"Yes."

"A second time." He regarded me for several long moments without speaking. When he began again, his voice held a note of regret. "My wife said you covered for Renate last summer—took the fall, so to speak. I suspected as much myself."

I was glad he knew the truth.

"Last time, the evidence was circumstantial. This is different. There are witnesses."

My heart sank. Damn her! I wouldn't take the blame for her, not this time.

"Why would she try to leave Germany? What is she running from?"

"How would I know?"

My uncle's gaze narrowed, then he nodded. "I will say this. The scheme was quite amateur. Hoping we'd give a cursory look so she could sneak past us. Young girls attempt deception that way. I have daughters, so I know. Now a man, his deception is different."

During the silent minute that followed, I could barely breathe. Finally, Onkel Edmund spoke again. "Unless evidence to the contrary arises, I say you're blameless in this, Werner. I read your face. You were as surprised as I was."

A mix of emotions coursed through me. Relief at my godfather's unexpected reaction. Rage toward Renate. And guilt. My Catholic upbringing and my old promise to Vater wouldn't let me forget the guilt.

"You are the sole heir to the Müller name, Werner. A strong name, Müller. Long, distinguished history. You alone must forge its legacy for the next generation. But there's a problem. A huge one. As I said, there are witnesses."

I held my breath.

"Renate has sealed her fate, so there's nothing to be done there. I always thought—still think—you are too soft. But you're it. The only heir my late friend has. You, I can help."

My knees threatened to buckle.

The two Gestapo agents who had hauled me in reentered, closing the door behind them. The witnesses.

Onkel Edmund strode to his desk, his leather chair crackling as he sat. The two agents moved to flank him. I froze, facing the wall formed by three uniformed men.

My godfather's expression changed. Gone was the man who spoke my family name with pride moments before, the uncle who sliced the goose for Christmas dinner and tried to stay involved in our lives after Vater died. The Gestapo officer was present. His pronouncement was swift and official. "A few days in prison will do you good."

I needed help to walk to the cell.

A week later, exhausted from sleepless nights on a filthy cot while inmates raged wailed nearby, I was led back into his office. Stinking of anxious sweat, I stood quaking and rumpled to face my uncle and his two henchmen. Onkel Edmund asked, "So what have you learned?"

That I will never return to prison. That to stay out of prison, I will do anything, *anything*. That I was a fool for trusting my sister. My voice shook, but Vater forgive me, I told Onkel Edmund my conclusion. "Renate must pay for her actions."

"She will."

What did that mean?

"As for you, these two"—he gestured to the men standing beside him—"have agreed to forget your presence at the incident in question."

I glanced at the two stone-faced men. "They have?"

"For a price, of course."

Ah. Money. "How much?"

"Five hundred mark."

Almost half my annual salary! I stammered, "Where will I get, how can I…"

Onkel Edmund laughed. Yes, laughed! "Your wages will be garnered until the debt is paid."

"My wages," I repeated.

"You like children, ja? I remember you were good with little ones. Want to help children, protect them?"

"Well, yes, but…"

One of the henchmen spoke up. "Hope he does a better job protecting them than he did protecting his sister." I cringed.

"That will be your job," my uncle said.

"My job."

"You're to leave Munich tomorrow."

"Tomorrow."

My godfather slapped his hand on his desk. "Stop repeating me! Take your orders like a man."

I stiffened and saluted. "*Jawohl*!"

"You've been granted a position in a new program. Lots of chances to protect children, since you do it so well." Here all three men snickered. "Plus, it gets you out of my hair." He shook one finger at me. "I don't ever, ever want to see you in this office again. Do we understand one another?"

"*Jawohl*!"

"If I see you back here for any infraction—and I do mean *any*—I won't save your scrawny neck again. As of this moment, you're Himmler's problem. Off to the chicken farmer you go."

I'd come out of the meeting with a future! I'd feared the worst—demotion, disgrace, retribution, *Sippenhaft*. More filthy prison. I would have done any job, any at all, to show my loyalty to the winning side. Thanks to a fat roll of bills and my Onkel Edmund's influence, I was an official member of the Lebensborn program.

I telephoned Anna with the good news, but before I could speak, she demanded that I come to her father's office.

That meant they already knew.

I stumbled past Herr Doktor Albrecht's receptionist and closed his office door behind me. He rose, ensuring I saw his full Party uniform, complete with military insignia from the Great War. Beside him stood my lovely Anna, wearing the uniform she'd worn as BDM troop leader, crisp and fresh. I looked down at my own garb, wrinkled and musky.

The doctor's pronouncement was swift and brutal. "For the sake of your Onkel Edmund, I was willing to overlook a great deal. But this second incident with your sister is too much. My daughter will not risk *Sippenhaft*. She will not bear children into the family of a traitor. I forbid it." With those words, he crossed his arms and turned his back to me.

After a shuddering breath, I faced Anna, my girlfriend of over a year, my fiancée, my connection to a secure future, my means of showing undying loyalty to the Reich. Without a flicker of hesitation, she, too, spun on her heel and turned her back to me.

For over five years, I worked in the Lebensborn program. Starting in the program's early days at the home in Steinhöring, I helped establish the heart of our nation's breeding program.

SS officers were encouraged to produce purebred offspring with as many approved Aryan women as they wanted. Then with the adults off serving the Reich, those offspring were raised in the Lebensborn homes like the one in Steinhöring. The Reich supplied the offspring's care, nourishment, and education. They learned to be proud of their heritage which prepared them for their role in creating the glorious Thousand-Year Reich. Perfect specimens for building the master race. It was all part of the vision for our country's future. Himmler's vision.

What I wouldn't give to have a child of my own among them.

Oh, Anna.

Instead, I threw myself into work. I seldom took days off or requested leave. There was no one to go home to. Renate had been arrested. Mutter had contracted the same disease that took Tante Gerde. She died in Hamburg in '39. And Anna. Anna didn't want me.

In late '39, the Lebensborn program expanded and my role changed. My assignment was to travel to distant villages within the expanded borders of the *Großdeutsches Reich*. My work ensured the Reich would be pure and strong well into the future.

I scoured our lands for blonde-haired, blue-eyed Aryan children. I gathered them from the far corners of Europe and accompanied them to the Fatherland to claim their rightful place in the Reich.

That part of the job was enjoyable, sitting on the train beside nervous children, singing songs to them in German, pointing out landmarks as we passed from their pitiful homelands into the glories of their future. When I delivered them to the Lebensborn home in Steinhöring, I knew they'd be nurtured by our loyal educators and nurses.

The mothers didn't understand. Fathers either. Their child was special, chosen. Part of a champion bloodline, precious to our leaders, deserving the best the Reich could provide. Our work demanded the utmost efficiency and discretion, so my attentiveness to detail was valued. We were creating the ultimate human race.

All that wailing and clinging. Desperate grasping. Pah. I protected those children.

No, that's a lie. As I stand at death's door with these two women forcing the truth to the surface, I must tell the truth.

I kidnapped children. Hundreds of them. I stole them from their homelands, from their families.

I destroyed their identities. I planted them in a foreign land among strangers.

My godfather's henchmen were right. The children didn't want to go with me. My version of protection destroyed their lives.

Chapter Twenty-four
Rennie

Munich, Germany
Near midnight, 3 January 1939

Beware the Ides of March pounded in my head.

The train was on the tracks when I arrived, a huffing hunk of black steel awaiting permission to move. The platform sported several neat rows of suitcases. Each piece of luggage was taped shut, already inspected, sealed, and numbered by officials. I rested the bakery's pushcart alongside the luggage, not daring to glance at the apple basket and its precious cargo. Petra was silent. I hoped and prayed she was all right.

In the Hauptbahnhof's crowded waiting room, the odor of bodies, wet wool, and anxiety clawed at my throat. Children from chubby toddlers to lanky teens and everything in between huddled alone or in small groups, some chattering, others silent. Young children clutched personal treasures like teddy bears and blankets. Around each child's neck hung a number, the specific and impersonal means of identification so they could connect with their numbered bag once in England. Near each child was a rucksack, probably filled with food and other essentials for the journey.

The adults in the room snuggled children on their laps or hovered near them with a hand on a shoulder or anxious glances. Poor, desperate people. My heart broke for them. Like

Sophie, like Frau Lunka and Bruno and little Petra, like the real Esther Kauffman, they were targets of propaganda and violence. These adults were caring for children the only way they could—by breaking up their family to send the children out of the country.

These children were about to travel to a foreign land without their parents and then live in the home of strangers who spoke a different language, ate different food, and practiced a different religion. These parents could only hope their own paperwork came through quickly.

Through the waiting room window, I saw uniformed officers patrol the train's perimeter. They walked right past my cart and its apple basket cargo. Getting the basket to Sophie should be easy: I'd warn her that Werner was checking papers at boarding. She'd see where he was and enter a different train car. I'd just slide the basket onto that car.

I scanned the waiting room for Sophie and spotted a pair of wooden crutches propped against a wall. Facing the crutches, back turned to me, was the hunched figure of a thin girl. She was partially hidden by those standing nearby, but I knew it was Sophie, her short hair now blackened with shoe polish. From my angle, I couldn't see the plaster cast that I hoped temporarily replaced her leg brace.

I tapped my waistband. The journal entry that vindicated Werner was with me. I prayed it wouldn't be needed.

The waiting room door pushed open, and my brother's high-pitched voice intruded. He waved a hand at a small sleeping child. "I need that chair." A frowning man lifted the child and cradled him against his chest. Werner spun the chair and climbed on it. All eyes turned to look up at him when he used a bullhorn to demand from his perch, "Everyone quiet."

I moved beside him and asked, "Aren't you supposed to be at the train doors?"

"Onkel changed his mind. Guards will double-check there." He jerked a thumb to the train. "I'm to process here with the ticket taker."

That would place Sophie literally right under his nose!

If I'd been able to use the picture frame's magic just then, I knew what I'd see—of the two paths in front of me, safety and loyalty, only one could save Sophie.

But what about Werner? I couldn't leave him the way he was, so lost to himself. I needed to be loyal to him and get Sophie on that train at the same time.

Nudging Werner onto his path of joy wasn't going to happen, I knew that now. But I might still find a way to get him onto his green path headed toward safety. If I could do that, I would have saved Sophie from the Nazis and I would have saved Werner from himself.

What could I do to help sweet little Petra?

Another line from *Julius Caesar* popped into my head. *Cowards die many times before their deaths. The valiant never taste of death but once.*

I took a steadying breath and ducked into the washroom.

The bullhorn's blared instructions followed me. A name would be called. The child was to step forward with papers and rucksack in hand. Once checked, the child was to proceed to the train.

I anchored clothing pads on my shoulders, my torso, my hips, and struggled into my blouse and skirt. When I tucked the red leather book in my waistband again, I realized I'd miscalculated. The top button of the skirt wouldn't close. No time to adapt. A bit loose, but it would have to do. Once Mutter's coat was over the top, the bulge of the book wouldn't be seen anyway.

My reflection showed a girl with a thick, almost stocky frame. I anchored the black shoulder-length wig with a dozen hairpins. Dark pencil thickened my eyebrows, and a bit of putty added a bump to my nose. A bit of face powder covered the most obvious flaws in my quick makeup job. Perfection didn't matter. I was the diversion.

With the rucksack containing the Romany's satchel over one shoulder, I slipped into the waiting room. "No adults on the train," Werner was saying. "Say your goodbyes here or on the platform." He glanced at his list. "Number One. Abitz, Helena."

A pale girl not even ten years old rose and clutched her rucksack. She leaned against the woman beside her, who in turn wrapped an arm about the girl's shoulders. They walked together toward the train official and Werner, their hips bumping as if connected by a rubber band. "*Bitte*," the woman said as Werner inspected the girl's papers and checked his list, "I need to see my daughter settled on the train. She is traveling alone, you see."

"*Nein*!" he shouted before turning to the room. "Next person who questions me will have their travel permit revoked."

Faces tight, Helena Abitz and her mother slipped out the door and onto the platform, now empty of suitcases. The pair walked past the pushcart with its precious cargo, then paused for a long embrace. With a gentle push, the woman urged her weeping daughter forward to the waiting officer. After he gave her papers a cursory glance, the girl climbed the train stairs. Her blotchy face appeared at a window, one hand pressed to the glass. Her mother moved forward to do the same, but the officer waved her off. Head bowed, the woman stepped back a meter or two and waited.

"Number Two. Binzer, Ursula."

I inched closer to Sophie.

"Number three, Dachstein, Isaac. Four, Dohler, Elfriede."

As each name was called, one child and an adult or two moved closer to Werner. The former scene repeated—papers checked first by my brother and the ticket taker, then by an officer at the train door. Each child boarded alone, the adult stepping back, sometimes with a false smile, other times in obvious distress.

I was halfway around the room. No one paid me any mind. I wasn't sure Sophie even noticed me.

Each child out the door meant the Ks drew closer. By the time "Grunau, Ruth" was called, I was beside Sophie. We'd shared so much—memories that stretched back ten years, our cooperative effort to get her photos to England last summer, our recent reunion. I leaned over to speak to her.

A brisk "Heil, Hitler!" caught my attention. It was Anna, dressed in her nurse's uniform, black medical bag in hand. She sidled up beside my brother.

And I'd thought things couldn't get worse.

"What are you doing here?" Werner snapped at his fiancée.

If she was offended by his tone, she didn't let on. "Vater got a call from Berlin. A Jew on the last transport arrived in England sick. Typhus." Concerned murmurs spread among the adults in the room.

Werner lifted the clipboard to cover his nose and mouth, then held it away in midair as if the paper itself might hold the germ. The last child called stood at Werner's feet, a grizzled man close behind. They seemed unsure if they should wait there or sit back down.

No doubt enjoying the fuss she'd brought, Anna smiled. "I'm to do quick checks on passengers. Make sure they're not contagious."

"Of course. Don't want to give the Brits reason to cancel our export of riffraff." He resumed control. "Over there," he told Anna, pointing to the area farthest from him. The very spot where Sophie and I were.

Beside me, two adults lifted sleeping toddlers from a bench. Faster than I thought possible, Sophie grabbed her crutches and hopped into a corner. I moved alongside her. Anna was so caught up in her own self-importance that she didn't seem to notice any of this.

Werner's command followed her to the impromptu exam area. "Anna, we need to process these Jews—and quickly. Get them out. For the benefit of the Reich."

With Anna's attention on examinations and Werner's on his list, I checked the rest of the room. Everyone's focus was elsewhere. Crutches stuck in her armpits, Sophie leaned against a wall alone. I approached her. "You dropped your hat."

Her attention flitted to me. "But I…"

I didn't wait for her response, just plopped the hat on her head. "It's a fine hat, well-made. I saw the label."

She blinked, her expression first one of surprise, then recognition, then obvious confusion at my thin disguise. "The *label* tells you everything inside." I scanned those close to us for possible eavesdroppers, but no one paid us any mind. "Check the *label* yourself." I turned to face her and relaxed my expression. After a moment's hesitation, she did the same and nodded. She understood.

With any luck, a casual observer would interpret our movement and conversation as friendly, just two teens passing time as we waited for our names to be called. That is, until Sophie took in my half-hearted disguise and hissed, "What are you doing?"

I slid off my rucksack and placed it beside hers on the floor. Feigning a stiff neck, I rolled my shoulders, then squatted so my crouched form blocked the two rucksacks from view. I made quick work of stuffing the infant's satchel of needs into Sophie's rucksack.

"What are you doing?" she asked again, this time in a whisper.

"Getting you on the train. You and…" I used my chin to indicate the basket on the platform. Sophie gave a quick nod. Apparently, she knew the basics of Frau Lunka's plan.

In no time, Werner set up a new routine. When he called a number and name, the child stepped forward where he and the ticket taker checked paperwork. The child then moved to Anna's corner where she shone her little flashlight into eyes, ears, and mouth and listened to heart and lungs. From name call to train boarding, the process took one minute per child, tops. If the train was to leave on schedule, and in Germany trains always left on time, the procedure had to hurry.

Then I heard it. "Number eighteen. Esther Kauffman." My stomach lurched.

Hunched over her crutches with her plaster cast just off the floor, Sophie crutched toward my brother. I knew she wanted to be invisible, to be behind her camera, to be anywhere but there. And yet there she was, a bona fide traitor trying to escape the country right in front of the very man she betrayed.

Anna the unpredictable would look her right in the eye. Having been Sophie's Jungmädel leader and then her student nurse at the polio hospital, Anna would recognize her. My best friend was in imminent danger.

The limelight had to be mine. I shouldered my way in front of Sophie. "Excuse me," I said, my papers outstretched to the ticket taker.

As I hoped, Sophie froze.

Werner's focus narrowed. "You." I peeked up at him from under my dark wig. But he was not looking down at me. His scrutiny was turned fully on Sophie. "What's wrong with your leg?" he asked her.

She did not meet his gaze. "I…I broke my foot."

"Doing what?"

She hesitated, then said, "Chasing my dog."

"Your name?"

Sophie was silent. Terrified, no doubt.

"I am speaking to you."

With obvious reluctance, Sophie turned a bit, just enough to acknowledge Werner's question without meeting his eyes. "Esther Kauffman."

Werner scowled and stretched out his hand. "Papers."

The ticket taker looked from my papers to the ones now in my brother's hand. They exchanged a nod. "What do we have here?" Werner said. "Two girls claiming to be Esther Kauffman." He gestured to a nearby wall. "Stand over there. We'll deal with you once the others are processed." The room filled with mumbles of confusion and concern.

"Ready for the next Jew!" Anna called out from her darkened corner. We ignored her. Werner continued down his list.

Taking advantage of the moment, I whispered to Sophie, "They found out." She stared at me, her mouth opening and closing in silence. I nodded.

She took in my dark wig and eyeglasses, my padded physique. Her expression was part alarm, part confusion. "So now you want to leave the country?"

Did I ever.

"I want you on the green path," I said. "Safety. You and the little one." I lifted my chin toward the platform, where, blessedly, the apple basket still sat undisturbed, little Petra awaiting her salvation. My smile quivered and threatened to break. "And hopefully him." I lifted my chin to my brother, still bossing people around from his chair-top perch. "Eventually."

"And so you..."

"Quiet over there!" Werner ordered us.

We obeyed for a moment or two. Once his attention returned to his task, I whispered, "He'll recognize me, or Anna will. I'll be the stowaway they're looking for. You are Esther Kauffman."

"Oh, Rennie. You can't..." Deep creases formed between Sophie's brows, but before she could finish, the train whistle blew.

The response was instantaneous. People jumped to their feet, grabbed rucksacks and the hands of small children. Waving papers, they pushed en masse toward Werner, voices raised. Several children began to wail. Werner clapped his hands. "I'll have order! Quiet!"

The room's volume softened a little, but the forward movement of dozens of people continued. They crowded Werner's chair, shoving papers at him and the ticket taker.

"Please, sir, let my daughter get on board."

"My nephew must go. His parents are already dead."

I felt their desperation, agreed with it. Sophie shifted on her crutches and took a couple hops closer to the door.

Anna left her post and stood beside Werner's chair. "What's the meaning of this? There will be order!"

The pleas continued. "This is the only chance my son has. Please."

"Take my ring. Real gold with a diamond chip. Just get my little girl on the train."

Anna stuck her head out the door and hollered down the platform. Moments later, two SS officers entered, boots slapping the concrete floor. They saluted, then rested hands atop hip-holstered guns. The crowd hushed and fell back.

Werner beckoned us with a crook of his finger. "You two." We moved beside his chair perch and handed our papers to a frowning SS officer. He examined both sets of papers, sheet by sheet, side by side. "The papers are identical," he announced, handing them back to Werner.

"So." My brother climbed down from the chair and stood in front of us. "Either one of you is lying, or you're both in cahoots. Let's take a look."

That's when Onkel Edmund pushed through the door.

Chapter Twenty-five
Werner

West Palm Beach, Florida
2005

I am surprised to be among the living, still in the same hospital room. Two figures are slumped in chairs on the other side of the room. One of the figures snores.

I must make a sound because both women rouse and come to my bedside. Sophie uses a wheeled walker now. Guess she'd have to, weakness from long-ago polio. I feel no anger toward her, not anymore. I do feel something though. Undefined. Unfamiliar. It's hard to breathe.

Sophie settles on one side of me, Susanna on the other. "Better?" Susanna asks.

"Thought…dead."

She looks over my shoulder to the monitor. I follow her gaze to a screen where colored lights flash and squiggles dance. "The doctor was in. He said"—she looks at Sophie, who nods—"he said we need to speak our peace and leave you to rest."

Sophie pulls out that old paper and gestures with it. "There's not much more to the letter Rennie sent to England. Do you feel up to it?" I take a wheezing breath and nod.

And now, S, the hardest part. My path divides from yours tonight. This breaks my heart. I am afraid to go it alone. But I must be true to the role I'm given.

You are the star, mine is a supporting role. I'll play my part to the best of my ability. When the curtain falls, I'll be in the wings applauding your success.

About the last-minute addition to our cast: her family will attend a future performance on her overseas tour.

Your friend always,
R

Sophie allows the paper to fold into its well-worn creases, returns it to the envelope, and secures them away.

"My family never made it to England," Susanna says, wiping away a tear. She must see the confusion on my face because she continues. "I was the last-minute addition. That night, at the Hauptbahnhof. The night you saved my life, Werner."

All I did that night was process paperwork and allow my sister to be hauled away by the Gestapo.

Susanna folds her hands and begins. "Since I was but a babe, I don't remember it. Sophie told me the story enough times that I can picture it all." She sighs. "You see, my birth mother asked for help finding safety for me and my brother. She approached a farm woman she knew, but that good soul already had taken in two others. Pretended they were nephews living there as farm help.

"Then my mother met Beatrice Ellende, a British national employed as a social worker in Munich. The two struck up a friendship, and Frau Ellende agreed to help get my brother and me out. Legally, of course.

"But legal paths to freedom took time. And money. And a country had to agree to accept you. That wasn't happening for Romany children. As my people were targeted more often, my mother grew desperate, and Frau Ellende worried for our safety."

Sophie chimes in. "By then, I was hiding in Frau Ellende's flat. Her brother arranged it." She and Susanna exchange another smile. "And both of them were trying to figure out how to get me out of Germany. Not easy, since I was wanted on treason charges."

Susanna picks up the thread. "To make a long story short, Frau Ellende left Munich and went to England to re-establish her homestead. As a British citizen, she was to provide a temporary home to a German refugee named Esther Kauffman. Rennie created Sophie's disguise."

Sophie gives a small, sad laugh. "My disguise was pretty thin. It only worked because Rennie's was worse." She shakes her head. "I've never met anyone more courageous, more loyal than your sister. Never."

Silence follows. I must fill it with sound. I focus on the irregular mechanical beep overhead, hallway voices that approach my door and pass by. Anything to drown the painful questions hammering at my skull.

Susanna resumes her tale. "The day before the transport, my birth mother wired England to ask if Frau Ellende would take me too. Too late for proper paperwork, of course. And too late for a foolproof plan. But the pressure was increasing, and my family was in imminent danger. So, desperation ruled. It was winter, and I was a babe." She pauses. "The frau said if I could reach England, she would indeed take me in." She smiles at Sophie. "That's how Frau Ellende became Auntie Beatrice to both of us."

"We were raised as sisters."

"Fifteen years difference in age."

"And we look nothing alike." Both women laugh.

"We were fortunate," Susanna says. "The war took our families, but Auntie Beatrice gave us a good life. She was gentle and kind, and we loved her dearly. We helped care for both her and her brother, our Uncle Peter Massey, until they passed."

"Get back to the train, Susanna."

"Sorry. So just before the transport, we presume my birth mother met Rennie and asked her to get me onto the train."

"All I'd been told was to watch for a special package being loaded onto the train," Sophie said. "The package would contain a baby, and I was responsible for keeping the baby safe until we crossed the border."

Susanna flashes her smile filled with gratitude. "I slept in the bottom of a basket, right there on the platform while the other children boarded the train, while the Gestapo…"

I replay the scene in my mind. I'd stood in stunned silence and watched Onkel Edmund pull off Renate's wig. As his henchmen clicked handcuffs onto her thin wrists, I did nothing. Nothing! Just stood there gaping like a fool.

I'd gone to the station to watch for a stowaway with false papers, and what did I find? My sister! In disguise and trying to leave the Fatherland! Her actions made no sense.

And while I stood there staring like an idiot, the other Esther Kauffman, Sophie in disguise, as I figured out long ago, boarded the train.

"Once I was on board," Sophie says, "I was powerless. All I could do was watch." She closes her eyes a moment, then resumes. "With the little Rennie managed to tell me in the waiting room, I assumed the baby was in the basket. Which was still on the platform. As I said, I couldn't do anything but watch from the train. When they shoved Rennie into the Gestapo car, she dropped this book." She indicates the journal.

"As the train readied to leave, I saw a figure on the far side of the platform. Thin, adolescent. The figure hurled an object toward the train, and when it landed on the platform, it splattered. An apple, I suspect. Werner, that apple seemed to rouse you, as if you awakened from a dream. You walked toward the basket, and as you did, you picked up the book Rennie dropped. You plopped it on top of the basket and slid the basket and all its contents through the train doors before they closed." She rubs the back of her hand across her eyes.

I remember. I wanted the Jews to have rotten apples.

Susanna smiles. "You put the basket on the train. Yes, you did, Werner. And in doing so, you saved my life."

It was not intentional.

Sophie lifts the weathered book and gives it a shake. "Obviously, Rennie intended the letter in here to vindicate you right away. Instead, it went with me to England." She shrugs, then continues. "When I realized it, well, returning the book wouldn't have helped Rennie. It may have helped you, Werner, but I was angry with you. The way you stole my photos. The way you stood by and let them arrest your sister. Your wonderful, loving sister." She shakes her head. "Keeping the book was my sad attempt at retribution.

"Years later, you led Erich back into my life. That's when I forgave you." She smiles. Contentment is clear on her face.

I am tormented.

Both women are silent a few moments. Susanna resumes her tale. "I know little of my birth family. Auntie Beatrice didn't have much information about them, travelers as they were. She'd never even been told the name I was given at birth." Sophie squeezes Susanna's arm. "But I have the picture frame Rennie sent in the basket." She taps it. "Old Romany magic there." She sits back in obvious relief to have finished her tale. "So, Werner, now you know. By putting the basket on the train, you saved this small piece of my heritage. And as I said before, you saved my life."

I didn't do it to be kind. I did it to be cruel, to tempt the children on board with food that smelled wonderful but was practically rotten.

At least I think that's why.

Just as I didn't tell Erich where Sophie had gone because I wanted them to find one another. I did it to torment him.

Didn't I?

They're making me out to be kind. I was not kind. Never have been.

Although Renate held a different opinion.

I lick my lips and try to gather air. It's hard to do; there's pressure in my chest. But I must know. "Renate…"

Sophie takes over. "Of course, Werner. How rude of me." She taps the leather-covered book again. "I used this to document my efforts to find your sister. Susanna read some entries to you while you slept." She seems distracted as she flips through the pages, then shakes her head and resumes her tale.

"During the war, I used Auntie Beatrice's name and address and wrote Rennie at your home. Letters were returned unopened with a black **X** across her name." She shakes her head. "After the war, I placed newspaper ads, checked refugee bulletin boards. No leads. I even traveled to Munich late in the '40s and dug up the old pickle jar." She laughs. "Believe it or not, that thing was still there, rusty lid and all. Inside was a note signed *Evelyn D* with a phone number in Hamburg. It seems she and Rennie had been bunkmates at Ravensbrück."

My breath catches. Several beats pass before breath resumes on its own.

"I spoke with Evelyn by telephone, and we met for a long weekend. They'd become friends at Ravensbrück, Rennie and Evelyn. Shared a love for stories and acting. Kept everyone's spirits up doing little skits, right there in that horrible place." Even behind her specs, I see Sophie's eyes glisten. "Amazing. Rennie could bring sunshine to the bleakest of circumstances."

She draws a breath and continues. "It seems Rennie told Evelyn about her life, what she'd done to end up in the camp. Even about the old pickle jar and where it could be found. They made a pact, those two. If Evelyn survived and she did not, I should be told how she lived her last days." Her gaze intensifies. "You and I should both be told, Werner. Evelyn searched for you but couldn't find you."

Of course, she couldn't find Werner Müller. He didn't want to be found.

I don't know if I can take more. I want to shut them out.

But I'm spellbound.

"When Evelyn and I met, I wrote everything she could remember right here in this book." Again, Sophie shakes the old volume. "Dear, sweet Rennie died in Ravensbrück early in '45. Hung on a long time. Always did love life."

While I worked the ratline to reach Italy and escape the ruin of the Reich, my sister lay dying in a hellhole concentration camp. I can't bear it. It's all my fault. Forgive me, Renate. I am so, so sorry. I didn't protect you.

Vater, I let you down.

Renate, sweet little Rennie, you were right. Back when you told me you missed me, the real me, you were right. I sold the Reich my very soul.

I've wasted it. This one life of mine, wasted. I hid from everyone and everything that truly matters.

I'm so, so sorry.

I gather whatever energy I have left in this dwindling life. In my mind and heart, I form the needed words. "Bless me Father, for I have sinned. It has been many decades since my last confession. Forgive me, I beg of you, Father God, Almighty One. I am a kidnapper. I am a thief…"

There's a series of loud beeps. An alarm sounds, monotonous.

I'm aware of a shift, a blur of air and space and time. I'm moving somewhere both brand-new and utterly familiar. Then I'm above the bed, looking down on white sheets tucked around a shrunken waste of a man. Two women lean over the man, then step back as three other figures race in.

No need. It's fine.

Let me go.

I turn from the man in the bed. Before me is brightness. I should be blinded by it, but I'm not. It draws me, and I move toward it without effort. Floating, gliding. Easy.

There's no rush. I am content. Neither here nor there. I am without location, without time.

The uniform brightness ahead is marred by a small dark spot. I can't tell if I move toward it or it moves toward me, but either way, it grows closer, larger. It is a figure. I am not afraid.

I see the figure is a teenage girl with an outstretched hand. I accept the hand and grasp it. Recognition charges through me.

Rennie says, "Welcome home."

Chapter Twenty-six
Susanna

West Palm Beach, Florida
Two days later, 2005

There was no real mourning. His family was long gone; he'd never married or had children, had no nieces or nephews. Sophie and I stayed beside the urn for the two-hour visitation.

A handful of people attended, mostly hospital staff. A couple older gentlemen too, former colleagues from the greyhound track. The visitors asked no questions of us; we offered no information. They signed the book, shook our hands, paused in front of the urn and its accompanying unframed photo, then moved along.

When all was done, I handed Sophie the photo. She smiled. "We've waited a long time. Let's do it together."

I pulled the frame from my purse and settled it on a table. Sophie slipped the childhood photo of Rennie and Werner into place. We both sighed in relief.

Because in the image, the two young figures were holding hands, their feet planted on a single spot. That spot was as green as summer leaves.

Glossary

Altstadt: Old Town. The Medieval center of many German cities, including Munich and Nuremberg
Bäckerei: bakery
BDM, Bund Deutsche Mädel: branch of Hitler Youth for girls ages 14-18
Bitte: please
Brauhaus: an informal German restaurant and brewery
Danke: thank you
Dya: Romany for mother
Felderrnhalle: the Field Marshall's Hall which faces a large public square in Munich. It is the site of Hitler's attempted overthrow of the government, the so-called Beer Hall Putsch, on November 8th and 9th, 1923. After a night of public speeches and drinking, Hitler and his cronies faced 130 armed state police on the site, resulting in the death of four police officers and sixteen Nazi party members. Hitler was arrested and imprisoned for his role. When he became chancellor in 1933, a monument to the slain Party members was erected nearby and a reenactment of the 'march on the Felderrnhalle' was conducted annually on November 8th and 9th.
Fräulein: Miss
Geheime Staatspolizei, Gestapo: the State Secret Police
Grossdeutsches Reich: The Greater German Empire
Gutes neues Jahr: Happy New Year
Hauptbahnhof: main train station
Ja: yes
Jawohl: Yes, indeed
Jud: Jew
Jungmädel: branch of Hitler Youth for girls ages 10-14
Kaesespaetzle: a German dish of homemade noodles, cheese, and caramelized onions
Kaputt: broken, out of order
Kinder: children

Kinder, kirche, und kuchen: Literally, children, church, and kitchen. This phrase was often used to define a woman's role in traditional German life.

Lebensborn: Literally, fountain of life. A program founded by Reichsführer Heinrich Himmler in 1935 to promote the so-called Aryan race in Germany and beyond. See Author's Notes and Bibliography for more information.

Lebensraum: Literally, living space. Additional territory considered to be needed for national survival, used as an explanation for expansion of Nazi Germany over its borders.

Mein Schatz: my sweetheart

Mischling: Literally, hybrid. The term was used to identify people of mixed racial and/or religious heritage

Mitte: center, the middle of a city

Mutter: mother

Mutti: mom

Nein: no

Nicht: Literally, not. When added at the end of a question, it is translated as 'no,' as in 'she lives here, no?'

Oma, Opa: Grandmother, Grandfather

Onkel: uncle

Pfennig: a small unit of currency, a penny

Pimpf: branch of Hitler Youth for boys ages 10-14

Reichsführer: Literally, leader of the empire. Both title and rank given to the commander of the SS, most often associated with Heinrich Himmler who held the title from 1929-1945. And yes, Himmler was often denigrated by others for his previous profession, that of a chicken farmer.

Rotes Kruez: Red Cross

SA: Abbreviation of Sturmabteilung, literally Storm Detachment, also called the Brownshirts. This militia-style group formed under the leadership of Ernst Röhm during the 1920s was notorious as street thugs. The SA played a significant role in Hitler's rise to power by providing protection during rallies. Members often physically fought against those who resisted the Nazis and actively intimidated and targeted minorities. The SA grew in number and influence until Hitler believed the organization to be a threat to his supremacy and his army. In 1934, Röhm and dozens of other SA leaders were murdered in what became known as the Purge or The Night of Long Knives. The SA continued to exist until the end of the war, but in significantly diminished numbers and influence.

Schadenfreude: literally, malicious joy. The sense of pleasure derived from someone else's pain.

Scharführer: Master Sergeant

Schwein: pig

Sieg, heil!: Hail, victory!

Sippenhaft: literally, collective punishment. The notion that a person's guilt may be spread among family members, even across generations.

SS: Abbreviation of Schutzstaffel, literally Protection Squadron, easily recognized by their all-black uniforms. Formed in the 1920s as Hitler's personal bodyguards, this unit grew to about 50,000 members by the time he took office in 1933. As the SA's influence diminished after the 1934 Purge, the SS continued to grow, eventually splitting into four main groups. One of those groups was the General SS which dealt with local and 'racial' matters. The notorious Gestapo was a division of this group.

Tag der Deutschen Kunst: Day of German Art, an annual arts festival in Munich

Tante: aunt

Uhr: Literally hour. Similar to military time, Germans use the 24-hour clock.

Vater: father

Verlaust: lousy

Viktualienmarkt: a large, open-air market in Munich

Volk: translated as 'the people' or 'folk,' used both to describe an ethnic group and a crowd.

Was ist los? What's wrong?

Wehrmacht: German Armed Forces

Willkommen: traditional German welcome, often translated 'you are welcomed with open arms'

Zigeuner: Gypsy, the pejorative term for people who are Roma and Sinti

Author's Note

When *Risking Exposure* was published in late 2013, I was satisfied that I'd told a complete tale of Sophie, Rennie, Werner, and Klaus. Some readers, including my own mother I should add, contacted me to say, "And? What happened next?" Even though I was delighted that readers wanted to spend more time with my characters, I dismissed requests for 'the rest' of Sophie's story. I needed a respite from the darkness of Nazi Germany and happily moved on to other writing projects.

A year or so later, I had one of those otherworldly experiences which creative types call 'a visit from the muse.' I awoke with an unknown character's voice in my head. The narrator was an old man, quite a grouchy one at that. Without knowing who he was or why he was in my head, I dutifully recorded his words. About five hundred words into his dictation, I realized he was an unrepentant Nazi. After another five hundred words, I recognized the character as an octogenarian version of Werner, the antagonist in *Risking Exposure*. The seed for *The Path Divided* had been sown. The rest of the story took shape over the next three years.

I've long been fascinated with the power of choices we make every day. Each choice we make does indeed lead to new possibilities and different outcomes. For over a decade, I've toyed with the idea of a Romany picture frame which visually shows choices and their potential results. After several failed attempts to integrate it into stories, I hope readers will agree it has found a home in *The Path Divided.*

All four of my grandparents emigrated from Germany during the 1920s. When I was a child, one set of grandparents lived in the apartment above ours in NYC. A few years after we moved to the suburbs, my other grandmother moved in with us. The language, music, food, and culture of Germany were shared with pride, but Germany's dark role in twentieth-century events was never openly discussed.

As an adult, my curiosity about those events led me to a treasure trove of literature and film, both fiction and non-fiction. Most novels and films set during the Nazi era take place during the war, that is from 1939-1945. My interest lies in the years just before that, the pre-war Nazi era of 1933-39. What was it like to grow up in Germany then? What did the average person see? How much did they know of what their government was doing? If my grandparents hadn't emigrated, how would the lives of my parents, teenagers in NYC during those same years, have been different? My search for answers has yielded these two novels.

Some historical details about people, programs, and events referenced in *The Path Divided* are presented here in the order found in the book's narrative.

Romany or Romani: Because their heritage and lifestyle run contrary to the Nazi concept of Aryan perfection, the Romany people were some of the earliest targets of Nazi aggression. Untold numbers of Romany men, women, and children were persecuted, imprisoned, and sent to concentration camps. An estimated quarter of a million of them died. The terms Gypsy and its German equivalent Zigeuner are considered pejorative.

Lebensborn: Literally, 'the fountain of life,' this program began under Himmler's direction in 1935. Its goal was to create a racially pure aristocracy in Germany. It was essentially an SS breeding experiment.

Women determined to be racially pure and free from genetic defects for six generations were encouraged to wed (or at least be impregnated by) SS officers who had previously met the same standard. Children born from these relationships were technically the property of the SS. If born out of wedlock, the children were raised in one of the ten Lebensborn homes throughout Germany under the supervision of dedicated Nazi nurses and teachers.

After Germany's invasion of Poland in September 1939 and the subsequent invasion of other countries, the program expanded. SS officers were trained to spot 'German blood' in those countries, that is, blonde-haired, blue-eyed children. The officers were charged to 'return those children to the Fatherland' without concern for the child's actual genetic ancestry or the family's protests. It is estimated that 200,000 children from occupied countries were kidnapped in this way, some literally from their parents' arms.

If the child were 6-12 years old, he or she would go to a German boarding school and/or Hitler Youth camp where indoctrination could begin. If the child was under six years old, he or she would be raised in a Lebensborn home with a disciplined Nazi doctrine. The children's documents were falsified so name, birthplace, and other vital information was permanently altered to align with the Nazi-approved standard of Aryan race.

Identified to the German people as orphans, most of the Lebensborn children were eventually placed in foster homes or adopted by unsuspecting German families. The advent of ancestry databases and DNA testing in the early 2000s led to a surge in media exposure about this program as thousands of German adoptees searched for their true heritage.

Rat Line: Originally a nautical figure of speech, the term is applied to military activities of a 'last ditch effort' nature. Here it describes the underground escape route Nazi officers used to flee Germany during the last months of the war. So many fled, adopted aliases, or just plain vanished that only 24 senior Nazis faced charges at the Nuremberg Trials.

Even after the war, chaos on the European continent created opportunities for movement between countries and continents with surprising ease. South America was a favorite relocation site, especially Brazil and Argentina because of their sympathetic and corrupt governments. Adolph Eichmann and Josef Mengele were among the notorious Nazi criminals who escaped to South America along these transportation routes.

Nuremberg Rally: This week-long gathering of the Nazi Party faithful took place each September from 1933-1938. Hitler's favorite architect, Albert Speer, was tasked with designing and building the massive stadiums and surrounding grounds which served to showcase the Reich's size and scope. A propaganda feast of speeches, torchlight parades, military demonstrations, and patriotic songs, hundreds of thousands of Hitler Youth and Party members attended the Rally each year. The advent of war on September 1, 1939 effectively brought the annual event to a close.

Kristallnacht: The 'night of broken glass' was the first widespread demonstration of Nazi aggression against people of Jewish heritage. Across Germany and occupied lands on November 9 and 10, 1938, Nazis vandalized and burned Jewish homes, synagogues, schools, and businesses, killing almost 100. Additionally, 30,000 Jewish men were arrested, then imprisoned or sent to a concentration camp. Many never returned.

Within hours of these attacks, desperate families flocked to immigration offices around the country applying for paperwork which might allow them to emigrate. Because of a complicated mix of cost, quotas, sponsorship, and paperwork delays, many people who hoped to leave the country were instead arrested and killed in the months and years which followed.

Kindertransport: The 'children's transport' was a series of coordinated rescue efforts by rail, by sea, and sometimes by air between December 1938 and September 1939 when war began. In those ten months, about 10,000 vulnerable children were safely moved out of Nazi Germany and occupied lands and placed in homes in Great Britain and several other European nations.

Following the increasing aggression against Jewish people seen on Kristallnacht, British social welfare agencies and churches teamed up to create the program. Nazi Party officials approved and even encouraged the program, anxious as they were to rid the country of 'unwanted populations.' German social welfare agencies assisted with paperwork, opening the cooperative international program to all vulnerable children under age seventeen.

Most of the children on the Kindertransport were Jewish, their parents desperate to get them to safety. And yes, many of the trains did leave at midnight. The average German citizen did not witness this emotional rending of families.

My idea for Sophie's fictional escape was sparked by personal narratives of The Kinder, as they are now called. A number of Kinder were categorized as 'politicals.' To my knowledge, none of them was an accused traitor, but the potential for legal emigration of young political opponents of the Nazi regime existed, at least until the war began. None of the personal stories I read spoke of passengers in disguise. That element, too, was of my own making.

But a few escapes like Petra's did indeed happen. Several Kinder described caring for infants snuck on board in baskets of food, sometimes through windows of a departing train or when the train was stopped at a crossing.

I cannot imagine the fear that drove parents to place their unaccompanied children and infants on a train bound for a foreign land, sending them off to live with complete strangers a thousand kilometers away. These acts of pure, selfless love are both heartbreaking and heartwarming.

Of course, the parents planned to join their children in England once their own paperwork was approved. But this was Nazi Germany. Many of the children never saw their parents again.

A selected bibliography is included in this work to guide readers toward further exploration of topics of interest.

Acknowledgments

A novel is not created through the author's efforts alone. Many people influence the book's evolution from idea to finished product. For *The Path Divided,* I am indebted to:

- My beta readers, for their boundless encouragement and incredible feedback: Katie Barnett, Sandra Bush, Brinton Culp, Cindy Hospador, Michael Moran, Hildy Morgan, Nadine Poper, Jenna Rhoads, Nancy Walter, Susan Weintrob, and Stefanie Zych;
- My Pennwriters Rebel Writers critique partners: Sandra Bush and Cindy Hospador;
- My SCBWI critique group: Jill Bateman, Brinton Culp, Chuck Gaston, Nadine Poper, and Pradeep Velugubantla;
- My beach walking and writing retreat buddy, Hildy Morgan;
- My eagle-eyed editor, Dana Perrow Moran;
- My brilliant cover designer, Michael Rausch;
- The incredible librarians at the Library of Congress;
- My sister-in-law Kathy Moran who offered her home as my base during LOC research;
- Bea Green, who generously shared her personal memories of both Kristallnacht and the Kindertransport in vivid, harrowing detail;
- My late mother, Judith Grunau, for urging (okay, nagging) me to finish the story of Sophie and Rennie, and not to 'leave those poor children alone on the verge of war';
- The countless readers who contacted me after reading *Risking Exposure* and asked, "And then what happened?" Because you loved Sophie and Rennie as much as I did, your questions kept the characters alive in my head and in my heart;
- And of course, I'm indebted to Michael, who listened to and read more iterations of this story than I care to remember. Your encouragement and support mean the world to me.

Selected Bibliography

Some of the nonfiction resources used in creating this novel's historical backdrop are categorized and listed below. The list is by no means exhaustive, but it represents the variety of sources consulted.

Dozens of works of well-researched Nazi-era historical fiction I read and enjoyed are not included here. I encourage you to explore the world of historical novels as well!

Hitler Youth

Bartoletti, Susan Campbell *Hitler Youth: Growing up in Hitler's Shadow*. New York: Scholastic, 2005.

Heck, Alfons. *A Child of Hitler: Germany in the Days When God Wore a Swastika*. Phoenix: Renaissance House, 1988.

Heil Hitler: Confessions of a Hitler Youth, (HBO, 1991.)

Hitler's Children series: Adolf Hitler Schools, (Discovery Channel, 2011).

Kater, Michael H. *Hitler Youth*. Cambridge: Harvard University Press, 2004.

Mahlendorf, Ursula. *The Shame of Survival: Working Through a Nazi Childhood*. University Park: The Pennsylvania State University Press , 2009.

Tempted. Misled. Slaughtered: A Hitler Youth History (Museum of the City of Nürnberg, *Dokumentationszentrum Reichsparteitagsgelände*, 2010), CD-ROM.

Kindertransport

Bea Green, passenger on Kindertransport from Munich, personal email correspondence and interview.

Fast, Vera K. *Children's Exodus: a history of the Kindertransport.* London and New York: IB Tauris, 2011.

Fox, Anne L. and Eva Abraham-Podietz, eds. *Ten Thousand Children: True Stories told by Children who Escaped the Holocaust on the Kindertransport.* West Orange, NJ: Behrman House, Inc., 1999.

Gershon, Karen, ed. *We Came as Children: A Collective Autobiography.* New York: Harcourt, Brace, &World, Inc., 1966.

Golabek, Mona and Lee Cohen. *The Children of Willesden Lane.* New York: Warner Books, 2002.

Harris, Mark Jonathan and Deborah Oppenheimer. *Into the Arms of Strangers: Stories of the Kindertransport.* New York: Bloomsbury, 2000.

Into the Arms of Strangers: Stories of the Kindertransport. California: Warner Brothers, 2001, DVD.

Kaczmarska, Ela. *The Kindertransport,* podcast transcribed on National Archives, UK, from interview dated 2/26/2010.

Leverton, Bertha and Shmuel Lowensohn, eds. *I Came Alone: The Stories of the Kindertransport.* Sussex, England: The Book Guild, Ltd, 1990.

Milton, Edith. *The Tiger in the Attic: Memories of the Kindertransport and Growing up English.* Chicago: University of Chicago Press, 2005.

The Children who Cheated the Nazis. Directed by Sue Read. London: Golden Reed Productions, 2000, DVD.

The Kindertransport to Britain, 1938-39: New Perspectives. Andrea Hammel and Bea Lewkowicz, eds. Amsterdam and New York: Rodopi Press, 2012.

The website for the Kindertransport Association Archive. www.kindertransport.org.

The website for the Wiener Library Archive, London. www.wienerlibrary.co.uk.

The website of the Association of Jewish Refugees: *Refugee Voices.* www.wjr.org.uk .

The website of the United States Memorial Holocaust Museum: *Oral histories.* www.usmhm.org

The website of the Wollheim Memorial. *Norbert Wollheim.* http://www.wollheim-memorial.de/en/home

Lebensborn

Associated Press website, "Documents detail Nazi drive for racial purity," by Melissa Eddy, April 6, 2007.

Associated Press website, "Sixty of Hitler's children met," November 5, 2006.

BBC News website, "Nazi Past haunts Aryan children," by Kate Bissell, June 13, 2005.

Catrine, Clay and Michael Leapman. *Master Race: The Lebensborn experiment in Nazi Germany.* London: Coronet, 1995.

Jewish Virtual Library website, "Stolen children: Interview with Gitta Sereny," 1999.
http://www.jewishvirtuallibrary.org/stolen-children

Joshua Hammer, "Hitler's Children," *Newsweek International,* March 20, 2000.

Lebensborn, the fountain of life, from "History's Mysteries," (History Channel, 2013).

"Nazi program to breed Master Race," by David Crossland, *Der Spiege*, March 8, 2007.

"Nazi Selective Breeding," *The Times* (London), Dec 14, 1943.

Schmitz-Köster, Dorothee. *Lebenslang Lebensborn.* Munich: Piper Verlag, 2012.

"Stolen by the Nazis," *Daily Mail* (London), January 9, 2009.

The Last Nazi: Children of the Master Race - Lebensborn (PBS, 2009).

"Third Reich Poster Child," by Titus Chalk, *ExBerliner,* November 22, 2010.

VonOelhafen, Ingrid, Tim Tate, and Dr. Dorothee Schmitz-Köster. *Hitler's Forgotten Children.* New York: Berkley Caliber, Penguin-Random House, 2016.

Nuremberg Rally

Rawson, Andrew. *Showcasing the Third Reich: The Nuremberg Rallies,* Spellmount, Gloucestershire, England, 2012.

The Nazi Party Rally Grounds, (Museum of the City of Nürnberg, *Dokumentationszentrum Reichsparteitagsgelände*, 2010), CD-ROM.

The website for Documentation Center of Nuremberg; Nazi Party Rally Grounds. https://museums.nuernberg.de/documentation-center

The website for World Future Fund. *A Guide to the Annual Nazi Party Congress ("Parteitag") in Nuremberg, 1938.* http://www.worldfuturefund.org/

Wykes, Alan. *The Nuremberg Rallies: Ballantine's Illustrated History of World War II, campaign book number 8*. New York: Ballantine Books, 1970.

Ratline

After Hitler: The Untold Story. National Geographic documentary, 2016.

Carlson, John Roy. *Under Cover: My Four Years in the Nazi Underworld of America.* New York: EP Dutton, 1943.

Goñi, Uri . *The Real Odessa: How Peron Brought The Nazi War Criminals To Argentina.* New York and London: Granta Books, 2002.

Lightblau, Eric. *The Nazis Next Door: How America became a safe haven for Hitler's men.* New York: First Mariner Books, Houghton Mifflin Harcourt Publishing, 2015.

Romany people

Cooper, Patrinella. *Gypsy Magic: A Romany Book of Spells, Charms, and Fortune-Telling.* San Francisco: Red Wheel/Weiser, 2002.

Crowe, David M. *A History of the Gypsies of Eastern Europe and Russia.* New York: St. Martins Griffin, 1994.

Fings, Karola, Herbert Heuss and Frank Sparing. *From Race Science to the Camps: The Gypsies during the Second World War, volume 1.* England: University of Hertfordshire Press, 1997.

Fonseca, Isabel. *Bury Me Standing: The Gypsies and Their Journey.* New York: Alfred A Knopf, 1996.

Hancock, Ian. *We Are the Romani People.* England: University of Hertfordshire Press, 2002.

Kenrick, Donald, editor. *In the Shadow of the Swastika: The Gypsies during the Second World War, volume 2.* England: University of Hertfordshire Press, 1999.

Kenrick, Donald, editor. *The Final Chapter: The Gypsies during the Second World War, volume 3.* England: University of Hertfordshire Press, 2006.

Lewy, Guenter. *The Nazi Persecution of the Gypsies.* England: Oxford University Press, 2000.

Milton, Sybil H. "'Gypsies' as Social Outsiders in Nazi Germany." In Gellately, Robert, and Nathan Stoltzfus, *Social Outsiders in Nazi Germany.* Princeton: Princeton University Press, 2001.

The website of Patrin: East Midlands Gypsy Heritage Project, http://www.patrin.org.uk/

Ramati, Alexander. *And the Violins Stopped Playing: A Story of the Gypsy Holocaust.* New York: Watts Publishing, 1986.

Rosenberg, Otto. *A Gypsy in Auschwitz.* London: London House, 1999.

Tebbutt, Susan, ed. *Sinti and Roma: Gypsies in German-speaking Society and Literature.* Part of the series *Culture and Society in Germany.* New York and Oxford: Berghahn Books, 1998.

Sinti & Roma. United States Holocaust Memorial Museum pamphlet.

Winter, Walter. *Winter Time. Memoirs of a German Sinto who Survived Auschwitz.* England: University of Hertfordshire Press, 1999.

Yoors, Jan. *The Heroic Present: Life among the Gypsies.* New York: Monacelli Press, 2004.

Nazi Era History

A Walk through the 20th Century with Bill Moyers: WWII, The Propaganda Battle. PBS, 1984, DVD.

Beer, Edith Hahn and Susan Dworkin. *The Nazi Officer's Wife: How one Jewish woman survived the Holocaust.* New York: William Morrow and Company, 1999.

Benz, Wolfgang. *A Concise History of the Third Reich.* Berkeley: University of California Press,2006.

Berenbaum, Michael. "A Mosaic of Victims: What About Non-Jewish Victims of the Nazis?" In *The Holocaust and the Christian World: Reflections on the Past, Challenges for the Future,* Edited by Carol Ritnner, Stephen D. Smith, and Irena Steinfeldt. New York: Beth Shalom Holocaust Memorial Centre, Yad Vashem International School for Holocaust Studies, Continuum International Publishing Group, 2000.

Bishop, Chris and David Jordan. *The Rise and Fall of the Third Reich: An Illustrated History.* London: Amber Books, 2005.

Bruhns, Wibke. *My Father's Country. The Story of a German Family.* New York: Alfred A Knopf, 2008.

Dodd, Christopher J. *Letters from Nuremberg. My Father's Narrative of a Quest for Justice.* New York: Crown Publishing, 2007.

Domarus, Max. *The Essential Hitler: Speeches and Commentary.* Wauconda, Illinois: Bolchazy-Carducci Publishers, 2007.

Dumbach, Annette E. and Jud Newborn. *Shattering the German Night: The Story of the White Rose.* New York: Little Brown and Company, 1986.

Faber, David. *Munich, 1938: Appeasement and World War II.* New York: Simon and Schuster, 2008.

Friedlander, Henry. *The Origins of Nazi Genocide: From Euthanasia to the Final Solution.* Chapel Hill: University of North Carolina Press, 1995.

Friedman, Ina R. *The Other Victims: First-Person Stories of Non-Jews Persecuted by the Nazis.* Boston: Houghton Mifflin Company, 1990.

Gallo, Max. *The Night of Long Knives: June 29-30, 1934 - Hitler's Purge of the SA.* New York: Harper & Row, 1972.

Germany, Politics and Government, 1933-1945. Library of Congress archives of prints and photographs online. http://www.loc.gov

Hunting Hitler, TV series, History Channel, 2015-2018.

Johnson, Eric A and Karl-Heinz Reuband. *What We Knew: Terror, Mass Murder, and Everyday Life in Nazi Germany.* Cambridge, Massachusetts: Basic Books, 2005.

Large, David Clay. *Where Ghosts Walked. Munich's Road to the Third Reich.* New York: WW Norton and Company, 1997.

Lobel, Anita. *No Pretty Pictures: A Child of War.* New York: Greenwillow Books, 1998.

Marks, Jane. *The Hidden Children: The Secret Survivors of the Holocaust.* New York: Fawcett Columbine, 1993.

McBride, Robert Medill. *Towns and People of Modern Germany.* New York: Robert M. McBride & Company, 1936.

Neuman, Ralph. *Memories of my Early Life in Germany: 1926-1946.* Berlin: German Resistance Memorial Center, 2006.

Newsweek magazine, multiple articles September 1938-January 1939.

Owings, Alison. *Frauen: German Women Recall the Third Reich.* New Brunswick, New Jersey: Rutgers University Press, 1995.

Phayer, Michael. "The Response of the German Catholic Church to National Socialism." In *The Holocaust and the Christian World: Reflections on the Past, Challenges for the Future,* Edited by Carol Ritnner, Stephen D. Smith, and Irena Steinfeldt. New York: Beth Shalom Holocaust Memorial Centre, Yad Vashem International School for Holocaust Studies, Continuum International Publishing Group, 2000.

Read, Anthony and David Fisher. *Kristallnacht: The Nazi Night of Terror.* New York: Random House, 1989.

Ruins of the Reich. Shannon and Company productions, 2007, DVD.

Secret Lives. New York: Aviva Films, 2002, DVD.

Shirer, William L. *Berlin Diary: The Journal of a Foreign Correspondent.* New York: Popular Library, 1961.

Sophie Scholl- The Final Days. New York: Zeitgeist Films, 2005, DVD.

Stargardt, Nicholas. *Witnesses of War: Children's Lives under the Nazis.* New York: Alfred A. Knopf, 2006.

Taitz, Sonia. *The Watchmaker's Daughter: A Memoir.* New York: McWitty Press, 2012.

Tec, Nechama. "A Glimmer of Light." In *The Holocaust and the Christian World: Reflections on the Past, Challenges for the Future.*

Edited by Carol Ritnner, Stephen D. Smith, and Irena Steinfeldt. New York: Beth Shalom Holocaust Memorial Centre, Yad Vashem International School for Holocaust Studies, Continuum International Publishing Group, 2000.

The Holocaust. United States Holocaust Memorial Museum pamphlet.

The Nazis: A Warning from History. London: BBC, 1997, DVD.

The Restless Conscience: Resistance To Hitler in Nazi Germany. Film by Hava Kohav Beller, 2006, http://www.therestlessconscience.com/

The Third Reich in Ruins: Munich. Captioned pre-war and post-war photos in and around Munich. http://www.thirdreichruins.com/munich.htm

The Third Reich, produced and distributed by A&E Networks and the History Channel, 2011, DVD set.

The Times (London), various articles 1934, 1938, 2003.

The website archive of the *New York Times*, multiple articles, 1934, 1938.

The website of Axis History. *Axis History Factbook.* http://www.axishistory.com

The website of Calvin College, *German Propaganda Archive.* http://www.calvin.edu/academic/cas/gpa/

The website of the City of Munich. ThemenGeschichtsPfad (History-themed trail): *National Socialism in Munich.* https://www.muenchen.de/rathaus/dam/jcr:e6012757-0206-4728-9bf4-25c85ed762fe/national-socialism-in-munich.pdf

The website of the German Historical Institute. *German History in Documents and Images: Nazi Germany.* http://www.ghi-dc.org/

The website of the History Learning Site, UK. *The Night of the Long Knives.* http://www.historylearningsite.co.uk/nazi-germany/the-night-of-the-long-knives/

The website of the History Place, *Nazi Germany: 1933-1939.* http://www.historyplace.com/

The website of the Holocaust Teacher Resource Center of the Holocaust Education Foundation. *Hitler's Unwanted Children*, by Sally Rogow. http://www.holocaust-trc.org/

The website of the Munich Documentation Centre for the History of National Socialism. http://www.muenchen.de/Rathaus/culture/museums/Documentation_Centre/188431/index.html

Voices of the Holocaust. Part of the series *Literature & Thought.* Logan Iowa: Perfection Learning Corporation, 2000.

Volkischer Beobachter, (Munich newspaper), multiple articles, 1934 and 1938.

von Halasz, Joachim, series editor. *Hitler Youth: An Introduction for American and British Readers.* First published in 1936 as *German youth in a changing world.* London: World Propaganda Classics, Foxley Books, 2008.

von Halasz, Joachim. *Hitler's Munich.* London: Foxley Books, 2007.

vonMoltke, Helmuth James. *Letters to Freya: 1939-1945.* New York: Alfred Knopf, 1995.

To learn more about the author or to arrange a school, book club, or library presentation, please visit
www.jeanneemoran.weebly.com

Contact the author directly
authorjeannemoran@gmail.com

If you enjoyed *The Path Divided,*
please leave a review
or tell a friend.

Made in the USA
Monee, IL
04 October 2020

43608750R00173